RUTHIE PEARLMAN

FOUNDLING

MENUCHA PUBLISHERS

Menucha Publishers, Inc.
©2018 by Ruthie Pearlman
Typeset and designed by Rivkah Lewis
All rights reserved

ISBN 978-1-61465-656-2
Library of Congress Control Number: 2018937947

No part of this publication may be translated, reproduced, stored in a retrieval system, or transmitted in any form or by any means, electronic, mechanical, photocopying, recording, or otherwise, without prior permission in writing from both the copyright holder and the publisher.

Published and distributed by:
Menucha Publishers, Inc.
1235 38th Street
Brooklyn, NY 11218
Tel/Fax: 718-232-0856
www.menuchapublishers.com
sales@menuchapublishers.com

Printed in Israel

TO ALL THE GOOD PEOPLE who foster children the way the Reeds fostered Yael. Okay, it didn't work out so well for her in the end, but their intentions were good. Like ours were good when we fostered a little boy many, many years ago, which also didn't end well. However, I wrote *Daniel, My Son*, a novel based on our experiences as foster parents, which has, I think, helped some people come to terms with their own fostering experiences.

ACKNOWLEDGMENTS

I HAVE A TERRIFIC editor in Chaya Silverstone. She goes through my books with a fine-tooth comb and picks out all the anomalies, then nags me until I straighten them out. I really need someone like her in my life as a novelist!

Special thanks to *Ami* magazine's teen section, where *Foundling* was first published as a weekly serial.

CHAPTER 1

ON YAEL REED's twenty-first birthday, she woke up depressed. In the past year, since the mysterious and traumatic case of the trafficked Russian babies had been solved and Yael had been covered in glory as well as other less pleasant substances, both Nena and Shuli, her two single friends, had gotten married. They had both moved to Israel for their new husbands to learn for a while. Rosie had a gorgeous baby girl, whom she and Zalmy had called Yudit.

The four of them, who had gelled as a group at school and had stuck together, more or less, since, were now split in four different directions, and only she, Yael, was still alone. Rosie a wife and mother. Nena and Shuli, both glowing new brides. And Yael? A twenty-one-year-old private investigator with an impressive CV of daredevil cases to her name, but no husband, and no prospect of one.

The case of the missing babies had earned her an impressive reputation as a supersleuth. Naava Schwartz, the schoolgirl who had first employed her when she'd been suspicious of the family she'd babysat for, couldn't compensate her sufficiently for her work on the case, but Naava's parents, on hearing the whole story, had managed to raise over fifteen thousand pounds to pay Yael for her services. The Jewish community in Golders Green, relieved and pleased that this ghastly practice of baby trafficking and its even more ghastly perpetrators, Vladimir and Sylvia Bolkin, had been removed from their midst and were both serving lengthy prison terms, had happily put their wallets on the line for Yael.

She was suddenly a celebrity, where previously she'd been a nobody. Business was picking up and she was no longer wondering where her next rent payment, both for her apartment and her office, was going to come from. Even if the day-to-day work that came her way wasn't as exciting as the cases that had made her name, it paid her bills and she even had some left over to put in the bank.

Yael was getting so busy, in fact, that sometimes she didn't have time to realize how lonely she was.

Her single-girl apartment block in Golders Green, the brainchild of a local entrepreneur, was a migratory affair, with single girls coming and going at a rate of knots, most hardly living there for a year before their own personal *basherts* came and swept them off on the back of a metaphorical white stallion, or in the passenger seat of an orange Renault, the modern version. She was the longest-staying tenant there by far, and was becoming increasingly embarrassed by the fact. It also meant that she couldn't really make friends with the girls living there, as they were gone, it seemed, almost before they arrived.

Her detective friends and gurus, Colin and Leora Sommers, or rather Leora on her own, had been working on a *shidduch* idea for Yael during the babies case. But somehow the very daredevil aspect of Yael's personality had proved too much for the prospective young man to contemplate. He wanted a nice, normal sort of girl, not one who put her life on the line on a regular basis. Leora had been hoping he'd be more open-minded to Yael and her lifestyle, but it appeared not.

So when the local *shadchante* approached Yael in the grocery store, she couldn't help feeling a frisson of hope that her own *bashert* could be on his way at last.

She'd been browsing the ready meals, wondering if her new-found increase in income could run to spoiling herself every now and then, rather than subsisting on canned soup and pasta, when the woman, known as Rebbetzin Hoff, approached her and watched while the young woman made her choices.

"Can't cook won't cook?" she commented finally.

Yael looked around and saw the *rebbetzin* observing her. She had a vague idea that this woman was a matchmaker, but so little had this particular profession impacted on her life so far that she didn't put two and two together and think she was being deliberately targeted.

Another girl might have realized she was being assessed, and made up some story about her culinary expertise, but Yael wasn't made of such stuff.

"I heat up a mean can of soup, and I can slice sausages into it like a pro." She grinned. "My apartment has very limited cooking facilities and I'm mostly at work, so I haven't had the time or inclination to learn."

Rebbetzin Hoff tilted her head to one side like a bird as she looked Yael up and down. "Your parents listening?" she said.

"Listening to what?" Yael asked naively, never having heard this phrase.

The other woman frowned. "I mean, are they taking suggestions? For you, for a *shidduch*."

"I don't have parents," Yael said, and thinking the conversation over, turned back to the shelf of chilled meals.

"Oy, *nebach*!" Rebbetzin Hoff exclaimed. "A poor orphan! My favorite kind to get married off! Such a big mitzvah."

"If you say so," Yael said, without looking around.

"All you have to do is give me some details of your parents when they were alive," the woman said, taking out a notebook. "*Yichus*. People want to know that sort of thing. Where you come from. From whom did you stem. You know."

Yael turned to the woman. "I was found in front of a hospital, in a basket, abandoned by my parents," she said. "I was brought up by foster parents and eventually in a children's home."

"Oy! *Nebach*! What a story! Bound to get the sympathy of prospective in-laws, I'm sure!"

"Whatever," Yael said, getting irritated.

"But your real parents. They must have left you some details, some way you could trace them. No?" the woman persisted, still holding the notebook like a policeman ready to take down one's particulars.

"I found my mother, eventually. She's remarried and lives in America. But I wasn't able to find my father. I think he's presumed to have died in a hit-and-run accident. I'm not sure. Details are a bit vague on what happened to him." Yael didn't add the part about her mother being decidedly hostile at being found and wanting nothing to do with her. Her *yichus* was bad enough without elaborating on it.

"Oy!" Rebbetzin Hoff said again. "I shall make it my personal job to find you the perfect *shidduch*! But you need to find out more about your father. The other side will want to know. Is he alive, or dead for sure? I presume if he's alive he gave your mother a kosher *get*? If he's dead, can you find out where he's buried? And if he is alive, where is he now and what is he doing?"

"I don't think he's alive. I heard the hit-and-run story from my mother, and my foster parents." This wasn't strictly true. Yael wasn't entirely sure where she'd heard it from, it had entered her mind by osmosis, but she had definitely heard it from a source that was more than rumor.

"If he's dead, a *chevrah kaddisha* somewhere must know where he's buried," persisted the woman, tapping her notebook with her pen.

She was by now seriously getting on Yael's nerves. Yael's theory on *shidduchim* was: *If someone wants me, he'll take me, warts and all, no yichus and all.* But by the same token, this theory, admirable though it was, was flawed in its execution, as here she was at twenty-one with no marriage prospects in sight. It was the only thing that stopped her blowing her stack at Rebbetzin Hoff, which she was sorely tempted to do.

They parted company having exchanged contact details. Rebbetzin Hoff had heard of Yael Reed's achievements in sleuthing, but hadn't put her fame to the face in front of her. She seemed both impressed and bemused by the reality of the young woman behind the reputation.

"I'll try and find out what I can about my father," Yael said.

"And I'll work on some ideas," the woman said. "But if I can make a suggestion? Why don't you go get your hair done. You're not making the best of yourself, and competition is fierce out there, even for a girl who's achieved as much as you have."

Yael stared after her with a slack jaw and raised eyebrows. She ran her hands through her mop of unruly curls and once again thought, *He'll take me the way I am or not at all.*

After the woman had gone, Yael grabbed a bunch of the nearest and probably priciest ready meals on the shelf. She'd freeze most of them, and be sorted for weeks. She had work to do that did not involve getting paid by others, or cooking. She was going to find out the truth about her father. Whatever it was, it couldn't be as bad as not knowing.

CHAPTER 2

NOW THAT YAEL had this mission in life, she could honestly not understand why it had taken her so long to begin to wonder about her father. All her formative years, and indeed her young-adult years, he had been so far out of her realm of interest that he might as well never have existed. And now she was borderline obsessed with the prospect of her journey of discovery.

Was it only *shidduchim*, or the lack of, in her life that had kindled this intense interest? Or was this foundling finally, albeit rather late, fascinated by her biological roots and what had made her the way she was? She had been so unlike her foster family, and had fit in there so badly that eventually they had thrown her out. She was very dissimilar to pretty much all her friends too. They put her differences and daredevil nature down to endearing eccentricities and loved her for it, but sometimes now, in the dead of night as she lay awake wondering about the origins of her genetic makeup, she wondered how she could be so very different from just about everyone she knew.

She hadn't actually met her mother, but had tracked her down in America and had spoken to her on the phone, and could not understand her personality either. To finally find a long-lost daughter, and to so comprehensively reject her out of hand, was to Yael beyond all reasonable behavior. Mind you, she herself had very lukewarm feelings toward the trafficked babies in her most recent case. But perhaps Yael was so super-duper extraordinary that how could anyone *not* want to get to know her?

So if she wasn't like her mother, and wasn't like any so-called normal, regular person of her acquaintance, there was only one possible alternative.

She must be an absolute chip off the old paternal block.

This made her father, instead of a shadowy figure she had very little interest in ever finding out about, the core of her curiosity and fascination. He had to be the person who had shaped her personality. As such he had to be someone very special.

Of course, being as he was probably dead, it made it a little more difficult to assess his character—but someone, somewhere out there, had to know what he was like. And wasn't she, Yael Reed, the private investigator par excellence who had solved mysteries that had baffled even the most brilliant of detectives?

Well, maybe that was somewhat of an exaggeration, but now that she was deeply involved in her own personal mystery, she had far more reason to find out the truth. He wasn't some random stranger she was investigating. He was her flesh and blood, part of the reason she was on this earth.

In the cold light of day, Yael sat at her office desk, fiddling with the mouse and checking her e-mails, and wondering how to go about this search. As usual, she decided to consult her guru, Colin Sommers, the top detective now after having worked several cases together—albeit he and his wife Leora had been extremely exasperated by Yael's reluctance to listen to sensible caution when going on one of her daredevil missions.

She called Colin at work. He was out on a case. Well, why should he be sitting twiddling his thumbs waiting for her to call? She called Leora at home. Same result; she was in Lambeth, home to the Forensic Science Laboratories.

Yael sat and thought about what to do next.

Since she had managed to at least partially ingratiate herself with Colin, aka the cops, she had been granted access to certain databases not available to the general public. She decided to start the search there.

She realized that she had no idea even what her father's name was, but she did know what her mother's name was, and thought about calling her to ask about her father. But, as it was too early to call the US given the five-hour time difference, she'd have to do this on her own, at least for now.

The database listed Yael's mother as Elisheva Trent of Brooklyn, New York. Yael knew that already, so she delved deeper. Elisheva Trent was listed as having only one child, a girl, who certainly wasn't Yael. Had she successfully managed to wipe all traces of Yael's birth from her life? She needed another database, one that went further back in Elisheva Trent's life, to before she remarried whoever this Trent guy was.

Colin had a computer expert called Ho Kai Ming, a talented Chinese man who had been involved in many of Colin's cases before Yael had gotten involved, but she had met him, and admired him a lot. He'd been the subject of false accusations in the past, had had to leave his post in London and move to Milton Keynes for a while, where Colin and Leora reconnected with him for the case of Carers Ltd., but now had been fully exonerated and decorated with honors for his work for the Metropolitan Police.

Ho Kai was now in charge of a whole team of computer techies and ran the police databases with fantastic skill. He, in turn, admired the feistiness and determination of Colin's recalcitrant new "trainee"; it was so much like his own. He'd made the (possibly hasty) decision to give Yael his cell phone number so she wouldn't have to go past the dragon lady on the switchboard. It was this number that Yael now called.

Ho Kai was delighted to hear from Yael. She'd never abused his trust in her in giving her his private number; indeed this was the first time she'd called. After discussing niceties, she honed in on the purpose of her call.

"I thought Jewish young ladies liked to get married young," Ho Kai commented, after hearing about why she wanted to find out about her past. "Me, I only got married at thirty. My wife was twenty-eight."

"Seems like I'm heading in the same direction," Yael said cheerfully. "Maybe I was meant to be Chinese. Anyway, who'd have me? I'm much too high maintenance."

"You have to find a Jewish boy with a bit of fire in his soul. A bit like Colin and Leora, really. They're both very fiery people."

"Yeah, and not so many of those around. That's why I'm calling. The matchmakers in our culture, they like to know about a client's background. As you might know, my background is shrouded in mystery, and that's not helping me get a suitable match. I need to find out about my father, Ho Kai, and my database stops dead at my mother's second marriage. She's called Elisheva Trent and she lives in Brooklyn. I need to find out about her first marriage. I don't even know my father's name. I was called Reed after my foster parents."

She heard Ho Kai let out a long breath. She held her own breath, hoping this wasn't going to be a no.

"Yael Reed, you certainly know how to give someone a challenge," he said at last. But there was a smile in his voice and she released her breath in a sigh of relief.

"So you'll help me?" she asked.

"Of course I will. I'm as curious as you are to find out who made you so crazy anyway! It should be interesting, finding out about your father and maybe even meeting him."

"Be warned," Yael said. "To all accounts, he's dead. Hit-and-run. No idea when. My mother, when I tracked her down, was, shall we say…less than communicative on all fronts, didn't want to know me. So I wasn't able to ask her anything about him."

"Ah," Ho Kai said. "But you have no documentation to prove it one way or the other, right?"

"Right."

She could hear him tapping on his computer in the background.

"Leave the database search with me," he said. "Alive or dead, I'll find him. Even dead men leave trails. But you're not just going to sit back and leave *everything* to me, I hope, are you?"

"I thought you said…?" Yael was puzzled.

"I said I'd do the database. But I want you to phone your mother and try and persuade her to give you whatever knowledge she has. After all, it'll make life so much easier than just fumbling around in the dark. She was married to him, after all. Presumably she knows his name and what happened to him!"

Yael knew when she was cornered. Her reluctance to repeat the distressing phone call to her mother was acute, but Ho Kai was right. She couldn't expect him to do all the groundwork and her to just sit back and wait for results.

She waited until it was about eight in the morning in Brooklyn and then put in the call. Her hands were trembling and her palms were damp.

Her half-sister answered the phone. Yael decided not to identify herself to the girl, who obviously didn't know of her existence, but just asked to speak to Elisheva Trent. The girl bellowed, "Mom, it's for you! ... No, I don't know who it is!" and Yael heard the handset being banged down. She waited for what seemed like an interminable time, irritated by the mounting costs, before her mother finally came on the phone.

If there was one good thing about the ensuing exchange, it was that it hardly added to the cost of the call. Yael explained her mission, and hoped maybe the off chance of her mother being pleased that her long-lost daughter might get married as a result of her information might soften her toward Yael.

"If you think I'm gonna give you information about that no-good so-and-so, you've got another thing coming!" she said in a perfectly adopted Brooklyn drawl. "You're best off forgetting you ever had a father, take it from me!"

Wow, Yael thought, *when did you learn to speak Americanese? You had a British accent last time we spoke. I'm guessing you're immersing in the culture...*

"I don't want to get to know him," Yael protested untruthfully. "I just need to know about my roots. You know, for *shidduch* purposes. Surely, as my mother, you owe me that much?"

"Like I told you last time you called," Elisheva Trent said harshly, "I don't owe you nothing, and I don't want you to call me again. But I'll tell you this for nothing, and it's the last motherly thing I'm gonna do for you. After this I'm gonna hang up and I don't ever wanna hear from you again, d'hear? Don't go nosing around into your father's past. Some things are best off buried forever. You might not like what you find."

CHAPTER 3

YAEL PUT THE phone down slowly; her ear was still ringing from the force of her mother's hang-up.

"Don't go nosing around into your father's past. Some things are best off buried forever. You might not like what you find."

Buried forever? Did that mean her father was definitely dead? Or that what he was, or what he had done, was best not looked into? It was all so ambiguous. *You might not like what you find.* Yael imagined the worst-case scenario—that her father was a hardened criminal. She couldn't envisage he would be, but she tried to make herself believe it for a minute.

Then she wondered if she'd rather know or not know. If that unlikely scenario was true, she'd probably be destined for eternal spinsterhood. Having that on her resume wouldn't do her *shidduch* chances with Rebbetzin Hoff any good. She couldn't see anyone, anywhere, writing that one off as, "Oh well, never mind, it's the quality of the girl herself that matters."

If it was true, wouldn't it come out one way or the other eventually? And if she was already married when the awful truth about her father came out, would her husband, however adoring, stick by her? She doubted it somehow.

So, Yael concluded to herself, it had to be better to know than not to know, no matter how horrible the truth proved to be. And her mother telling her to keep her nose out of it just made her all the more determined to find out everything and anything she could.

She called Ho Kai back with the summary of her phone call. Ho Kai sighed.

"Shame," he said. "I mean, I didn't have the greatest mother in the world, but I doubt she'd have been quite *that* bad. And it doesn't sound as if your dad was up to much either."

"Yeah, seems I drew the short straw when they were handing out parents," Yael said, trying to sound cheerful, while wiping big self-pitying tears away from her cheeks. She didn't often feel sorry for herself, but on this occasion she made an exception. She was feeling relentlessly, mercilessly sorry for herself.

"So will you help me now, please, Ho Kai?" she asked, and despite her best attempts, he could hear the tears in her voice.

"I will help you," he assured her. "But you're prepared not to like what I find, right?"

"I've prepared myself for my father to be a hardened criminal. So anything better than that will be a plus," she replied. Yael tried sounding brave, while inwardly quaking at the prospect of uncovering dark secrets of her paternal past.

"I'll keep you as updated as I can so the news can be absorbed gently," Ho Kai said. "But again, I'm not going to do all the work for you."

"I understand," Yael said. "And thank you."

By those words, it was understood between them that he would do the job as a favor to her; no money would change hands. His time was immensely precious and Yael knew it, but Ho Kai wanted to help her so he'd stay late, pull all-nighters if he had to until he found out what he could.

Yael Reed was not normally one to sit back and let others do her work for her. If she was on a case, she got involved to the point of ridiculousness—as previous cases, and Colin and Leora Sommers' extreme exasperation with her, went to prove. She could never just "keep out of it and let the police do their job," like Colin had insisted. But somehow, when it came to her own father, with her mother's unpleasant rejection and nasty words pounding in her ears, she felt like *anyone* other than herself could do the job better than she.

Sitting the following morning at her desk, contemplating her work schedule (temporarily blank) and drinking tea, she fought against this feeling of apathy. It was *so* not Yael Reed.

Her phone chirped. It was Ho Kai with the first bit of information he had managed to dig up.

"Your parents had gotten divorced before the hit-and-run happened," he told her.

"Oh!" Yael said, wondering whether to be surprised. "That no-good so-and-so" was hardly the affectionate expression of an ex-wife who had managed to stay civil. "So do you have a name for him?"

"Yes. His name was Alan Katz."

She breathed. Alan Katz. So her birth name was Katz. She rolled the name around her head trying to make it sound familiar, but it didn't. She was Reed, always had been, even though the Reeds had kicked her out in the end.

"Okay, Alan Katz. It's a common name, which makes it somewhat difficult to research, but I can try. Do you maybe have a date for his death? I might be able to do some investigating on my own if I have that."

"That's where it gets a little weird," Ho Kai said. "According to this database, I have two death certificates for a Mr. Alan Katz, fourteen and a half years ago. But not the same date, and not the same cause of death either."

"Well, with a common name like Alan Katz," Yael surmised, "one of them at least needn't have been my father, no?" Her head was beginning to hurt.

"That's what I thought," Ho Kai agreed. "This is what I've got: two Alan Katzes dying on two different dates, in the same month, of the same year. And living in the same country too."

"Oh?" Yael had forgotten to ask about her father's geographical origin. She'd just assumed it would be London for some reason.

"Yes. Apparently your father lived, and died, in Jerusalem. That's what has made it difficult for me to find things out about him. I had to plunder the international databases."

"He was Israeli?" Yael asked, shocked. She'd had very little to do with Israel. It was, to her, just an amazing place somewhere she had to visit one day, but she'd never thought of her roots coming from it. She was very rooted in the UK, mostly to do with financial restrictions.

"I haven't found a birth certificate for him yet," Ho Kai said, "so I'm not sure where he was born, but he certainly spent some time in Israel, even if it was only a few months or a year. I seem to remember Colin telling me that Jewish young men often go there to study religious things in Israel for a while. Yesheeevah or something?"

"Yes, yeshivah. So he went to a yeshivah in Israel, possibly. And married my mother and died in Israel. But I was born in the UK. It doesn't make sense."

"That's all I've managed to find out for now. Here are the two dates." Yael wrote them down. "Now I have work to do. The kind that pays my bills."

Foundling 19

Yael was instantly contrite. "Go, go, thanks so much. You've been amazing and given me a lot to think about. I'll see what I can find out from here."

"I'll see if I can dig up a birth certificate, when I have some free time," Ho Kai said with emphasis on the last phrase, and disconnected.

Israel. Yael's father had lived and died there.

A hit-and-run would surely make the newspapers, even in a country with as bad a reputation for its driving as Israel. Traffic accidents were one thing, but a hit-and-run took callousness to a whole new level.

Yael got up from her desk and lifted her handbag. She was going to do some research at the Newspaper Library in Colindale. It had copies of every newspaper published anywhere in the world.

She was going to find the report on the hit-and-run.

CHAPTER 4

THE NEWSPAPER LIBRARY at Colindale, a neighborhood close to Golders Green but not an enclave of Orthodox Jewish life, was something Yael had heard about but had never visited. So imagine her disappointment when she discovered it had permanently closed in 2013. Luckily she had researched it before setting out for this famed archive. She stared at her screen.

"British Library Newspapers at Colindale closed in November 2013 and the print newspapers were moved to the new Newspaper Storage Building at Boston Spa, West Yorkshire, while the newspaper microfilm collection was moved to the British Library's St. Pancras site. A full newspaper service is now available via the British Library Newsroom at St. Pancras."

"Drat," Yael said aloud, then leaned back and put her hands behind her head, thinking. There was no way she was going to West Yorkshire, but St. Pancras was just a subway ride away in the center of London. Colindale would have been a subway ride away, only more local. She didn't need the original print versions anyway, just the microfilm would do. She could get photocopies of the microfilm papers if she found anything.

Fired up with enthusiasm as she was, it had to be that day. She looked at her work schedule. Since the babies case, Yael had never been without work, but it was still slow and unexciting even though it paid the bills. The upside of this was that there was nothing on her books that couldn't wait a day.

She e-mailed Ho Kai and told him what her plans were. He approved. "The newspaper reports of the hit-and-run should be very useful in identifying what happened," he said. "But it'll probably just be in a Jerusalem or Israeli paper, and possibly not in English. How's your Hebrew?"

"Terrible to nonexistent," Yael replied honestly. "Let's hope there's an English-language report, otherwise I'll be lost."

Ho Kai tutted. "You English and your inability to speak any languages," he said. It seemed a particularly British failing; probably due to the colonization of half the world, therefore expecting everyone to speak English rather than learning the indigenous language. "We Asians wouldn't have gotten half as far as we have in the world, if we'd expected everyone to speak Mandarin."

"You do speak an excellent English," Yael conceded.

"And Hebrew is meant to be *your* language too," Ho Kai said, rubbing salt into the already embarrassingly open wound. Yael winced obligingly and made some kind of empty promise to try and better her knowledge of the Hebrew language. Little did she know how soon this promise would be needed in fulfillment.

Yael didn't much care for the London subway system, better known as the "Tube" by locals. It was crowded, claustrophobic, and not very well ventilated, to put it mildly. She liked the buses better. At least on a bus she had a view of the outside world. But she had to admit, with London traffic the way it was, congested and slow, the Tube made more sense, even if she did have to strap-hang the entire way to Kings Cross/St. Pancras. From Golders Green it was a direct line; no changes necessary. So she took her e-reader and jogged to the Tube station at Golders Green, only a short walk from her apartment facing Golders Hill Park.

Emerging at Kings Cross/St. Pancras into bright sunshine, but wet pavements from a recent shower, she asked around where the British Library Newsroom was, and jogged there. Asking for help from the information desk, she was informed that in order to use their facilities she'd need a reader's pass.

The bespectacled woman at the issue desk frowned at Yael over her glasses. "I'm sorry," she said, "we don't issue reader's passes to anyone under the age of eighteen."

Yael frowned back. "I suppose one day I'll find that flattering, but right now it's just tiresome and annoying," she said. "I'm twenty-one."

Surprised, the woman smiled at Yael, transforming her face from stern to pleasant. "Believe me, my girl, you *will* find that flattering, sooner than you think. Show me some ID and proof of your address, please."

Yael produced her PI license, which had both her date of birth and address on it. The woman scrutinized it and looked up at her.

"A private investigator at such a young age!" she said. "Most impressive! So you need to research here for a case, I presume?"

"Actually, this is personal," Yael admitted.

With her reader's pass proudly in her possession, she went to sit down at one of the many desks, to access the vast database of over sixty million newspapers printed since the 1600s.

"Sixty million." Yael sighed, opening up a *How to Research Newspapers* help guide. "Talk about needles and haystacks." The guide told her that the library did not index articles by subject matter, so the researcher should have come with a lot of information already at her fingertips, like the probable date of the article and which newspaper it was likely to have appeared in.

Yael felt despair at this. She had the two possible dates of Alan Katz's death, whichever Alan Katz it was, but she had no idea which newspaper. She didn't even know the names of any newspapers in Israel. She should definitely have done more research.

However, she was resourceful and determined. She called her friend Rosie Gutstein, and in a library-style whisper asked her what newspapers she could think of that were published in Israel.

"*Frum* or secular?" Rosie whispered back. She wasn't sure why she was whispering; she was pretty sure no one in the British Library could overhear even if she talked at full volume, it was just instinctive to do so.

"No idea," Yael whispered. "Not sure this place archives *frum* newspapers, so you better just give me the most likely general one. Or maybe give me the name of a *frum* one just so I can see if they do have it."

It quickly became clear that *frum* weekly newspapers were not held by the library, but it did hold *The Jerusalem Post*, and some Hebrew-language papers. Yael decided to research *The Jerusalem Post* for the dates on or shortly after Alan Katz's hit-and-run.

Or his death due to an asthma attack.

Depending on which report one believed.

Both in the same month. Both in Jerusalem.

Well, an asthma attack would hardly make the news, but a hit-and-run might. So she'd better concentrate on that.

So she started looking up *The Jerusalem Post* from fourteen and a half years before. It was the usual diet of Israeli politics, foreign news, and sport, interspersed with terrorist attacks that made Yael sigh with despair.

She quickly realized that if there was going to be a report, it would be on the first three pages. That speeded up the reading to breakneck rates. She read through so many papers in microfilm format that her eyes were beginning to hurt and run with tears. She had serious doubts whether she'd spot any relevant articles.

It was a fruitless task. It wasn't in there.

And then, suddenly, it was.

CHAPTER 5

AN ENGLISH-LANGUAGE ISRAELI newspaper of the right timeline ran a story on page three that stated: "Jerusalem resident mown down by out-of-control teenage driver." That was the headline. The story went:

Alan Katz, forty, of Ramat Eshkol, was run over and killed by a hit-and-run driver as he crossed the Golda Meir Boulevard at Sanhedria last night. Witnesses reported the driver of the car, a Mazda, appeared to be a teenager on a joyride. There were several more teenagers in the car with him and loud music was blaring from the open windows. After the victim was hit, the car swerved around him and made off at speed toward the Tel Aviv turnoff.

No one managed to get the license number as witnesses said the car was so filthy from a recent dust storm that the plate was illegible. Said Yehuda Brief from Ezras Torah district, "I can't help wondering if the joyriders deliberately covered the license plate with dust or grime so they shouldn't be apprehended. Hatzalah and MDA came to the man's aid quickly, and we saw him taken off in an ambulance, but I guess it wasn't quickly enough."

We are happy to take part in a campaign to track down the perpetrators of this horrible hit-and-run. Any information that will help achieve this could lead to a reward of ten thousand shekels, which has been raised by distraught neighbors of the deceased.

Yael read this over and over. There was so much in this report that was meaningless to her. The streets and areas of Jerusalem mentioned—she'd heard of none of them. Not that this was surprising; the only area of Jerusalem she had heard of was the Old City and the Kosel. What was MDA? She knew what Hatzalah was because it existed all over the world. She searched for MDA, and after a lot of false leads, added "Israel" to the search, and it came straight back: MDA—Magen David Adom. The Red Magen David, equivalent to the Red Cross ambulance service in the UK. Ah, that made sense.

Yael sat and looked at the report and thought about what to do next. Then she went to the front desk and asked for a printout and a copy. This duly done, and the printout safely stashed in her bag, she did a search on "Alan Katz Jerusalem," but only the same article kept coming up. It seemed that was the only report of the hit-and-run.

But she had something to go on—witnesses, one even named. With that she could look up police reports, or get Ho Kai to do so.

She needed to find out more. And she couldn't do that sitting in London.

Slowly the idea was galvanizing in her brain. *I need to go to Jerusalem to find out what happened to my father.*

Yael Reed had never, in the twenty-one years of her life, as much as traveled to Wales, Scotland, or Ireland, let alone France or anywhere "really abroad." She didn't even own a passport. Thinking about that fact now, as a Brit living on a small island, it seemed silly that she had never gotten around to getting a passport. It was just that she had never needed one.

I might have been asked to go abroad on a shidduch, she scolded herself, *and had the chance slip away from me because I had no passport. This is really stupid. I must get one, and ASAP.*

She would set the wheels for that in motion. But while that was happening, she had "eyes on the ground" in Israel who might be able to help her. Nena and Shuli, both newlyweds, both living in Jerusalem—although Yael had no idea what area—and both, Yael presumed naively, probably bored out of their wits as they had no kids yet, so what on earth could they be doing all day? Just waiting for their husbands to come home for lunch and dinner? Yael had no doubt they'd have acres of spare time to help her investigate this matter.

She left the British Library and took the Tube back home. It was the middle of the day, so out of the rush hour, and quieter, and she actually got to sit down for the entire journey. At Golders Green Station she jogged back to her office, sat down at her desk, and switched on her computer.

Then, ignoring her PC, she looked up the phone numbers of her two friends and put in a call to Nena first. Nena had always been slightly more sympathetic than the tough-as-nails Shuli. Shuli, due to being largely neglected as a child and teen by her outreach-working, globetrotting parents, had built a protective wall around herself so that no one could hurt her the way they had. Nena was the only one of the quartet of friends who came from a stable home environment, even though she'd had her own issues, being in the Witness Protection Program at one time.

"What a messed-up bunch of girls we are, to be sure," Yael said to herself as she waited for the call to Nena to go through. "Rosie with her broken home, Nena having witnessed a murder, Shuli with no homelife, and me, with no life altogether!"

Nena finally picked up the phone. She sounded somewhat harassed, but also pleased to hear from her old school friend.

"Yael Reed! Talk about *techiyas hameisim*! I haven't heard from you in years! You didn't come to my wedding." This last part was said in accusatory tones. Yael blushed. Nena's wedding had been in Israel, due partly to the Witness Protection issue, and partly as it was cheaper, especially as her new husband was an Anglo-Israeli, born of British *olim* but himself a sabra.

"I know, Nena, and I'm so sorry, but I don't have a passport, and I couldn't have afforded to fly to Israel for a wedding even if I'd had one."

Nena was instantly contrite. "Oh, of course, how insensitive of me. I didn't think that you wouldn't have a passport. I thought only Americans were so insular that they thought the world began and ended on their coastlines. We Brits live on such a small island, I'd have thought everyone had a passport."

"I'll probably have to get one, and sharpish," Yael said. "Which is the purpose of the call, really. Nena, until I get a passport and probably come out to Israel, how do you feel about me appointing you as deputy PI for me out there? Fancy doing some investigating for me in your spare time?" Thankfully, Yael didn't add "I'm sure you have plenty of spare time" because Nena sounded frazzled at the idea.

"Oh, Yael, I don't know… I'm so busy, I barely have a second to spare. Yitzy comes home from *kollel* for lunch every day, and it's the main meal of the day here, so I have to cook him a proper meal. That means I have to shop and cook in the morning. And clean the apartment. And do the laundry. And I don't drive, so everything has to be schlepped home on the bus in my folding cart. It's quite stressful. Then in the evenings I'm trying to earn some money to support us by editing some technical papers for someone. I collapse into bed around one, and get up at seven to make Yitzy breakfast, and it starts all over again…"

Yael was silent for a moment. Then she said, "You have to clean your apartment and do laundry every single day? You have absolutely no spare time?"

Nena paused, too, and then said, "I'm not doing anything harebrained or dangerous, Yael. I know what your cases are like and I don't want to get involved in anything like that."

"No, no, it's not really a case. It's about me finding my father."

Yael filled her friend in on why she had embarked on this mission and what she had achieved so far. Nena drew in a sharp breath and let it out in a long sigh.

"I'm so pleased you're finally taking *shidduchim* seriously, Yael," she said. "Before you were like, 'Take me as I am or else.' Which isn't a very helpful attitude."

"Oh," Yael said cheerfully. "I'm still like that. But according to Rebbetzin Hoff, I need to know my *yichus*, terrible though it is. I have to find out what happened to my father or the whole shebang isn't ever leaving the starting gate."

"So what do you want me to do?" Nena asked, with a sinking feeling that she was probably going to regret this question.

"Thing is," Yael said in a businesslike tone, "I don't know any areas mentioned in the newspaper report; they're all meaningless to me. But there was one witness to the hit-and-run mentioned by name, and he's from Ezras Torah."

"Ezras Torah is just across Golda Meir Boulevard from me," Nena said. "I live in Ramat Eshkol."

"You do?" Yael asked excitedly. "That was where the Alan Katz mentioned in the report was from."

"Interesting," Nena said.

"Ideally I'd like you to try and find this named witness, see what he knows, whether he can fill in any blanks. That's all."

"I can try," Nena said. "Although a lot of people live in Ezras Torah. What's his name?"

Yael consulted her printout. "Yehuda Brief."

"You're kidding me," Nena said. "You have to be kidding."

"Why?" Yael asked. "Do you already know him?"

"I'll say I know him," Nena said. "I'm Nena Brief now. Yehuda Brief is my father-in-law."

CHAPTER 6

IF IT'S THE right Yehuda Brief, that is," qualified Nena. "It can't be such an uncommon name in Ezras Torah. Or indeed anywhere in the Jewish world."

"I wouldn't know, as I know nothing about Ezras Torah," replied Yael, stunned at the news. "I mean, what a coincidence! And I don't believe in coincidences. Maybe the whole reason you came into my life when we were fourteen, became my friend, and married Yehuda Brief's son was so that I could find out what happened to my father one day in the future! Imagine that!"

"Yes, imagine that!" Nena said drily. This conversation was taking somewhat of a ludicrous turn, so Nena tried to turn it back into logical sequence. Her friend was obviously getting carried away and Nena suddenly really wanted to get off the hook and get on with her household chores. She glanced at her watch and had a mild attack of panic. "Look, Yael, as I said, I don't really have time, and to be honest, nor the inclination, to be your PI agent in Israel. I'm sorry, but I don't. You enjoy running around solving mysteries; I'd rather stay home safe and sound, and curl up with a good book if I ever had a spare moment. But what I can do is speak to my father-in-law, or maybe to Yitzy and find out if he remembers his father commenting on that hit-and-run. He'd have been only about nine years old, so it's kind of a long shot."

"Then don't bother talking to Yitzy about this," Yael said, undaunted. "Much as I'm sure he's an excellent husband and has made you very happy, he's undoubtedly useless for this purpose. Cut out the middleman and go straight to source. Speak to your father-in-law."

Nena sighed. There was no getting off this particular hook, at least not without doing this small favor for an old friend.

"Okay, I'll speak to my father-in-law."

"Can I call you back tonight and you'll have an answer?" Yael asked enthusiastically.

"Tonight? Gosh, Yael, you don't give a girl much of a break, do you?"

"Every minute wasted means I'm getting closer to twenty-two," Yael said with devastating logic.

"I'll try and call him at lunchtime. If not, this evening. Don't call me before nine thirty my time. That's seven thirty back in England, I think. Unless the clocks have gone back or forward or whatever they do, annoyingly, every now and then and confuse us all."

"Yes, it's two hours' difference. I'll call you at seven thirty on the dot. Bye, Nena, and thanks so, so much!"

The call was disconnected with Nena left feeling somehow she'd been bamboozled into doing something she hadn't really wanted to do. It was a small enough favor, looking at it from the outside. But with Yael Reed, nothing was ever what it seemed on the surface, and Nena had the feeling she had no idea what she was getting herself into.

Seven thirty was an age away and Yael was restless, so she called Ho Kai Ming—who sounded somewhat fed up with the constant disturbance to his real, aka paid-for, work. Yael felt embarrassed and worried that she was at risk of ruining a very useful contact by overuse.

"I'm really sorry for disturbing you," she said hastily. "Forget I called."

She expected Ho Kai to say, "No, no, it's okay. What did you call about?" Instead he said, "Okay, bye," and hung up, leaving Yael staring at her phone and wondering why anyone wouldn't be as excited as she was by the progress she was making. What kind of amazing coincidence was it that Nena was the daughter-in-law of the only recorded witness to her father's hit-and-run?

"Ho Kai must be really busy," Yael told herself sternly, and tried not to mind the abrupt disconnection too much.

NENA THOUGHT ABOUT THE IMPLICATIONS of Yael's request. A simple phone call to her father-in-law asking him about that newspaper report almost fifteen years ago. Nothing too taxing there. You'd think.

But Nena knew that anything with Yael's involvement was never simple. Much as she loved her old school friend, she'd been following her career and knew what scrapes she'd gotten into. She trembled as she picked up the phone at lunchtime, wondering what she was going to unleash.

Nena had never really hit it off with her father-in-law, which was another reason for her reluctance. The *shidduch* between her and Yitzy had progressed smoothly enough, but it hadn't been without its side issues—her having been in the Witness Protection Program being the main one. Why would a boy want a girl with even the slightest shadow on her past, when he could take a girl with an unblemished reputation and an innocent upbringing?

Having witnessed a murder between two members of the Russian Mafia when she was fourteen was hardly a shining star to add to her resume, and Nena knew it. Yehuda Brief and his wife, Esther, had made quite a song and dance about it when the *shidduch* had come up. But they'd reckoned without the enthusiastic response from their son Yitzy, who understood perfectly that the whole incident had been none of Nena's fault, and added to her fascination as a potential life partner. However, his parents' negativity had lingered and persisted into the marriage, making them regard their new daughter-in-law with suspicion and wariness. And making it hard for Nena to feel at home with them too.

Nena sighed as she dialed her father-in-law. *Yael Reed, Yael Reed*, she thought, *what are we going to do about you?*

"Hello, Nena, how are you?" came Yehuda Brief's wary voice. He never sounded pleased to hear from her; he was always probably on his guard that her past could resurface at any time and bite the whole family where it hurt most.

"I'm fine, thanks, Dad. No worries here," Nena was quick to reassure him. She knew he wasn't asking after her health. She could almost hear her father-in-law relax.

"So, what's doing? I have to go to the office soon." Brief had successfully managed to establish a work-learn balance that enabled him to sit in *kollel* all morning and run a thriving business in the afternoon. As a workaholic in both fields, he didn't believe in small talk. Time was money, and time was his bank up on High as well.

Nena explained her quest in as short a paragraph as she could muster. When talking to him, she had mastered the art of the no-schmooze way of putting things—just getting to the point as quickly as possible. She likened it, in her head, to being on a phone-in radio show where the presenter would cut you off before you'd even made your point, if you waffled on too long. She told him about Yael, and her search for her father, whom she believed had been the victim of the hit-and-run he had witnessed almost fifteen years previously. And that Yael would like to talk to him about it if possible.

Then she stopped, conscious that she had probably overrun her thirty seconds of allocated "radio phone-in" time.

There was a silence on the other end of the phone. It stretched out to the point where Nena wondered if her father-in-law had heard anything she had said to him. Maybe she'd been talking to dead air and the connection had been cut sometime during her thirty seconds.

"Dad?" she said at last. "Are you there? Did you hear what I asked?"

"I heard," he said.

"And?" she asked, breathless with nerves. The tone of his voice had not been at all friendly. Indeed, it was as hostile a response as she had ever heard from him.

"Tell your friend," Brief said in slow, measured tones that sent a chill down Nena's spine and a flush of heat to her face, "that I never witnessed any hit-and-run. I never spoke to any reporter in *The Jerusalem Post*. As far as she and I are concerned, the matter is closed, and I do not want to discuss it ever again."

This time the connection really was severed. Nena's phone showed the home screen.

She stood there looking at her phone, trembling in shock and humiliation. Despite what her father-in-law had just said to her, there was one thing very clear in her mind.

He was not telling her the truth. *Something* had happened almost fifteen years ago; she was almost certain now, that he, Yehuda Brief, was involved in it up to his neck.

CHAPTER 7

NENA SAT TREMBLING for a long time. Her brain was whirling with all the implications the phone call had brought up.

That her father-in-law wasn't Mr. Perfection.

How could that be? Yitzy, her husband, was such a great guy, and he had such high regard for his father. Always showed him the greatest respect and spoke warmly of him to Nena; something she had found a little hard to swallow, especially as Yehuda Brief hadn't shown his new daughter-in-law the same warmth when she'd come onto the scene. She'd tried her best to see the side of him that Yitzy saw, but all she perceived was a cold, blank wall when she made her friendly approaches to him.

Nena had no mother-in-law issues with Esther Brief. Indeed, she barely knew her. Her mother-in-law was a meek woman, totally overshadowed by her domineering husband. She just sat on the sidelines, listening to her husband holding forth on this or that topic, as was his wont; when something needed saying, Yehuda Brief said it, at length. When she wasn't trying to placate her husband, Esther was serving meals almost in silence.

Her children, Yitzy included, showed her the respect and love she deserved, as they should have, but Nena sometimes wondered how such well-adjusted children had emerged from such a strange combination of parents. Maybe the balance between too much personality and too little had resulted in "just right" children. Nena certainly thought Yitzy was "just right"; she couldn't believe her own luck at having landed such a perfect husband.

Nena's thoughts continued to tumble around her head. If her father-in-law had something in his past he'd rather keep hidden, didn't that make him not that different to Nena herself? Nena had been the innocent witness to a horrible crime, and had been seen witnessing it, putting her own life at considerable risk. From the reaction Nena had heard Brief give to her questions, she wondered if his involvement in the crime was not totally innocent.

And maybe that was why he had those negative feelings about his daughter-in-law.

She couldn't quite work out the progression of his thoughts in this matter, but if that was why he'd never taken to her, it made some kind of twisted sense. To him if not to her.

One thing Nena was sure about—she had to speak to Yael *now*. There was no way she was waiting until the evening. Not with this sitting on her head like an elephant.

As she waited for the connection to happen, she worried about how she was going to put it to her friend without it coming over like *lashon hora* or *motzi shem ra* on her father-in-law. After all, she had no real proof of anything. Just a very real and disturbing sense of foreboding.

Yael had not been expecting Nena to call her back. She had her eye on the clock, waiting for it to be seven thirty. The routine work she was doing barely touched the sides of her consciousness even though she knew it was wrong to be so distracted. This mundane work paid the bills, and the quest for news of her father would not. She felt guilty for not giving it her full attention, but this was Yael Reed on a mission. Once she became obsessed with something, she thought of little else until it was solved.

So when the phone rang, she even thought of not answering it at first, thinking it was probably someone trying to sell her insurance. But then, glancing at the caller ID, she stopped in her tracks and snatched it up.

"Nena?"

"Yes, it's me. Can you talk?"

"Sure I can, I just hadn't expected…"

"Nor did I, I can assure you," Nena said in such a meaningful tone that Yael's heart started pounding.

"Have you found my father?" Yael just had to know upfront if this was the reason for this precipitous phone call.

"No, no, nothing like that, I'm afraid," Nena said guiltily, realizing what the other young woman must have been thinking and that she had led her along the wrong path.

"Oh." Yael's voice drooped in disappointment.

"I'm sorry, Yael. But something weird has happened, and I didn't want to wait until this evening to tell you." At this point in the phone call, Nena still had no idea how she was going to shape the words. She just prayed for Divine guidance.

"Go on," Yael said in a slow voice, even though inside she was burning with impatience. "You spoke to your father-in-law, yes?"

"Um, yes, I did," Nena said, matching Yael's pace of voice, "but it didn't go exactly as planned."

"What do you mean?" Yael asked. "He wasn't the right Yehuda Brief, right? That must be it." She laughed in a high voice, panic overtaking her. Nena's father-in-law not being the right person was the best-case scenario that she could think of, so she hoped against hope that was it. Nena's next words dashed that hope.

"No, that wasn't it. He was the right person. It's just that...his reaction wasn't what I'd expected."

"What do you mean, exactly?"

Divine guidance seemed to be hiding somewhere. Nena sought desperately for the right words and they eluded her.

"I don't know how to tell you this, Yael..." she began.

Yael took a deep breath. This was obviously going to be very bad news. She prepared herself to hear that her father was dead and the trail was cold. That there was nothing more to be done, nothing more to find out.

"Look, Nena, you and I have been friends a long time," Yael said, trying to control her rising panic, "so whatever you have to tell me, tell it to me fast. It'll be easier that way."

"It's not what you think," Nena said. "I have nothing bad to tell you about your father, except that I haven't been able to find anything out about him. But...well...my father-in-law...he..."

"He *what*?" Yael shrieked down the phone, relieved that there was no news about her father, good, bad, or indifferent, but something was still very, very wrong.

"He knows more than he's letting on," Nena said. "And it's put me in an impossible situation. You must understand that. I cannot possibly continue being your PI by proxy. I'm married to his son. We're very happy, and even though my in-laws and I don't really click, it hasn't affected our marriage, at least so far, thank G-d. But this situation, it's incendiary."

"Incendiary?" repeated Yael. It seemed a very strong word to use.

Nena said, "Yes, I don't think 'incendiary' is too strong a word to use in this context. I'm bowing out as of now, Yael. I'm really sorry, but there it is."

Yael was confused and hurt. Nena was letting her down, and badly.

"So you're just throwing in the towel and refusing to help me? What, at *all*?"

Nena sighed, hearing the hurt in her friend's voice, and said, "I think your best bet would be to come out here and deal with it yourself."

After the phone call Yael sat in shock for a few minutes, trying to assimilate the information, or rather lack of information, she'd been given. There was no doubt in her mind that she would have to fly to Israel.

She called Colin Sommers.

"Colin, can you help me get a passport quickly? I need to fly abroad. To Israel, actually."

"I don't work for the passport office, Yael," he said, sounding irritated.

"I know, but you can pull strings, I know you can," she said, undaunted.

And he could. With a sigh, Colin knew he was onto a loser trying to fight this with reason or expressions like "I have real work to do." He capitulated and told Yael what she had to do.

She had her photo taken in a local booth, dropped it in to him, and he pulled strings like he was running his own puppet theater.

Six hours later, Yael was holding her very own, very first biometric passport in her hands. She stared at it for a while, then booked the next day's flight to Ben Gurion.

CHAPTER 8

SHE WAS GOING abroad! For the first time in her life, Yael Reed was stepping off British soil and into the unknown! And not just any abroad, but Israel! She could hardly believe how excited she was. She had to temper this excitement in the crazy rush to get herself ready to leave the next day. The flight was in the afternoon, so no crack-of-dawn trip to the airport, but even so. So much to do, so little time to do it in!

First, she had to clear her calendar. She had no idea how long she'd be away. It could be a few days; it could be a few weeks. She e-mailed all her clients, apologizing and telling them that unforeseen circumstances meant she could not handle their cases for the next while. She knew she'd get a few snarky replies, and she did, but she tried to handle them as diplomatically as she could. Yael had *never* been off the radar before; she'd always been at her clients' fingertips, ready and willing to do whatever they wanted, whenever they wanted.

"Am I not allowed to go on holiday?" she asked herself angrily, as she tried to pour oil on yet more troubled waters with a response to another rude e-mail: "How could you go away *now*, in the middle of our case?" The case in question was not urgent, or Yael would have moved heaven and earth to try and sort it out, during the night if necessary. But as it could easily wait without the skies falling in, she didn't feel too guilty. Except for the shortness of notice, Yael felt perfectly within her rights to disappear for a week or two.

She did need every last one of her clients, good, bad, indifferent, and the users. They paid her bills and her rent, and put food on her table. She was going to Israel on the cheapest ticket she could find, and she planned to scrounge a bed at Nena's place if she had space, but it was still all expenses and no earnings at the end of it. So she'd have to eke out her money very carefully.

She called Nena and shamelessly begged to be allowed to stay. "You won't even know I'm there."

"How can I not know you're here?" Nena responded drily. "I have a two-bedroom apartment that's about eighty square meters altogether. One bathroom. We'll be falling over each other wherever we go. I'm not sure how Yitzy's going to take the idea of having another female in the house too. I'll have to ask him."

"I'll try and be out whenever he's home," Yael said.

"What, like all night?" Nena asked. Then she softened. "Look, I'm sure it'll be okay. I'm just not used to having house guests. It's our *shanah rishonah* and we're quite territorial about our privacy. I know you'll be out all the time; you're not coming to laze around my apartment, driving me nuts, that's for sure. And you're going to want to see a little of Jerusalem at the same time as looking for your father."

"A little of Jerusalem?" Yael shrieked. "I've never been abroad, and this is Israel! You won't see me for dust!"

"That's good," Nena said honestly. "I'll get you a Rav-Kav. It's like the Oyster card we used back in London; it'll allow you on the buses and trains."

"Thanks, that'll be great!" Yael said, then asked, "What's the weather like in November? I've got to know what to pack! Summer or winter?"

"Wet and cool," Nena said. "It's been pouring a lot recently. Our davening for rain over Sukkos must have really worked! You won't need much in the way of summer clothes, unless you go to Eilat." Yael, who had fondly imagined Israel as a place of permanent summer, and herself lying around a swimming pool somewhere, was rather disappointed at that news.

Apparently Yitzy capitulated as long as certain privacy and *yichud* elements were kept to. Yael now had a plane ticket and a place to stay. She quickly began packing.

She barely slept that night through excitement and worry about what she might be missing. "Passport, ticket, I have those. Israeli money...I don't have any of that. I'll change some at that change place along Golders Green Road opposite Kosher Kingdom," she told herself at around 2 a.m.

At three o'clock, after dozing a little, she sat bolt upright in bed. "How am I going to get to the airport?" Unable to sleep, she searched for directions and saw she could go by Tube. Okay, that would work, except she'd have to schlep all her stuff on the underground by herself. Luckily Yael lived very close to Golders Green Station. She could make it work. She'd have to.

At around three thirty Yael finally fell asleep. She awoke at eight o'clock, feeling like she hadn't slept at all. But adrenaline made up for the exhaustion. She got herself ready, finished off her packing, and took the bus down Golders Green Road to the change place, to change as little money as she could get away with. Then she stocked up with some food for the journey at Kosher Kingdom, and made her way back home to get her stuff and start her Heathrow Airport–bound journey.

"I'm going to give myself tons of spare time," she said as she locked up her apartment. Dragging her suitcase behind her, and hefting her knapsack onto her back, she set off for the Tube station. "I wouldn't want to miss my flight."

Yael had never been to Heathrow, or any airport. She'd considered flying easyJet from Luton, which would have worked out cheaper, but without transport, it was too difficult to get to.

When she arrived, she looked around and finally asked for help in finding the right check-in desk for El Al. Thrilled and excited, she joined the line at security, which wasn't very long yet as she'd arrived so early. She told anyone around her who would listen that this was her first trip to Israel—indeed, her first trip abroad. Yael was childlike in her wonder and awe at what was happening.

The security officer looked at her passport and ticket, then at her.

"It's new!" Yael said with a smile. "I just got it yesterday! I've never owned one before!"

The security officer did not smile back. Instead she said, "Wait here a minute, please," and went off to talk to a colleague.

Yael stood there, smiling and looking around her for confirmation that this was a normal thing to happen. Her fellow passengers did not smile back at her; they looked away and shuffled uncomfortably.

Yael stopped smiling.

Something was wrong. Had Colin messed up with her passport? Wasn't it valid?

The officer came back. Her expression was grave.

"I'm going to need you to come with me, please. We have some questions to ask you. A security issue has been flagged up."

Yael went with the officer, heart pounding, not understanding what was happening, but at the same time fully aware that everyone around her was looking at her thinking she was a terrorist.

CHAPTER 9

THE SECURITY OFFICER took Yael off to a side room. It seemed to Yael that she was deliberately going as slowly as possible. Yael was almost screaming with impatience by the time they closed the door behind her and bade her sit down.

Yael looked at her watch pointedly. The security officer ignored the gesture, sat down opposite her, and started shuffling papers with agonizing and painstaking slowness. Yael couldn't stop herself; she started shifting around on her chair and looking around the room to see if there was a clock (which there wasn't) that might tell a slightly less worrying time than the time her watch was telling her.

"Why do you want to go to Israel?" was the first question.

"Why not?" Yael said. "I'm Jewish, it's my country, and yours, presumably, so I want to go there. As it happens, I'm a private investigator, too, and I'm on a case."

The security officer scrutinized her closely after this remark. "Yes, I have details here that you are a private investigator. This has been flagged up by our security advisors as worrying. I do not think you need to do your investigating in Israel. Why do you need to be there?"

Yael was stunned by the direction this conversation was going. At no time did she even dream that her work as a PI would be an obstacle to her going to Israel. Surely there were other Jewish PIs who traveled safely to and from Israel without all this fuss?

"I'm looking for details about my father, who lived and died in Israel," she explained. She tried going into details about Nena and her father-in-law, but the officer didn't seem interested in the minutiae.

The officer interrupted Yael quite rudely and said, "I feel sure you can get someone in Israel to investigate your father's death for you. You do not need to go there personally."

"What if I just wanted to go there as a tourist?" Yael asked, getting angrier by the minute.

"I'm not comfortable that's all you'd do there," the security officer said. "I'm sorry, but we have to do some more investigations before we allow you to go there."

"But I'm missing my flight already!" Yael burst out, suddenly jumping up in agonized impatience. The woman's face was impassive.

"We've already taken your name off the flight list, pending further investigations," she said.

"You've what?!"

"You are not flying today. Go home."

"But I paid for my ticket! I can't afford to lose the money!" Yael cried stupidly.

"You'll be reimbursed for your ticket. In fact, it's already in your bank account," the officer said, peering at a computer screen. "Go home. You are not flying today."

Yael didn't cry very often, but this was an exception. This was way beyond any disaster that had ever befallen her, most of which were her own doing and therefore hers to fix. This one seemed to be so grossly unfair and unreasonable, and so not as a result of anything she had instigated, that she was left literally reeling with helplessness.

The entire way home on the underground, she sobbed unashamedly, uncaring of other passengers' curious gazes. What was more frustrating was that there was no cell phone coverage in the Tube tunnels, so she couldn't even contact anyone. Which she was desperate to do.

At Golders Green Station she just ran home, dragging her wheelie case, barely able to see through her tears. She was too hysterical to phone anyone just yet anyway.

In her apartment, she dumped her suitcase and knapsack in her bedroom, and switched on her PC at once. She stared at her blank computer screen. She had cleared the next couple of weeks of all commitments. She had literally nothing to do. She wasn't supposed to be there.

When she'd composed herself enough to phone anyone without sobbing, she called Colin. At the sound of his voice, she broke down again, and he could hardly hear what she was saying.

Colin was puzzled by her call. Wasn't she supposed to have been on an El Al flight to Israel?

"Whoa, Yael, calm down. I can't hear a word of what you're trying to tell me! Why aren't you on the plane? Did you manage to miss your flight? I don't know what you expect me to do about that, if you were late to the airport!"

Yael instantly stopped crying. That was *so* unfair of him to assume!

"I got to the airport with *plenty* of time to spare!" she said, outraged. "Far too early, in fact!" The power of her anger carried her through the telling of what had happened to her. Once she'd finished, she broke down again.

Colin was shocked to hear this piece of news. His brain whirled, trying to make sense of it.

"Yael," he said slowly, "I want you to think carefully before you answer this. Are you *absolutely sure* the person who took you aside was a security officer and not an imposter? Because the whole thing sounds totally unreasonable."

"It *was* unreasonable!" Yael bawled, glad to have someone finally on her side. Then she stopped and thought. "Look, this person was the one who was checking everyone's passport before mine. And she took me into a room at the airport that…oh wait…it was locked and she had the key to it."

"Hm, that sounds genuine enough. How weird. Well, there's one way to check. I'll find out if your name has indeed been taken off the flight list. In fact, I'm checking now as we speak. Hang on…"

Breathless moments passed, and then Colin's voice came back on the line grim and gray.

"Well, you aren't on the flight list, so she must have been who she said she was. I just wonder what on earth had precipitated this."

"Surely me being a PI wouldn't have?" Yael burst into fresh tears.

"Of course not, not unless you were a real troublemaker." There was a slight pause while the implications to that remark sunk in on both sides. "I mean a potential troublemaker to Jews in Israel, obviously, which is patently ridiculous."

Yael's sobs had reduced to sniffles. She was thinking.

"Colin," she said, "I have an idea that someone out there doesn't want me to go to Israel because I might find out something they don't want me to know about."

"Oh? And what might that be?"

"Something about my father. I spoke to Nena, remember her? My old school friend?"

"How can I forget Nena? She was in the Witness Protection Program, wasn't she?"

"Yes, that's her. Well, it turns out that her father-in-law, Yehuda Brief, was the only one to witness the hit-and-run that killed my father. And for some reason Nena won't go any further in questioning him about it. She said I have to come and find out for myself. Which leads me to believe, and Nena has more or less confirmed this, that he knows much more than he has let on."

"That's very interesting," Colin said slowly. "And it sounds like just the sort of case that terrier-with-a-bone Yael Reed would love to get her teeth into. Leave this with me. Don't cry, don't despair, and whatever you do, don't unpack. I'm going to find out what's behind this, and if I don't manage to find out exactly what's going on, and you can do that when you get there, worst-case scenario I'll get you on that plane tomorrow if the whole Golders Green police force has to escort you on board. Do you hear?"

"Yes, Colin, I hear. Thank you so much." Yael smiled through her tears. She felt vindicated and validated.

But if Yehuda Brief didn't want her there, and would go to such lengths to fabricate issues against her, to stop her going, what could happen to her once she actually got to Israel? And what on earth was behind her father's hit-and-run?

CHAPTER 10

AFTER HER PHONE call to Colin, and time to calm down, Yael's next call was to Nena. Nena was puzzled at first to hear from her friend; according to her timetable, Yael should have been three thousand feet in the air and therefore not really able to make the call. Unless she was using one of those extremely expensive phones you made calls from the plane on, and Nena doubted Yael had the funds for that kind of expenditure.

"I missed the flight!" Yael said. "And before you accuse me of idiotic tardiness, no, I *didn't* leave home too late. This was a deliberate and premeditated move to get me taken off the flight. I was taken aside for questioning by El Al security on some spurious excuse."

"What happened?" Nena asked, looking at the bed she had just made for Yael and wondering if this meant she should take the linens off. "This really sounds awful."

"I was taken off the flight list, as some kind of security risk," Yael said. "*Me*, a security risk! It's so unlikely as to be ridiculous, isn't it?"

Foundling 53

Nena thought secretly that based on Yael's track record as a PI, it wasn't quite the stretch Yael thought it was, but she held her counsel on that point. However, she was sure something more sinister was going on than Yael's reputation traveling before her. So she answered her friend in a soothing tone.

"It does sound a spurious reason, yes," she said. "I wonder what on earth…?"

"I need to know *exactly* what your father-in-law's reaction was when you asked him about the hit-and-run," was Yael's reply. "Word for exact word, please."

Nena was stunned into silence by this, her mind joining all kinds of dots like a flame racing along a fuse toward an explosive device. The picture formed by the dots was not a pretty one.

"You think my father-in-law had something to do with you not being allowed on the flight?"

"Only you can answer that, Nena. I wasn't privy to what he said, remember? I was just assuming, based on your reluctance to tell me exactly what he said, that it could be the reason. Am I right or way off the mark here?"

Nena paused, desperately searching for the right words. Everything, at this stage, was guesswork and conjecture. She couldn't say anything bad about her father-in-law. He could have a perfectly innocent and plausible reason for the way he reacted to her bringing up the topic of the hit-and-run. Unlikely, but…

"Your silence gives me all the answers I need," Yael said at last.

"I'm sorry, Yael, right now I can't say anything more. So you're not coming? We were planning to come and meet your flight." Nena had already started unbuttoning Yael's duvet cover.

"Oh, I'm still coming," Yael said, and Nena started buttoning it again. "I'm on tomorrow's flight. Colin Sommers is arranging it for me. He said he'll give me a police escort if necessary to make sure I'm on the plane. Just do me one favor, Nena. Don't tell your father-in-law, and maybe don't tell Yitzy either. If he's thick as thieves with his father, he's bound to tell him."

"Yael," Nena said slowly, having finished buttoning up the duvet cover, "as I said. I have a tiny apartment. How do you plan to keep your presence hidden from my husband, exactly?"

"One favor, part two," Yael replied. "So it's actually two favors, sorry. I can't stay with you, obviously. Can you ask your friends if anyone can host me? That way I'll be there, but your husband and father-in-law need not know. I'll do my investigations under the radar. Tell Yitzy that for some strange reason, your friend isn't coming, and leave it at that. Then he's bound to tell his father, who'll relax and assume the threat is over. If, as I'm assuming, he's behind my being taken off the flight."

"You want me to find you somewhere to stay?" Nena repeated dumbly, thinking of her local friends, such as she had any, at this early stage in her marriage and move to Israel, and the sizes of their apartments. She started unbuttoning the duvet cover again. If she'd hoped by her tone that Yael would hear her reluctance, and jump in with "Oh, don't worry, I'll ask around myself, don't trouble yourself!" she was to be sadly disappointed.

"Yes, please," Yael said, cheerfully oblivious to the strain she was putting onto her friend, and indeed, their friendship, by this request. "I'm only one person. Shouldn't be too difficult. And tell them I have no idea how long I'll be staying. Weeks, probably."

"Weeks," Nena repeated, stunned.

"Yes, and say I'm really sorry but I can't offer to pay any rent because I can't afford it," Yael added, knocking yet another nail into the coffin of the likelihood of Nena finding such a place.

"I'm sure people will be lining up to offer you somewhere to stay," Nena said drily.

Yael, totally missing the sarcasm in her friend's remark, said, "I know. It's amazing! Jews are known for their hospitality the world over, aren't they? *Mi ke'amcha Yisrael* and all that, huh?"

"I suppose you can offer to cook them dinner every now and then," Nena suggested.

"Oh, I can't cook," Yael said. "Unless they're happy with mac and cheese. That's the extent of my culinary expertise. I suppose you do have canned soup and sausages in Israel?"

"Yael, this isn't quite the third world country you think it is. We do have basic foodstuffs here. I don't make porridge out of gruel every night."

"Well then!" Yael said. "That's sorted!"

Nena took a breath. "Yael. I've only been here a couple of months. I don't know many people yet. And *kollel* couples here tend to have very small apartments and not a lot of money. You're not really offering them much of an incentive to host you for weeks on end, and I presume you'll want feeding, and Shabbos, and so on. Do you have any idea what you're asking?"

"Oh," Yael said. "I suppose I've been single too long. All my earnings go on myself. I didn't really think about what it's like to be married and struggling."

"No, you aren't thinking. I honestly don't think I can ask any of my friends to host you without pay, for an indeterminate time. I'm sorry, it's asking too much."

"It's okay," Yael said in a small voice. "I'm sure I'll find a park bench somewhere. Israel, even in November, can't be as cold as London. Maybe I can just come to you when Yitzy is out, to shower and wash my clothes?"

Nena sighed, hugely and audibly. This friend of hers took high maintenance to a whole new level.

"I don't have a washing machine. I go to the Laundromat. As

can you. But as to the park bench idea, don't be so ridiculous. There has to be another answer."

Yael's brain started whirling. "How about if you tell Yitzy, and therefore your father-in-law, that I'm definitely not coming. So they won't be expecting me at all, will they? So, if I come, completely openly, but as someone else entirely, how are they to know who I am? I've played undercover before, as you know. I've been a schoolgirl when I was nineteen, and gotten away with it."

"I think that'll be stretching coincidence somewhat, telling Yitzy you're not coming, then you come, and you're someone else," Nena said. She'd stopped unbuttoning the duvet cover again. "I don't think even Yitzy will fall for that one."

"Well, think of something, because I'm coming tomorrow and need somewhere to stay if you're sure park benches aren't suitable!" Yael said, troweling on the emotional blackmail. "Shall I call you back in an hour?"

"An hour! Yael, I do have a life, surprising as it may seem!"

"Two hours?" Yael asked in a pleading voice.

"Three," Nena said firmly. "I have to make dinner. Yitzy will be home soon."

When the call had been disconnected, Nena sat at her small kitchen table, head in her hands. Having Yael on her doorstep, even if not in the house, was going to be challenging, to say the least.

She finished making supper for herself and Yitzy before she did anything about Yael's accommodation. She was just looking through the latest *Pirsumit*, the weekly advertiser, to see if anyone was looking for a free lodger, unlikely though it would surely be, when her husband walked in, *sefer* under his arm. He smiled at her, but his smile didn't reach his eyes.

Nena looked at him, trying to judge what he was thinking. "Hi, Yitzy, good *seder*?"

"Dad called me in the middle," her husband said. "He wanted me to go over to hear some news."

"Oh?"

By the look on his face, the news wasn't good. "Mum. She was diagnosed a little while ago, but they kept it quiet."

"Diagnosed with what?" Nena's heart was sinking, wondering what the implications of all of this were.

"MS. Early stages, but MS isn't something you get better from."

"Oh no!" Nena said, clutching the chair she had just sat down in, her legs unable to support her.

"The good news," Yitzy went on, "if there is any, is that multiple sclerosis can go into remission, sometimes for years. But the reason Mum got tested was that she's had a few falls. Once when she was alone in the apartment. Apparently she had to struggle into a chair, but it took her quite a while, and then she just sat there until Dad came home to get her. Luckily she had her phone with her, or heavens knows how she'd have been able to contact anyone. She doesn't get many visitors."

Nena was instantly ashamed that she didn't visit her mother-in-law more often. Esther Brief was hardly an attractive proposition to visit, but even so… Nena felt guilty and wanted to put things right.

"She's going to need some help," Nena said, an idea forming slowly in her mind. "Someone around to take care of her, at least part of the time."

"Yes, I think so," Yitzy said. "Maybe even a live-in, although it seems a bit early for that."

"Part-time live-in might just fit the bill," Nena said. Her brain was whirling.

CHAPTER 11

When Yitzy had gone back to yeshivah for evening *seder*, Nena wasted no time in calling her parents-in-law. She hoped her father-in-law wouldn't answer the phone. After their last conversation she didn't imagine she was in his good books. She was lucky. Esther Brief answered the phone and sounded shaky. And not very welcoming either.

"So now you call," was her opening gambit. Nena felt like slamming down the phone, but she reminded herself that she had been in the wrong for not calling or visiting enough, and also she wanted to help Yael.

"Mum, please forgive me." Humble-pie eating was something Nena did quite well and she almost choked on a huge slice at that moment. "It was very remiss of me not to visit or call you very often. I'm so sorry."

The older woman wasn't letting Nena off the hook quite so easily. "Very often? When was the last time? I can't seem to recall, exactly…"

Wow, Nena thought. *How did I get myself into this?*

"That fall must have been really scary," Nena went on, swallowing the sarcasm.

To her surprise, the empathetic remark went down well, and Esther Brief audibly softened.

"Yes, it was very frightening," she admitted, and it sounded to Nena as if she was stifling a sob. "Until I got into that chair I thought I was going to lie on the floor until your father-in-law got home. And that can be pretty late, believe me. Not that you'd know, because you're never here," she added, the snarky remark obviously irresistible.

"Mum, please don't. I'm really sorry, and I'm going to do better." Nena thought groveling without making any excuses was the only way to go.

"I'm sorry for being so irritable," her mother-in-law said surprisingly. "This MS is starting to bite and it's scaring me half to death, I must confess. That's why I'm so aggressive and nasty. I accept your apology and I hope to see you more often. I'm afraid my husband is more absent than present, and the fact that I have MS doesn't seem to have changed that much. He says if I'm going to need more medical care, the bills will go up so he has to work more. Fair enough, I suppose," she added doubtfully.

Privately Nena didn't think it was fair enough at all. *If your wife has MS, you be there to look after her!* she thought angrily, but kept quiet. She needed her in-laws on her side for what she had in mind.

"I was wondering, Mum," she said cautiously, "if you might benefit from part-time live-in help? Someone to be around some of the time—but not all the time, not at this stage; it's much too early."

"A live-in? Oh, I don't know. I don't like people around all the time. They get on my nerves."

"But Mum, you've said yourself, you fell and no one was

around. If this live-in had been around, she could have helped you up, sought help. And she wouldn't be around all the time. Just a few hours a day, maybe mornings. Then she could be free in the afternoons. And you could have someone to babysit Yonina in the evenings if you and Dad go out."

Yonina was Yitzy's little sister. At nine going on twenty-five she behaved like an only child, coming, as she did, so long after her older siblings. She was precocious and babyish all at once, and hated it when her parents went out. If she had to have a babysitter, it had to be an entertaining one, not one that just sat there and read. Nena didn't think Yael was maternal enough to be patient and loving, but she'd be good value on the entertainment front.

"That's true," Esther conceded. "Getting babysitters who meet Yonina's requirements is getting harder and harder. They want to sit and do schoolwork. She wants to be amused." There was a pause. "I think I could get used to someone being around, just in case my legs get wobbling again, and maybe doing some light housework, nothing backbreaking," she said at last. "What's the going rate for an au-pair-type person? I'll have to ask around."

Nena was taken aback. She hadn't thought of Yael being paid, just of her not having to pay for her room and board. This was a huge bonus for someone as broke as her friend.

"I have no idea, Mum. As you say, ask around. And I will, too, and see if I can find someone. Unlikely, but you never know."

"Thank you, dear." Esther sounded quite warm by the end of their chat. They disconnected with Nena promising to visit once every few days, if not more frequently.

She called Yael back at once. "I think I might have found somewhere for you to stay," she said. "And it comes with a bonus. A huge one."

"What, what, what?" Yael asked excitedly. Nena filled her in and heard her friend gasp. "I don't believe it. I just don't believe it! Wow and double wow!"

"So I guess you want to apply for the job?" Nena asked wryly.

"Are you kidding me?" Yael was jumping around the room as she spoke. Then she paused. "We must be careful though. It's entirely possible your father-in-law has researched me. I'll have to be someone totally different so he doesn't get suspicious that I really am the person he's trying to keep out of the country."

"Do you have any images of yourself online?" Nena asked.

Yael went straight to her PC and did a search online of herself. "No, only information. No pictures."

"That's good. At least you won't have to wear a silly disguise or false nose or anything—or a wig like when you were a schoolgirl."

"Yes, that wig was awfully scratchy," Yael recalled. "I'll just have to change my name for the purposes of the job. Do you suppose your father-in-law will be scanning the flight lists to see if I sneak in the country anyway? That could be more complicated because I don't think I can change my name for the purposes of the flight, and my real name is in my passport anyway. Hm, I'll have to keep my passport well hidden from him while I'm there."

"I doubt he'll go to those lengths," Nena said. "I'll tell Yitzy you aren't coming, he's bound to tell his father, and that will be that. Then you present yourself as a different name and background story, keep your passport hidden at all times, and hopefully all should be well. But Yael, I can't stress enough that my mother-in-law has MS, although very early onset. You can't treat her like a free hotel. You have to do your job there, which will involve housework, babysitting my little sister-in-law Yonina, and being there for my mother-in-law during your hours of employment. You can't just do what you usually do, go off at a moment's notice, to do your own thing, because something has occurred to you."

"I hear you loud and clear," Yael said. "Anyway, I'd be in the best possible place to do a lot of snooping round while I'm scrubbing the furniture or whatever."

"You'd better not *scrub* the furniture," Nena said worriedly. "My in-laws have some very expensive pieces in their home. Oh, I do hope you're not going to mess this job up and get yourself fired. It won't do my reputation with them any good, especially if you come with my recommendations."

"I was just using an expression, Nena. I'll treat their furniture with kid gloves, don't you worry."

"How much do you know about housework?" Nena asked, not reassured.

"Not a lot," Yael answered honestly. "My apartment consists of white Formica and plastic everywhere, so I just wipe down everything with a damp cloth. When I get around to it, that is. Most of the time I just leave it until the dust reaches a certain thickness and then I have a blitz."

"Oh dear," Nena said.

"Don't worry," Yael said. "I'll be a sterling au pair. They won't know what hit them."

"That," Nena said, "is exactly what I'm worried about."

CHAPTER 12

"I'm Tamara Rifkind," said Yael Reed to Esther Brief. "I hope you'll find me a suitable lodger and caregiver. I love looking after people. I'm sure you've seen my resume." The latter, a particularly inventive piece of creative writing, was something Yael worriedly hoped she'd be able to live up to.

Esther sized up the young woman in front of her critically. "You look about twelve," she said at last.

"I'm twenty-one, actually," Yael said, not knowing whether to be flattered or insulted.

The older woman smiled. "An advantage I'm sure you can't see the benefits of now, my dear, but believe me, you will. Come in, come in. You have no bags?"

"I have," Yael said, blushing, "but I didn't want to be presumptuous and bring them with me in case I didn't get the job."

Esther visibly relaxed. "I like that. You're not assuming anything. Sign of good *middos*. Let's talk."

The fact that she had started off this whole exchange pretending to be someone else was hardly a sign of good *middos*, Yael thought, but she couldn't afford to let anyone know her real identity, even if her father was not called Reed but Alan Katz. It wouldn't take someone determined enough more than five seconds to track down the daughter of Alan Katz.

She followed Esther into the apartment. It was on the third floor of a nice, relatively new building, the communal areas of which had been completely annihilated by muddy strollers parked everywhere, equally muddy footprints, and dead leaves. As Yael had taken the elevator she'd wondered what kind of dump the place would turn out to be. However, once she stepped across the threshold of the Briefs' apartment it was like entering another world. It was clean, with white marble floors marked out in large square tiles, and tastefully furnished.

She was invited to sit on a pale creamy sofa, and did so gingerly, not wanting to dirty it. She had trekked there on a post-rainy, muddy day and had no idea if she was clean or splattered. Her first view of the capital had been disappointingly like Golders Green, at least as far as the weather was concerned. Only the difference in the buildings, with their construction out of golden Jerusalem stone, and the fact that they were all apartments, at least as far as she could tell, instead of single-occupancy Golders Green homes, made her realize she had indeed traveled three thousand miles and was now in the holiest city on earth.

"Now, my dear Tamara Rifkind," Esther said, and it took Yael a second or two to realize she was being addressed. "Tell me all about yourself. Your previous employment, your background. I want to know it all."

The piece of fiction that followed is not worth mentioning in its entirety, except to applaud its sheer creative imagination. Yael had made copious notes on her phones, both English and Israeli, to fill in the background of Tamara Rifkind, so she wouldn't slip up on details. Her main problem, she realized, would be to remember to actually answer to her new name when called, and not to turn around and say yes if anyone named Yael was called. That could be extremely dangerous, especially if someone (Yehuda Brief?) was becoming suspicious of her and was looking out for clues.

By the time she was finished, Esther was satisfied that the young lady in front of her was an experienced caregiver. How Yael was going to pull this off in practice, she had no real idea, but she reckoned it would be a breeze. After all, how hard could it be to look after a mostly independent older woman in the very early stages of MS?

"And of course there's my *bas zekunim*, Yonina. She's quite… highly strung."

Uh-oh, thought Yael. "I'd love to meet her," she beamed. "I love kids." *But I couldn't eat a whole one.*

"Of course! Yonina!"

A muffled answer, a thunder of feet, and the nine-year-old appeared. Yael's first impressions were of an overfed girl who was obviously indulged in her every whim. She looked at Yael curiously.

"This is Tamara Rifkind," Esther said. "She's going to come live with us and help Mummy, and babysit you too." Yael had not been aware she had been offered the job, let alone accepted the offer. It just seemed to be a foregone conclusion.

"I don't need a babysitter," Yonina said at once. "I'm nine. I can babysit myself." She glared at Yael.

"You can't, darling, not until you're much bigger. It's the law," her mother said.

"My friend Feigy is nine and looks after all her younger siblings." Yonina pouted. The use of the word "siblings" instead of "brothers and sisters" seemed incongruous to Yael, but she presumed that was how a kid who was always in the company of adults talked.

"Well, your friend Feigy's mother should be reported," Esther said firmly.

Yonina, obviously deciding not to pursue this argument, turned to Yael with a narrowed gaze.

"Are you good at reading stories aloud? Like, can you act them out? Some babysitters read me stories and they're all in the same voice."

"Oh, I'm a very good actress," Yael said with the utmost honesty. "Do you want to give me a story and I'll show you?"

"Yeah!" Yonina thundered off and was soon back with a book. Yael put on an award-winning performance with several different voices and the child was spellbound.

"Mummy, can Tamara Rifkind stay *forever*?" Yonina begged. "She can do Chinese and Pakistani and I've never known anyone who can do both those voices!"

And so it was, that, based on her ability to do Chinese and Pakistani accents, along with a resume that owed more to fiction than an entire anthology by Dickens, Yael Reed, aka Tamara Rifkind, got the job.

"Let me show you your room," Esther said smoothly after a salary was discussed that would happily keep Yael financially balanced, along with room and board, most afternoons off while Yonina was at *chug* (afternoon activities), and evenings when she wasn't required to babysit.

Yael was expected to cook simple suppers for the child and herself when babysitting, and this worried her more than anything, as she couldn't cook to save her life. But when Yonina begged to be the one to show Tamara her room, and once they were alone she whispered, "Please just make spaghetti and cheese with ketchup. Or order in pizza. I don't want anything else. And please, please, please don't try and make me eat healthy foods!" Yael knew she had the right job.

Foundling

Her room was simple enough, and a bit chilly, what with stone floors and no heat, but Esther soon supplied a plug-in electric heater that warmed the room up nicely.

Later, once Yael had fetched her bags and was comfortably ensconced in her new room, her duties began. Yehuda Brief came home for dinner late as usual, apparently, and eyed the new help with a jaundiced glance.

"I have no idea why my wife feels she needs live-in help," he said over dinner, "but if she does, your resume seems satisfactory enough. I'm out again after dinner and my wife usually retires early. Please keep an eye on her to make sure she doesn't fall, and entertain my daughter."

Yael thought his statement was contradictory—in one breath saying he didn't think his wife needed help, and in the next, asking the new paid help to make sure she didn't fall. She took an instant dislike to Yehuda Brief anyway, probably due to what had happened to her at the airport. He was overbearing and bombastic and seemed to have no time for his daughter whatsoever. The latter failing was one that Yael could identify with at least, as she wasn't that keen on children herself, but she presumed that her own would be different.

On Shabbos, she sat at the table with the family, only retiring to the kitchen when an important guest showed up and Yehuda Brief didn't want the paid help present. *Motza'ei Shabbos*, when Esther and Yonina had gone to bed, Yael crept out of her room and made a first snooping expedition of the apartment. Silent as mist, she opened drawers and closets, looking for she had no idea what. Something with her father's name on it. Anything. She found nothing incriminating.

Frustrated, she closed the last drawer, prepared to go back to bed and start again the following day, when a voice behind her said, "What are you doing out of bed, Tamara? And why are you opening those drawers? I can't sleep. Will you read me a story with your Chinese and Pakistani voices?"

CHAPTER 13

"ARE YOU KIDDING me? It's half past ten! Go back to bed!" Yael said, more shocked at being discovered snooping than annoyed at the child being out of bed. She'd hardly been a stay-in-bed kid herself, although to compare the unpleasantness of being in foster care, with the comfort of being in one's parents' home, was hardly valid either.

Yonina's chubby face took on a stubbornness that Yael found disturbingly familiar. In fact, Yonina, in her entirety, was disturbingly like Yael herself had been once, and probably still was. It was both endearing and intensely irritating at the same time—like looking in a mirror and seeing a reflection you didn't much like.

The child folded her arms and glared at her new babysitter. "I won't go to bed unless you either read me a story with your voices, or tell me what you were doing snooping in my parents' closets."

Wow, Yael thought. *She really is like me. That's pretty much what I would've said in her place.*

Either way I'm done for, Yael thought, looking at Yonina. *If I*

70 Foundling

read her the story, she'll realize I was doing something untoward. If I tell her what I was doing... Well, how can I?

"I'll do better than that," Yael said. "I'll tell you both. But because I'm telling you both, the story will only be a short version. Deal?"

The child's eyes gleamed. "Deal!" They high-fived.

"But you have to be in bed first. And the deal also is, no coming out after." *This will give me time to think.*

"What if I need the bathroom or a drink?" Yonina pouted.

"I'll bring you a cup of water. You go to the bathroom now while I get it. And that's it. Okay, young lady?"

It was doubtful that Yonina had ever been spoken to with such firmness. Her eyes grew round as she sized up her opponent. But her curiosity, and her wish to hear Yael using those voices, won her over.

"Okay," she said, and thundered off.

Yael went to the kitchen to fetch a plastic cup and bottled water. The last thing she wanted was Yonina coming down with some kind of parasite or bug because she poured it straight from the tap.

"Everything all right?" Esther called from her sofa, where she lay with her feet up, reading.

"Oh, Mrs. Brief! I thought you'd have gone to bed by now!" Yael said, surprised to see her there.

"I'm all ready for bed, as you can see," the older woman said, "and I'm just as likely to drop off to sleep here as in my bedroom. But I'd like to try and wait until my husband comes home so he can help. If he's not home by eleven, I might call you and ask you to assist me instead, or at least stand around while I get into bed, just in case I fall."

"Sure thing," Yael said, trying to sound servile. She decided not to squeal on Yonina and tell her mother that she was still up. She wanted to build a bond with the child, and playing snitch wouldn't go far in achieving that bond. Yonina was far too astute and far too nosy not to be taken seriously.

"If you're getting yourself a drink," Esther said, "use the bottled water. Heavens knows what's in the tap water. It's probably perfectly safe, but with me not being well, and Yonina being so delicate, you can't be too careful."

Privately, Yael didn't think Yonina was that delicate, but she held her tongue.

"I figured that most people drink bottled water here," Yael said, trying to sound immensely knowledgeable about Israel. "In the UK, the tap water is perfectly safe."

She took the plastic cup, and one for herself which she kept strategically hidden, so that her employer shouldn't ask why she had two cups, and made for the door.

"I'll just be in my room," Yael said. "I'll wait until after eleven before I go to bed, shall I? To see if you need me to help you?"

"Thank you so much," Esther called after her as she left the room, the second cup of water successfully concealed.

In Yonina's bedroom, the pudgy princess sat up in bed waiting impatiently, the book that required the voices open on her lap.

"What took you so long?" she demanded.

"Your mother was talking to me."

Yonina's round blue eyes narrowed. "I bet you told her what you were going to do. Snitch!"

Wow. Found guilty and executed without trial, Yael thought.

"Nope. Didn't say a word to her," Yael said proudly.

Yonina considered this, and then looked satisfied, and rather impressed. Yael had scored some brownie points.

"Hm. I believe you. If you had, Mummy would've been in here like a shot. Or as fast as she can move these days anyway." A shadow of sadness flitted over her face.

"It must be hard being the youngest of a family, and having much older parents," Yael said with genuine sympathy. To be nine years old, and have a partially disabled mother, couldn't be any fun.

"Yeah. When Mummy fetches me from *chug*, kids who don't know me assume she's my *savta*. I hate that. And she's not even fifty years old yet. But her illness makes her walk funny, so she looks older. And sometimes she walks with a cane. That makes her look about a hundred and I hate it."

"The cane is probably in case she falls," Yael said. "She's very afraid of falling."

"Anyway," Yonina said, tossing any passing sympathy for her mother's MS out the window, "we had a deal. I'm in bed. I've been to the bathroom. Here's my book. Now, what were you doing in my parents' drawers?"

"I was looking for my passport," Yael lied. "Your father put it somewhere for me and I realized I had left a slip of paper inside it that I needed. Nothing more sinister than that."

"My father has his passport in his safe," Yonina said. "Along with lots of other papers and things. Maybe he put yours in there too."

"Oh? Maybe that's where it is… Where is the safe?"

"You won't be able to get into it anyway," Yonina said without answering the question. "It's a combination safe. I don't even think my mother knows the combination. Only he does."

Yael thought this was strange, not allowing one's wife access to the safe. What if something happened to him and he was the only one who knew the combination?

As if reading her mind, the girl said, "My mother has her own safe. She keeps her jewelry in it. And I think her passport's in it

Foundling 73

too. She doesn't need to get into Daddy's safe."

Yael still thought it was strange, but decided this was not a topic to discuss with a nine-year-old. She would also find it very hard, after this conversation, to ask Yonina again where this safe was.

"The story now please, Tamara," the girl said, slamming the book into Yael's hands.

"Half," Yael said. "As agreed in the contract."

"Humph."

Yael's star-studded cast of voices more than made up for the fact that she read only half the story, however. The child was enchanted. "You should be an actress!" she breathed, enraptured.

"Oh, I definitely should," Yael said with feeling. "Now, madam, to sleep. It's nearly eleven, and at eleven I could be called upon by your mum to help her into bed. And then she'd definitely find you up."

Yonina thumped down into a prone position and pulled the covers up to her nose. "Good night, Tamara. And I'm glad you're here."

Yael's heart filled at those words. "So am I, Yonina," she said. "So am I."

And she meant it.

Just as her watch ticked over to eleven o'clock, which was, after all, only nine o'clock UK time, but still felt like the middle of the night to the exhausted new employee, Yael heard Yehuda Brief's key turn in the lock, heard the door open, and heard him come in and call for his wife.

"I'm here, in the salon!" Esther called out.

Yael sighed with relief. She was only just able to stumble into her room, get herself ready, and fall into bed before sleep overtook her like a dark blanket. Before she fell off that endless cliff her last thoughts were, *I have to find that safe.*

CHAPTER 14

Despite Yael's utter exhaustion, something woke her up in the night. She turned on her bedside light. It was 3 a.m.

It's 1 a.m. for me, she thought, then realized she couldn't keep translating the clock to UK times. She had to adapt to Israeli hours and that was that.

She supposed someone was using the bathroom. But then as she thought about it, she realized her employers had their own bathroom, so why would they be wandering around the apartment? Was Yonina out of bed again?

As Yael was meant to be in charge of Yonina, she got out of bed to investigate. Her feet landed on what seemed to be an ice rink, but was just the stone floor. Brr, it was cold! Even in her basic apartment in Golders Green, the bedroom floor had an old, tatty carpet on it, which made for comfortable feet when getting out of bed. She found her slippers and pushed her icy feet into them, flung on a robe, and, not wanting to disturb anyone, silently opened her bedroom door to peer out.

The apartment was spacious by Israeli standards, certainly much bigger than Nena's little matchbox-sized one, where Yael had left her suitcase while attending the interview with Esther Brief. Her medium-sized suitcase had almost dwarfed the available space, and Yael had, for the first time, realized what a sacrifice it would have been for Nena to have hosted her in that tiny, cramped space.

Despite the senior Briefs' much larger home, it was still small by London standards, and Yael peering furtively out of her bedroom door, with it open only a crack, gave her a view of the whole living area.

And of Yehuda Brief, in pajamas and dressing gown, feet thrust into slippers, standing by the bookshelf.

How intense, Yael thought. She'd heard of people this dedicated, but had never witnessed it herself. Getting up at three in the morning to learn Torah! Impressive! But then she saw that he wasn't getting a book out of the bookshelf. He was fiddling around with the shelf in such a way that the entire shelf swung outward, with the books inside it. He stood there, fiddling with whatever was behind that shelf.

Turning something this way and that.

It was the safe. He was turning the combination.

Yael was taken aback. Was it normal behavior to go ferreting around inside a wall safe at three o'clock in the morning? She tried to think of all the scenarios in which this would be considered normal; the only one she could come up with was that he couldn't sleep and had to get something, or put something back anyway, so decided to do it then.

She preferred the cloak-and-dagger scenario though. It was much more interesting. Yehuda Brief was up to no good, so he had to do his whatever-it-was at that hour to avoid detection—obviously totally underestimating, or miscalculating, who was under his roof and how brilliant a sleuth she was.

Try as she might, Yael couldn't tell what he was doing, and wouldn't be able to without literally peering over his shoulder, which, she presumed, might not be a great idea. She kept a very low profile, with the door still only open a crack, and tried to see what he was taking out, or putting back.

After a few seconds of combination fiddling, Yael heard a heavy door swing open and Yehuda Brief stepped forward to bend toward the safe. He crouched, so she couldn't see him at all for a while, and then he straightened up, and was looking at something in his hand that she couldn't see. *Show me what you got!* she willed him, but he put something slim and light into the pocket of his robe.

A booklet of some kind.

Like a passport? Was he sneaking off somewhere?

Then he leaned into the safe again, took out another item, and put it in the same pocket. From what Yael could tell, it was another similar-sized booklet.

Another passport? Was he taking his wife with him? What about Yonina? Were they planning to dump Yonina on Yael and disappear into the sunset? And was Esther Brief really well enough to travel anyway? Yael was filled with righteous indignation at the thought of her employers abusing her good nature in this way. Going off and leaving her with the child! She'd object and complain!

Or maybe she was on the wrong track entirely. Maybe they weren't passports. So the Briefs weren't going anywhere after all! Yael instantly relaxed at the thought of not having to babysit Yonina 24/7 while her parents swanned off somewhere.

Then Yehuda Brief leaned into the safe for a third time, and took out something different. By the way he hefted it, it was much heavier than the first two items. He lay the item down on a shelf out of Yael's line of vision, much to her annoyance.

He stood up then, closed the safe door, twirled the combination to lock it, and swung the bookshelf closed. Examining the evidence, there was no giveaway that it had ever been anything but a bookshelf in an Israeli apartment.

He stood straight and Yael heard some bones crack as he stretched. She winced; she'd always hated that noise and he was doing it again and again, with obvious enjoyment, to release the tension of the bending and stretching into the safe. Yael endured several seconds of this bone cracking before it stopped just as she was about to admit defeat and beg for mercy.

Then, looking around, which made Yael close the crack of the door even further, until she could only see a sliver through it, Yehuda Brief picked up the item that he'd put on a shelf, hefted it again in his hand…

And clicked it. The sound was unmistakable. It was the sound of a barrel being opened, checked for heavens knows what, and closed again.

Oh my, Yael thought to herself, her hand firmly clamped on her mouth to stop herself from gasping aloud.

It was a gun. Yehuda Brief, *frum* father, father-in-law of her friend Nena, toted a gun. And it didn't seem to be a peashooter either by the way he hefted it.

He put the gun into his other robe pocket and turned toward the bedrooms area. As he approached her room, Yael silently closed her door and dived into bed, lying there, robed and slippered, heart thumping so loudly she was sure Yehuda Brief could hear it through the door. Was he coming in to kill her? Had he already discovered who she was, and that, despite his best efforts, she had entered the country? And not only the country, but his own home, under false pretenses? Was the game up for her?

Just when Yael was reconciling herself with the idea that at least she would die in the Holy Land, Yehuda Brief's footsteps passed her bedroom and were on to his own. She leaped out of bed again, and reopened the door a crack, just to see him thankfully passing his daughter's closed door and entering his own room. At least he wasn't planning to shoot Yonina. Yet.

Once his own door was closed, Yael sat on her bed, bedside light on low, and thought about what she had seen. And tried to make sense of it. She waited a while for the sound of gunshots, but the house remained peaceful and still.

If he wasn't going to kill his wife, which it seemed he wasn't, thankfully, and he hadn't killed Yael herself, what was he doing with the gun?

CHAPTER 15

YAEL DIDN'T EXPECT to fall asleep again that night, after witnessing what she had. She was too nervous to leave her light on and too unsettled to leave her light off. Being unfamiliar with her surroundings, she was scared she'd injure herself in the dark. So, using the dimmer switch (why didn't all lights have a dimmer, she thought), she put her bedside light on as low as she could get away with, so that she could just about see, but hopefully no one could tell she had it on.

After a few moments she got out of bed again, and went to her door and locked it. Then, thinking about it, she unlocked it again. What if she was needed in the night and either Yonina or her mother came to get her and found her door locked? She was meant to be a caregiver, after all, and making herself unavailable wasn't really in keeping with that role. So she took her chances with the door open.

Lying in bed, she pulled the covers up to her nose, and, despite the electric heater, she was shivering with cold and fear. Until now, whenever Yael had been in one of her multitude of scrapes, she'd always had her own home to escape to—a safe haven to creep into to lick her wounds and regroup her thoughts. Now, though, she was living in the home of the person who had caused her to miss her flight, who toted a gun he got out of the safe in the wee small hours of the morning, and who was probably extremely dangerous. There was nowhere to escape to, except this room allocated to her.

She had to make sure, above all else, that she gave Yehuda Brief no reason to suspect her of being anything else other than Tamara Rifkind, slightly wacky caregiver, housekeeper, and babysitter from the UK. One whiff of suspicion, one word said or gesture made that she hadn't meant to say or make, and she dreaded the consequences in a way she had never dreaded any case she had been on before.

"I always say that, don't I?" Yael said to herself, pulling the covers up so high that her feet became exposed to the still somewhat chilly room. "Each case I'm on seems more dangerous than the one previous to it."

In her last case, the case of the trafficked babies, she'd been mistakenly imprisoned in a police van driven by and unbeknown to the baddies themselves. She had learned during those long hours in the cage, at the back of that van, how to make herself invisible and inaudible to escape detection. But now she couldn't be invisible and inaudible. She had to be right there, in the home of—and in the face of—the enemy, and she had to play a part without ever slipping out of role.

Yael shuddered as she remembered the sound of that gun being cocked and readied. Just to add complications to the mix, the man she was so afraid of was her good friend's father-in-law. How could she act impartially with that complexity thrown in? Then again, she reasoned with herself, nothing about this case was impartial anyway. It was about *her father*. She couldn't get much more personal than that.

Yael tucked her feet up under the cover, which was just slightly too short for the bed—rather, it was a perfect length for the bed as long as you didn't have the top end of it up by your forehead, trying to get warm despite the (now proving to be) inadequate heater.

Winters in Israel are no fun, she decided. She'd only ever imagined Israel as a warm summer destination, but now as she shivered in bed, listening to rain battering her windows and wind rattling them, trying desperately to get in (and succeeding, if the fluttery movement of items near the windows were anything to go by), she longed for the warmth and coziness of her London apartment, with its central heating, hermetically sealed windows she'd been so frustrated with in the summer, and tatty, old carpets on the floor.

Eventually, frustrated again but for a different reason than hermetically sealed windows, Yael got out of bed and put on two pairs of socks and a sweater. And a woolly beanie hat she was eternally grateful she'd thought to bring with. With all that outer clothing on, back in bed, she warmed up and eventually fell asleep.

She woke up because Yonina was shaking her awake. She'd slept right through her alarm on her phone! She presumed this to be because she hadn't set it properly so it hadn't gone off at all. Embarrassed by this faux pas on her first morning, she jumped out of bed.

"You look funny," Yonina said, eyeing Yael in her beanie, sweater, and socks on top of her pajamas. Having no mirror in her room, Yael had no idea how she looked, but the reflection in the window did look rather strange. Her hat askew, and her unruly curls sticking out at right angles all over her head underneath it, gave her a wacky elfin look, but not in a flattering way.

"What time is it?" Yael asked, trying to decipher her watch through her rheumy eyes.

"A quarter to seven," Yonina said.

"That's a ridiculous hour to wake me up!" Yael said crossly. "No wonder my alarm didn't wake me. I set it for seven o'clock, which is quite early enough, thank you very much!" She patted her phone apologetically for having misjudged it so harshly.

"I have to be ready for the school bus at twenty to eight." Yonina pouted. "And it takes time to get me ready."

"Fifty-five minutes?" grumbled Yael, who had managed gradually to shave time off her own out-of-bed-to-out-the-door schedule, right down to ten minutes.

Yonina put her hands on her hips and stood, feet apart, looking sternly at Yael. "Tamara Rifkind. Are you meant to be looking after me or not?"

Yael got out of bed without another word. The last thing she needed was a pint-sized pudgy antagonist in the ranks.

Yonina was already dressed for school, but needed help in braiding her hair. Yael's heart sank. Her own hair, an unruly mess most of the time, had always defeated her, and now she was expected to create masterpieces with someone else's? But Yonina realized that "Tamara" wasn't very good at hair, so helped her out, and under her tutelage and guidance, a reasonable single braid appeared.

Once Yael was dressed (one minute twenty seconds), washed (a further thirty seconds), and had dragged a brush through her own hair (ten seconds, then gave up), Yonina asked her to make her a packed lunch for school. She told Tamara where all the ingredients were and she managed quite an acceptable-to-Yonina brown-bag lunch, consisting almost entirely of unhealthy ingredients.

Once her young charge had disappeared on the school bus, Yael managed to daven and eat a bowl of cereal, the same sugary stuff as Yonina had eaten. It was then her job to help Esther get up and dressed. That was easy, as Esther wanted to retain her independence as long as possible, so Yael just had to stand around and make sure she didn't fall, and that her legs and hands didn't let her down, which, this morning, aside from being a little shaky, didn't happen.

Then she had to do some light housework in the apartment. Yael, mindful of Nena's warnings about expensive furniture, made sure to ask her employer what products she wanted used on everything. This pleased Esther. "I'm glad you're taking care of my things," she said. "I feel I can trust you. If you don't mind, while you clean, I'll go and have a little lie-down. I didn't sleep so well last night."

This was the chance Yael had been waiting for. Yehuda Brief was out and her nosy young charge was at school, so once Esther's bedroom door was closed, Yael whipped through the cleaning like greased lightning, and then turned her attention to the bookshelf.

Feeling around where she'd seen her employer do so, she quickly found the hidden catch that made the bookshelf swing open and reveal the safe. That was the easy part. She looked around nervously to ensure that Esther wasn't going to come out, but some light snoring from behind the bedroom door reassured her that was unlikely.

She took some photos of the safe and its make and model on her phone, but try as she might, she couldn't work out the combination. Which was the idea, presumably. Combinations weren't guessable like passwords. She needed to actually have some kind of way to watch Yehuda Brief opening his safe. Without him knowing she was watching.

But how? There was no way she could risk snooping on him in the middle of the night again, and anyway, the sleep deprivation would get to her and she'd perform her duties under par.

Most people on their first-ever trip to Jerusalem visited the tourist places, such as the Kosel. Yael had other plans in mind, although she wasn't sure how she'd find her way there, as where she wanted to be was hardly in a tourist guidebook.

She wanted to find a spy shop.

CHAPTER 16

SILENTLY YAEL SWUNG the bookcase back into place, covering the safe, and checked that no one could have told it had been moved. She listened out for Esther, and still heard the quiet snoring coming from behind the closed door. With a sigh of relief, Yael returned to her "housework," which involved flicking a cloth in the vague direction of the furniture, while keeping her eyes firmly peeled for anything pertaining to her father.

She found nothing. She became even more certain that whatever there was to find would be in that safe.

The morning dragged on. Yael was, after all, the ultimate free spirit, and she longed to be out there, in the streets of Jerusalem, looking for a spy shop. She had no idea how that might be achieved, but she reckoned a few pertinent questions asked in the right quarters would bring results.

But she had to wait until her official time off, and that was more than she could bear. As Nena had correctly surmised, Yael was used to doing her own thing whenever the whim hit her. It was hitting her squarely between the eyes right now, but she couldn't just give into it, or she'd be out of a job, which meant out of a place to stay too. She wondered whether Nena could be persuaded to take her in, after all; maybe it would be worth risking her job just to be out there and at it, instead of stuck in that apartment polishing the furniture.

When Esther emerged from her bedroom, holding on to whatever furniture was at hand, and obviously somewhat unsteady on her feet, she looked around the apartment and frowned.

"You haven't even started in the kitchen or bathroom," she said disapprovingly. "You seem to have been in the living area an awfully long time, Tamara."

"I'm sorry, Mrs. Brief, I'm just familiarizing myself with the apartment," she said and added to herself, *and its secrets*. "I wanted to do a really good job on the salon first."

"Nothing I can particularly notice," Esther said sniffily. "It doesn't look much different from before, to be honest." She went over to the shelf above the bookcase that Yael had been investigating, and wiped a finger over its surface. "Look, it's still dusty. What *have* you been doing all this time, Tamara Rifkind?"

Yael realized she was really not up to much as a cleaning lady. The only way out of this was to eat an extra-large slice of humble pie. "I apologize, Mrs. Brief. Things will get better."

Esther shot her a hard look. "Well, you'd better hurry up and improve, because I'm not minded to give you many more chances."

"Yes, Mrs. Brief," Yael said in as servile a manner as she could muster. She put on her best cleaning lady persona and proceeded to clean as she had never cleaned before. Literally. Her own apartment had never shone the way the Briefs' place sparkled by the time Yael was finished.

Esther had to admit she was impressed. Yael, on the other hand, was beyond exhausted and hating every minute of it. She was ready to jack in the whole thing, forget she ever had a father, and take the first plane back to the UK, her normal life, and a fatherless existence where she would get married or not—without depending on anything except her as she was, not where she had come from. She was a PI, for heaven's sake, not a housekeeper!

Luckily Esther judged only by results, not by motivation, so she praised her new employee's efforts, told her she had the next four and a half hours off, and gave her a key to the apartment. "In case I'm resting when you come back. Please, though, just check in on me when you come in. I do have your phone number and I will call you if I get into difficulties, but I'd still like you to check on me. Yonina will be back before you, but she has *chug* most afternoons. She gets herself there and back mostly, or has one of her friends' mothers fetch her, but I might have to ask you to fetch her once in a while. But not today. Today you have off until five."

At twelve thirty in the afternoon, five o'clock sounded a hundred years away to the "imprisoned" caregiver. She practically kissed Esther in gratitude, but decided an over-display of delight at her freedom might not go down too well. So Yael hammed up a desire to be back and help just as soon as she could, and skipped out of the apartment. Then skipped back in again when she saw the weather, and put her coat and beanie on. Finally, she was free.

Looking around the general population of Ezras Torah and its environs, Yael judged correctly that very few if any of the locals would know where to find a spy shop. If indeed they even knew what it was. She had no idea herself what it was called in Hebrew. She knew the twelve men whom Moshe had sent to spy out the land of Israel were known as *meraglim*. She knew that a shop was known as a *chanut*. *Chanut meraglim?* Didn't sound quite right. She needed someone with enough English to know what she was talking about and the ability to translate it too.

She finally found the perfect person striding along Golda Meir Boulevard—a young female soldier who had made aliyah about three years ago from Australia and knew exactly what Yael was looking for.

"It's called a *chanut rigul*," she told her with a grin. "You want to get some cool surveillance equipment, is that it? To spy on your siblings, make sure they're not stealing your stuff?"

"Yeah, exactly!" said the sibling-less Yael with enthusiasm. "They're such pains, especially the eight-year-old twins!"

After a brief sympathetic exchange on the absolute pain of having eight-year-old twin siblings, the young soldier gave Yael an address in the Kanyon HaAchim mall in Talpiot.

Yael had no idea where Talpiot was, let alone how to get there, but the girl was super helpful, wrote down the bus numbers for her and where to get off, and pointed her at the right place to pick up the bus. Using her Rav-Kav, which she topped up with credit once she boarded the bus, Yael was soon on her way.

She wasn't sure where to get off, but it being Israel, there were enough busybodies on the bus to ensure she got off at the right place, and to instruct her exactly where the spyware store was. She considered herself lucky that none of them accompanied her into the store and watched exactly what she bought and why.

Once in the store, on the middle floor of the mall, Yael lost herself for a while looking around at the deliciously subversive equipment on sale. The prices meant little to her, and even though the numbers seemed huge, she comforted herself by saying that this was shekels, not pounds, and it was really much less. However, once she found an English-speaking salesman to walk her through the various options, she realized that even though the shekel numbers were huge, the pounds weren't *that* much less.

"Oh dear," Yael said. "I don't think I can afford anything in this shop. Truth be told, I only need the camera once." She couldn't tell the salesman she wanted it so she could see what the combination of a safe was; there wasn't single reason why doing this might appear legitimate.

So she went with the twin-siblings story. "I'm sure they're messing with my stuff and my mother won't hear a word said against them," she explained. "I just need recorded proof of their guilt to show her, so they leave my things alone, and my mother realizes I'm right."

"Just once?" the salesman asked thoughtfully.

"Well, when I say just once," Yael qualified this, "I mean until I catch them at it. It might take a few days."

"I could rent you mine, if it's just to be used once," he said. "I don't usually do it, but…"

Yael reckoned he did it all the time, by the warp-speed way the transaction was set up and almost completed. The shekels were still eye watering in number, but a lot less than if she'd had to purchase the camera. Before signing on the dotted line, she considered buying one new, using it, then returning it for a refund, and suggested this to the salesman as a way of further saving money. The salesman knew when he was outfoxed, as this was a valid idea with a month's option for refund as long as all the original packaging came back, so he dropped the price for his own camera by two-thirds, making it considerably less eye watering. Yael wanted proof it was working perfectly, and this he provided in-store.

With his camera in a padded envelope in her bag, and her phone details left with the salesman, Yael left the store, the temporary owner of a high-resolution spy camera, which, she hoped, would record Yehuda Brief's next visit to the safe behind the bookcase.

CHAPTER 17

L00KING AROUND THE streets outside the mall, Yael realized she didn't have a clue how to get back to the Briefs. She called Nena in desperation.

"Do you even know their address?" Nena scolded her after giving her directions, and Yael blushingly admitted that she didn't.

"This is my first time in Israel, cut me some slack!" she begged. "I don't know where anything is in relation to anything else. A girl soldier gave me directions to Talpiot and told me what bus to get on to get here, but I have no idea where Talpiot actually is."

"You're going to have to sit down with a map of Jerusalem and study it, my girl," Nena said. "Especially if you'll be going off on all these jaunts. Talpiot is hardly a touristy destination. It's an industrial area and has a couple of large, sprawling shopping malls and a few furniture warehouses. Most people go there for driving lessons; there's a driving test center there too. And it's quite close to Arab areas. Why was that your first port of call on your first full day in Israel, for heaven's sake?"

Yael considered how to answer this. She tasted the idea of "I'm trying to catch out your father-in-law and what he has in his safe" and decided it may not go down too well. So she stuck as close to the truth as possible.

"There's a cool spy shop here and I need stuff for my work." That wouldn't say too much while not being an outright lie. Nena could deduce from that what she wanted to deduce.

Nena laughed and said, "Trust you to go straight to a spy shop on your first-ever visit to Israel rather than the Kosel!"

Yael laughed, too, and said, "Yeah, trust me, hey?" The situation was diffused with a joke. "I'll go to the Kosel now, actually," she decided. Yehuda Brief was at work and she had a few hours off; there was no point in hanging around the apartment. She'd only be given housework to do, which was a fate worse than death.

Asking a few locals in her pidgin Hebrew got her on the right bus, and soon, she was standing in the Kosel plaza, looking up at the holiest site in the world for Jews.

Yael Reed was, as everyone who came to know her soon realized, a very single-minded person. And right now her mind was focused in one direction only: finding out the truth about her father. So as she stood at the top of the plaza, before entering the women's division, she looked around at the men coming and going from their sectioned-off part, and wondered if any of them had ever known her father, might know how he had lived, and how he had died. She scanned the faces of the men hurrying past her as if she could read clues in their eyes. Aside from being cast some rather strange looks, she found no signs to read.

With a sigh, she went down to the women's section, picked up a siddur, and started davening *minchah*. As the space around the wall itself cleared somewhat, she was able, before starting the *Shemoneh Esrei*, to stand right at the wall and have one hand on the huge stones as she davened. She felt a rush of emotion as she did so, as if the stones had delivered an electric pulse through to her hand. It was among the weirdest and most powerful sensations she had experienced.

To her surprise, as Yael stood and davened by the wall, tears flowed unbidden down her cheeks. She prayed that she should find out the truth about her father, no matter how painful it might turn out to be. It was as if she was experiencing some of that pain ahead of time. She hoped it was not a portent of how things were going to turn out.

Turning away from the Kosel, backing away as she saw others doing until she was a safe distance, she decided the first thing she was going to do was speak to the *chevrah kaddisha*, and try and find her father's grave. She put in a call to Nena.

"How are you getting along?" Nena asked her guardedly, as if she didn't really want to hear the answer.

Yael was just as guarded. "Fine," she said. "All going well. Anyway, I have some time off now, and before I go back to your in-laws, I'd like to speak to the *chevrah kaddisha* to try and find out where my father is buried. Do you have their number?"

Nena made a noise that Yael found hard to interpret, then Yael heard Nena rifling through a phone book. "There are several *chevrah kaddisha*s," she said, "but here's the number of the main one in Jerusalem. They may have a database to search in case some other *chevrah* buried your father. I don't know. Thankfully I haven't had much dealings with burial societies. I think you might do better if you actually go and see them."

Yael wrote down the address, which wasn't that far from the Briefs'. So, with the spy camera in her pocket, and the prayer at the Kosel still in her heart, Yael picked up a bus back toward Ezras Torah. Listening, as she loved doing, to other people's conversations, she overheard two girls, obviously American, and obviously in seminary in Jerusalem somewhere, discussing the current terrorist situation and how they were too frightened to go anywhere near the Kosel at the moment, even though they knew their time in Israel was limited and they must go at some point.

Yael hadn't given a second's thought to the possible dangers of going to the Old City. Now, in retrospect, she realized why these girls were so nervous, but what was done was done, and she'd been. And maybe her prayer would carry further even than intended.

At the *chevrah kaddisha* offices, the man in charge looked rather disapproving at a young girl coming into this male enclave of bearded Jews. But when she explained her predicament to the man in charge, who happened to be an American expat, compassion overtook him and he asked her for as many details as she could supply. Yael was embarrassed to realize that she only knew her father as Alan Katz and had no idea of his Hebrew name, which was obviously the name they'd be looking for. But she had his date of death. In English dates. Also not so useful.

The older man looked at Yael's distressed face kindly. "Don't worry," he said. "You're not the first and you won't be the last person to have so little information when looking for a burial. I can look up his Hebrew date of death using the English date you gave me. As for his name, well, we can guess at Avraham."

It was somehow incongruous, although Yael had no idea why, to see a bearded Orthodox Jew so obviously skilled at searching on a computer database. His fingers fairly flew across the keyboard and his concentration was absolute. She waited patiently at first, then rather impatiently as time dragged on. Finally he turned and looked at her. His smile was kind, but Yael knew from his eyes that the news was not good.

"I've searched every database—not only our own—and every

variation on that name together with his date of death in the whole of Israel. If he was buried here, there is no record of it."

"I *heard* he was buried here. After a hit-and-run accident," Yael said, tears welling up in her eyes, and surprised by her own shocked response to this news. "He lived here, the accident was here, so why wouldn't he be buried here?"

"There's another possibility," the older man said. "He could still be alive."

CHAPTER 18

YAEL STARED AT the man in the offices of the *chevrah kaddisha*. "Alive?"

"It's a possibility. Who told you he was dead anyway?"

Thinking back, Yael wondered who indeed had told her. "I read a report in the paper," she recalled finally. "It said he had been in a hit-and-run accident."

"And you're sure it was him? And that the report was accurate?"

"How can anyone be sure about anything?" Yael said slowly.

The man shrugged and splayed his hands out, palms upward. "Well, if he died and was buried here in Israel, I'd have found a record of it somewhere. So there are two possibilities. Actually three, but the third one is much less likely." He started counting off on his fingers. "One: he died and was buried outside of Israel. But then why would the paper report it? It's hardly international news."

"Right," Yael said.

He continued. "Two: that someone else was in the hit-and-run, not your father." He looked at Yael quizzically.

"The likelihood of two men with the same name *and* the same date of death dying in an accident is remote," Yael said. "We've confirmed his date of death; that's accurate at least. But I just know him as Alan Katz, I never found out his Hebrew name. It could be something wildly different from a Hebrew version of Alan, of course."

"Not helping," the man said. "I put very wide parameters to the search, and nothing came up. So we come to the third and least likely possibility, one I've never before encountered: that someone has deliberately erased something from the records. But I'm simultaneously disregarding that option because it's outlandish and makes no sense."

"No, it doesn't," Yael agreed. "I heard of a case where some crook erased a murder from police databases so that it would appear the murder never happened. Some police friends of mine were involved in that case. That motive at least makes sense. But here it doesn't. It was an accident, not murder. At least I presume so."

"Some say hit-and-run is tantamount to murder," the man said. "Or at least manslaughter. But this is bizarre. I'm sorry, I don't know how to help you further." Again the splayed hands.

Yael shrugged back. "Okay, well, thanks. I'll be in touch if I find anything else out," she said. He gave her a card.

Outside, she thought about her next move. She'd hit a blank wall, and there was basically nothing to do until she came up with something new. She patted the camera in her pocket and decided to go back to the Briefs. Her free time was almost up anyway.

Back in the apartment, Esther Brief wasn't home. Yael was a little concerned, but she'd left a note: *Tamara, I've just gone down to the makolet. I won't be long. I'll call you if I get into difficulties.* Yael had no idea how far away the *makolet* was, but she presumed not far if Esther could get there. She decided to use the time judiciously. She would install the camera so it was pointing directly at

Foundling 97

the bookcase behind which the safe was. Then, hopefully, it would record the combination.

It turned out to be a much harder job than Yael had imagined. Trying again and again, and experimenting by filming herself at the bookcase, she saw the flaws. If the camera was pointing at the bookcase, and she had the safe exposed just to make sure she had the right spot, it was basically filming her back, not the combination. No matter what position she put the camera in, she couldn't get a clear view of the combination without it being blocked by whoever was opening it.

Yael shut herself in her bedroom and called the spy shop. She managed to get the same salesman who had lent her his spy camera.

"I know this is going to sound strange," she said, "but I wasn't telling you the truth about the reason I want the camera."

"The siblings-messing-with-my-stuff story?" the salesman said. "I didn't believe it for a second. So what do you really want it for?"

"I'm a private investigator," Yael said, "and I'm watching a suspect."

"Ah," the salesman said. Yael thought he didn't sound any more convinced than he had been by the siblings story.

"He has some very suspicious items in his safe and I'm trying to find the combination so I can access the safe myself when he's out. Do you have any kind of gadget, like those criminals use to copy your ATM PIN number, that could be fixed onto the safe so I could pick up the combination without him knowing?"

There was a longish pause, then the salesman said, "I've never heard such a request. You want me to give you something that'll tell you the combination of a safe? You have to be joking. I could call the police on you."

"I realize it sounds suspicious…"

"No arguments there."

"But my motives are honest."

"Look, forgive me for not falling at your feet, but I suggest you return my camera immediately, and stop bothering me, or I'll call the police."

"I'll return it tomorrow as I said," Yael said and hung up hastily. She was shaking. Thinking back on the conversation, she realized how it had sounded. The salesman did have her phone number. She hoped he'd think she was just some crazy and dismiss the call.

"Necessity," Yael said to herself, "is the mother of invention." She went back to the safe with the camera, climbed on a chair, and affixed it with some duct tape and a lot of pressure to the wall directly above it. She angled the camera down, so hopefully it would look over someone's shoulder rather than directly at their back. She was going to try it out when she heard a key in the lock.

She hastily climbed down and put the chair back, just in time to meet Esther, who thankfully walked very slowly due to her MS and the shopping she was carrying. Yael ran to relieve her of the shopping bags.

"You should have called me to help you," Yael scolded her gently. "You shouldn't be schlepping all this stuff."

Esther smiled apologetically. "It was nice to get out for a while. It isn't raining and the *makolet* isn't far. I hadn't expected to get as much stuff as I did of course. I only went out for some milk and bread."

"Isn't that always the way?" Yael grinned as she helped her employer put away four bags full of shopping. Her mind was on the camera perched high above the bookcase even as she chatted aimlessly with Esther. She hoped that no one would notice it and that it would work, as she had no time to experiment with it.

Yonina would be home any minute and then Yael would be on full duty until bedtime. Esther looked exhausted from her short foray to the grocery store, so Yael realized it was her job to take care of her, despite her desperate wish to try out the new angle of the spy camera.

"I'd love a cup of tea," her employer said, sinking into a chair in the kitchen. Yael busied herself with making tea, and some toast, which Esther appreciated, although she was too exhausted even to go to the sink to wash for the bread, so Yael had to bring her a basin and cup to the table.

"Next time," Yael said, "please let me do the shopping. This is obviously much too much of an effort for you."

"I want to be able to do it," Esther said, and tears welled up in her eyes as she ate the toast and drank the tea, "but I can see that my MS is getting considerably worse. I don't want to give into it, but I can't help it." She started crying piteously.

Yael patted her awkwardly and said meaningless platitudes, until a couple of moments later Yonina thundered into the apartment.

"What have you been doing to my mother?" were her first words. Esther was quick to disabuse her daughter of this assumption and assured her that Tamara had been nothing but kind and helpful.

"She's an absolute treasure," Esther said between sniffles. "I wish I'd have employed her much sooner."

Yael felt like the biggest fraud on earth as she patted her employer, smiled disingenuously at Yonina, and kept one eye on the spy camera taped to the wall above the bookcase in the hall, praying it wouldn't fall off onto someone's head. She couldn't wait for a quiet time to try it out, to see if the angle was good, but she might not get one. It would have to be that night. If Yael didn't return the camera to the salesman in the morning, heavens only knows what he might conclude.

She had one shot at this. Just the one.

CHAPTER 19

"ARE YOU *LISTENING* to me, Tamara?" Yonina asked, grabbing Yael by the arm and shaking her. "You made me spaghetti with ketchup but no cheese! I wanted cheese!"

Yael shook herself back into reality and looked at her charge. The plump red face looked angrily back.

"I'm sorry. I guess I'm tired. Still haven't got over the jet lag."

"Jet lag? What jet lag?" Yonina demanded. "It's only a two-hour time difference from here to London."

"Two hours is still two hours." Yael wondered how she was ever going to cope with this job interfering with her "real work." She was finding it increasingly frustrating not to be able to do what she wanted to do because she had to work for the Briefs—while at the same time realizing that the only reason she was inside that apartment, was that she had that job. It was a real catch-22 situation and she hated it.

"Well, I always want cheese on spaghetti, not just ketchup," Yonina insisted. "I told you so the first day you came."

That first day seemed about a hundred years ago, but it was

just a couple days ago, Yael thought wearily as she got the shredded cheese from the freezer and added it to the spaghetti mixture, dumping the whole dish into the microwave again. Yonina sat at the kitchen table, fork at the ready, looking like one of those comic book characters who sits waiting for their food with knife and fork held upward in anticipation. She looked so incongruous that Yael couldn't help laughing at the sight of her.

The microwave pinged, Yael got the dish out, burning her fingers as she couldn't be bothered to use an oven glove. The sight of her, "owing" and dancing around the kitchen trying to cool off her burned fingers under the tap, made Yonina laugh in turn. "Payback time for laughing at me," she said. "I don't like being laughed at, Tamara. Why *were* you laughing at me anyway?"

"You looked just like a guy on Shabbos waiting for the cholent to arrive!" Yael laughed.

To her dismay, huge tears started rolling out of Yonina's eyes, unchecked, down her cheeks.

"Oh, I'm sorry, Yonina, I didn't mean to upset you," Yael said, rushing to try and hug the child, but was shrugged off. "What *is* it? What's wrong?"

"I get teased in school for being fat," Yonina said, struggling not to burst into a full flood of sobbing. "Me and one other fat girl. I think I'm even fatter than the other one. I'm the fattest girl in my whole class. Probably the whole school. The whole of Israel, I expect."

Yael brought the dish of spaghetti to the table, and sat down next to her charge while she started eating. "That must be awful. I'm so sorry," she said.

Yonina looked at her with narrowed eyes. "And don't you dare say it."

"Dare say what?"

"Firstly, don't dare say I'm not the fattest girl in Israel. I know that. That was me having a pity party. But secondly, I don't want you saying, 'Well, why don't we talk about healthy eating?' I'm not interested in healthy eating. I *hate* vegetables and fruit. I only like spaghetti and cheese, and pizza and fries. I know exactly what I should be eating and I'm not going to eat it."

"What did you eat on Shabbos?" Yael asked, trying to remember what Yonina had eaten yesterday.

"Mummy always makes me schnitzel and fries. I don't mind that."

"You do eat an awful lot of fried food," Yael felt obliged to point out. She was thinking of her own rather poor student diet, consisting also mainly of pasta and cheese, with the odd can of soup as a variation.

"I know. Thing is, so do most of my friends. They all eat garbage, just like me, but none of them are fat. None. It's just not fair!" A deluge of fresh tears welled up and spilled over.

"Maybe they run around more than you do," Yael said.

Yonina considered this. "Yeah, I hate exercise. All that huffing and puffing."

Yael had not been employed as Yonina's nutritionist, so decided it wasn't her job to push this health issue. However, she felt she had to say, "Well, if you won't do anything about your weight, you can hardly blame people for teasing you about it."

"People should still be nice and not tease," Yonina said, shoveling in a mountain of spaghetti dripping with melted cheese and ketchup. Yael gave up. The child was right after all. There was no excuse for being mean and nasty no matter what the cause.

After Yonina's supper, Esther had rallied a little after her exhausting shopping trip, and prepared dinner for the adults. A simple affair of frozen meatballs and roasted potatoes, but it was still a culinary effort that Yael had never attempted. She watched intently as her employer put the frozen meatballs into a foil dish and added chopped onion, garlic powder, and a bottled sauce; covered it with foil; and put it in the oven.

Yael was also interested in how one made roasted potatoes, and ended up standing and peeling them for Esther, who'd used up her energy with the meatballs and was sitting down again, looking wan. Esther gave her instructions from her chair, and Yael followed them to the letter, creating her first-ever dish of homemade roasted potatoes.

She felt quite the chef by the time Yehuda Brief's key turned in the lock and he entered the apartment looking like a bear with at least two sore heads. He didn't greet his wife or his daughter, let alone "Tamara," but went straight into a small room he used as his study, and closed the door.

"He needs feeding, that's all," Esther whispered to her employee as Yael looked at him, puzzled at his frowning face. "Men, before they get fed, they're just irritable! Nothing to worry about!"

Yael, however, wondered what had happened during his day to make him so bad tempered. She had a strong feeling it wasn't just the lack of food. After all, she surmised, if he was that hungry, he could pick himself up a shawarma or falafel on the street. No, something else was bothering him. She hoped whatever it was, it would lead him toward his safe that night. She glanced up at the camera, which seemed to be holding its own up there on the wall. Yael once again prayed the duct tape wouldn't let her down.

Yehuda Brief eventually emerged from his study looking calmer, even smiling at his wife and daughter. He gave Yael a cursory nod as he sat down for dinner. Yael served everyone because Esther was still very pale and tired looking. Brief looked at his wife's pallid face with concern.

"Have you been overdoing it again?" he asked. His tone was slightly accusatory as well as worried.

Yael concentrated on her food and tried not to look as if she was as interested in the conversation as she was. Any clues as to Brief's moods and behavior would be useful and she was trying to read him. She was gratified to note his concern for his wife. *At least that*, she thought.

"I only went to the *makolet*," Esther replied. "I meant to get two items, but you know how it is. I ended up with a few heavy bags. Tamara helped me as soon as I came in, but in truth I should have called her from the store and asked her to come and help me carry them home."

"And in the future that's what you'll do," Brief said sternly. "Or even better, get the girl to do the shopping in the first place."

Yael resented intensely being called "the girl," but didn't comment on it. She just smiled, put on a willing expression and said, "Just leave me a list next time and I'll do all the shopping. I'm a strong girl." Slight accent on the word "girl" got her message of distaste across, she hoped.

After dinner, Yonina and Esther retired to bed early, and this time Yael was told to be on standby for the latter, having read another story to the former using a multitude of talent-laden voices that enchanted the youngster.

Yehuda Brief showed no interest in either his wife or daughter after dinner. He had some "very important matters" to attend to in his study. *What could be more important than looking after your sick wife?* Yael thought. But whatever. She did what she was told and bided her time. She was only waiting for Brief's next visit to the safe. She was ready for him. Or was she?

Yael had worked hard that day and was so tired. She'd also been woken up at what she considered to be the crack of dawn by her young charge. She wanted to wait up and see if Brief accessed his safe. But it was going to be a job and a half keeping her eyes open.

After the house was quiet, Yael went into the kitchen and made herself the strongest coffee she could tolerate. She wasn't a coffee drinker at all, so this concoction of a powerful shot of caffeine in a very small cup would certainly do the job. She was shuddering as she drank the bitter brew. Then a male voice behind her said, "Is there any special reason you're drinking such strong coffee, Tamara Rifkind? What are you trying to keep yourself awake for?"

CHAPTER 20

YAEL ALMOST DROPPED her coffee cup as she jumped. Yehuda Brief stood in the kitchen doorway, leaning nonchalantly against it in the most casual pose. If he'd been wearing a hat, which he wasn't, it would have been tilted over his eyes like a detective.

She had to think fast.

"I'm studying for a degree at the Open University," she said. "And the only time I have is late at night. Yonina woke me up very early this morning so I'm rather sleepy. So I decided to fill up on caffeine and do some studying."

Brief didn't move from his position. He barely blinked.

"A degree, hey?" he said. "I wouldn't have put you down for the studious type."

He's got that right, Yael thought.

She smiled and shrugged apologetically. "I'm not the studious type. Not at all. That's why I have to push myself."

"Hm…I see. And what's this degree in?"

Yael knew her answer was likely to get her into trouble, but she just couldn't help herself. She wanted to see his reaction.

Foundling 107

"I'm studying criminology," she said.

This time, Brief did blink. Definitely. Yael noticed a blink, and he shifted his position from holding up the doorpost, it seemed, to holding *on* to it.

"The next Sherlock Holmes under my roof!" Brief said with a laugh. "I'd better watch my step, hadn't I!"

Yael laughed, too, and said, "Yes, I guess you'd better!" in a light tone, but her glance remained as passive as she could keep it. She didn't want him suspecting anything. Not before she'd seen for herself what was in that safe.

"I'd be interested to see your study books," he said, recovering his composure.

Yael hadn't been expecting that. "I don't have study books as such," she said. "The Open University sends me stuff to do, I do it. Single tasks."

"I see." Finally Brief said, "Well, I mustn't keep a good Sherlock from her work. I've got stuff to do too. Important stuff. I'll be in my study." And he let go of the doorpost, turned around, and went into his inner sanctum, closing the door firmly behind him.

Yael sagged against the kitchen sink with relief. Whoa. That had been a seriously uncomfortable exchange. And the caffeine, while wiring her against being sleepy, also had the effect of making her extremely jumpy and nervy. Not a great way to be when closeted in an apartment with a possible criminal.

Despite her distaste for the stuff, she drained the coffee cup, gagged a little, then washed the cup very well. She didn't want anyone else questioning her motives. She put it away, and made sure the jar of coffee was exactly where she'd found it.

She went back into her room. Keeping the door open a crack, she put a chair next to it, and sat down to wait. From her vantage point, she could see the bookcase, and the camera taped to the wall above it. Wasn't it interesting, she thought academically, how things taped high on the wall became relatively invisible? No one had noticed it.

It was a good thing, though, she surmised, her brain fueled by caffeine working overtime as it had nothing else to do, that the camera was a neutral beige color and not black. A black thing on the wall might be noticeable. Like a spider. People always noticed a black spider on the wall, didn't they? Yael didn't care much for spiders, even though in school she'd always been the designated one chosen to dispose of any eight-legged creatures that had taken up residency in the dorm.

She was just marginally less terrified of them than anyone else. She was also compassionate, which her roommates liked. She refused to kill them; instead she'd coax them into a glass cup, slap something over the top, then carry the glass outside to release the arachnid in the flowerbeds. She had felt sure one day she'd be rewarded for her kindness in this matter. Maybe now was the time?

Despite her caffeine overdose, Yael's brain slowed down after an hour of tedious waiting for something to happen that wasn't happening. She was almost in danger of drifting into a light doze. "I drank a gallon of caffeine!" she said to herself, pulling upright. "How can I be getting sleepy?"

The "gallon of caffeine" amounted to an egg-cup full and if she'd read the label on the jar, she'd have seen that it said, in Hebrew, "Decaf." Esther Brief never drank caffeinated coffee; it affected her MS somehow, so she had the two jars side by side on the counter. Yehuda Brief couldn't possibly have known which Yael had drunk, and seeing her obviously forcing the bitter brew down her throat, he must have assumed she wasn't taking such a small dose of decaf. Why would anyone?

The placebo effect that made Yael think she was wired could

only last for so long. She was, after all, exhausted, and eventually she fell asleep right there in the chair. A deep, dreamless sleep that lasted an hour and twenty minutes. When she awoke, she had a painful crick in her neck, and her left arm, on which she'd inadvertently been leaning, had gone to sleep, with the effect that she had pins and needles getting the circulation back into her fingers; she was beyond furious at herself.

She got up, went to the door which was still open a crack, and peered out. The apartment was in total darkness. When she'd set up her spy hole by the door, the living area had been lit. And to compound her fury, she now heard snoring coming from behind the master bedroom door that was a whole different kind of snoring to the light snuffles Esther had emitted earlier. This was like an express train approaching.

Yehuda Brief was asleep for the night, and if he'd been to his safe, she'd missed it.

How could that have happened? Yael thought. *Am I immune to caffeine or something?* She knew that wasn't true; in school she'd tried coffee just to prove to herself that she hated it, and it had indeed kept her up all night. Silently, she opened her door and went into the kitchen. Using her phone as a flashlight, as the kitchen light would have flooded the living area, too, she examined the jar of coffee. Then, for the first time, she noticed its "fraternal twin" next to it on the counter. The caffeinated version of the one she'd used. She'd drunk decaf! Oh my!

Putting the two jars back, she went to where the bookcase was and looked up. The camera was still there. *You'd better have done your job, since I made such a mess of mine*, she thought. Silently climbing onto a chair, Yael pulled the duct tape until the camera fell neatly into her hand. She'd never thought duct tape coming off a wall could make such a noise. She stood still on the chair, not breathing, until she was reassured the express-train snoring was still in full throttle. Then she climbed down gingerly, holding the camera close, and put the chair back, again as quietly as she could.

Back in her room, Yael connected the camera to her laptop. Now she would hopefully see what the combination was. Then, when she was next alone, she was going to crack the safe and find out its secrets.

CHAPTER 21

CLUTCHING THE PRECIOUS camera tightly, Yael locked her door and switched on her light. She was too excited to sleep now, and anyway, she knew the next day she'd have to return the camera, or who knows what consequences would ensue?

She listened out again for any signs of life coming from the other side of the door, then turned to the screen of her laptop. At first she just stared at footage of the bookcase that seemed to go on forever. Then she realized she could fast-forward it while still watching, and could stop it when anything interesting happened.

"This," Yael said to herself, "is the definition of tedium. Watching a bookcase. I think paint drying would be totally fascinating compared to this. In fact, give me a film all about paint drying right his minute and I'll jump at it! I've never been so bored in my entire—hey, what's this?"

The time stamp was when she was out cold during her placebo decaf-coffee boost. She slowed the footage right down and watched it intently. Yes, there was Yehuda Brief, coming to the bookcase. He, too, stopped and looked around and listened for sounds like she had just done. Then he turned back and pressed the catch that released the bookcase's spring. It swung back silently on itself, revealing the safe. Yael leaned forward. Could she see the dials on the combination? Yes, the angle of the camera was spot-on.

Hardly daring to breathe, she slowed down the playback and watched every twist and turn of the dial, jotting down what numbers she could make out. It wasn't crystal clear, there was still a margin for error, but it was at least something she could try, and a whole lot better than trying to come up with the combination randomly, which she'd never have been able to do.

Trembling with excitement, she went into the kitchen and made herself some hot cocoa—*shoko*, they called it there. Whatever they called it, she hoped it would have the opposite effect of the coffee, even the decaf. Wasn't it all in the mind anyway? If Yael could talk herself into being awake even if she hadn't had any caffeine, she could surely talk herself into…

Yael shook herself awake. She was still sitting in the kitchen, holding a mug of cocoa that had almost spilled over her hands. That could have been disastrous! She was obviously tired enough to go to bed. Holding her cocoa carefully, she walked across the kitchen. Suddenly she was aware that the express-train snoring had stopped.

Yehuda Brief stood at the kitchen door, a tightly fastened bathrobe over his pajamas, looking pointedly at his watch. He didn't say a word; he just looked at his watch. And then at Yael.

Yael waved the mug carefully at him. "Coffee to keep me awake and now cocoa to get me to sleep!" she said in a high-pitched voice that she didn't recognize as her own.

"Much as I want to applaud your application and dedication in getting your degree, young lady," Brief said sternly, "you are first and foremost employed by us to care for my wife and daughter.

And I can't have an employee who is so tired from all her extracurricular activities that her performance, when it counts, suffers. Do I make myself understood?"

"Crystal clearly," Yael said, heart pounding. "I don't think you'll find my work will suffer, Mr. Brief."

"I don't see how it can't. It's three in the morning. And you're here drinking cocoa to counteract the effects of a heavy dose of coffee. All very bad for you, I might add."

Yael did her best to hang her head and look contrite. It worked. He gave her a last stern glare, wheeled around, and went back to his room, closing the door quietly.

For the second time that day Yael sagged against this kitchen counter, aware that she had experienced yet another close call. This whole thing was not fun. And it wasn't as if she was being paid by a client. She was, in effect, her own client and her own boss and she had actually chosen to do this. Why? Right at this minute, she couldn't think of a single valid reason for carrying on this investigation into her father. He was, after all, dead, and nothing could change that. Maybe she should just throw in the towel, forget the whole thing, give in her notice, and fly back to London. No one would care less if she did.

Hugging that thought to herself, Yael went back to bed comforted. There was a huge advantage to being one's own client and one's own boss: she could fire herself. She would give herself a stern lecture on her inadequacies as a home help, and tell herself that her services were no longer required—and that she'd be on the first plane back to the UK without severance pay to cushion the blow.

She gave a passing thought to poor Esther Brief, who really needed her help, but she dismissed that with the additional thought that people as useless as Tamara Rifkind were ten a penny; the Briefs would find someone better in no time. And Yonina would be far better off with someone who took her bad eating habits under control, rather than pandering to them for the sake of an easy life.

Giggling at the idea of dismissing herself from her own employment, Yael snuggled under the inadequate bedcovers, shivering in the chill of the room. *I could be back in my own bed tomorrow night*, she thought happily. *With central heating blasting until I can barely breathe. Sounds like heaven to me.*

Thoughts of home radiating through her like the heat the room was lacking, she fell into a deep, comfortable sleep. Even the thoughts of what the safe contained seemed of little importance to Yael on this new pink fluffy cloud she was floating on. She'd return the camera in the morning, and try and get the first plane home in the afternoon. She'd get back to some real, paying work. Work that did not involve living in the same house as the man she was investigating.

It seemed only five minutes later that she was being roughly awoken.

"Leave me alone, Yonina!" Yael grumbled, turning away from the insistent shaking of her shoulder. "My alarm hasn't gone off yet! Stop waking me up at a quarter to seven, will you?!"

"It's not Yonina, it's me," came an adult female voice. And it wasn't her employer's. Yael struggled to surface through the multiple layers of sleep deprivation that held her down. She opened one eye blearily and looked up at a familiar yet out-of-context face.

Nena stood there, shaking her. Her expression was one of extreme anxiety.

"Nena!" Yael said, sitting up sharply, then holding her head as it started thumping. "What are *you* doing here?"

"I came to tell you that my mother-in-law was taken to the hospital in the night," Nena said. "She's doing quite poorly, actually."

"Oh no! *Refuah sheleimah!*" Yael said, shocked. "I didn't think her MS would deteriorate that bad, that fast."

"It's not her MS," Nena said. "They think she might have had a stroke. In fact, they're pretty sure that's what it is."

"That's awful!" Yael gasped. "And your father-in-law is with her, presumably?"

Nena shook her head gravely. "No, he isn't. He vanished in the night, just after getting her settled at the hospital. No one knows where he is. His phone isn't even taking voice mail. Oh, Yael, everything is going so horribly, horribly wrong!"

CHAPTER 22

"So where's Yonina?" Yael asked, sitting up in shock.

"She's at my place. Yitzy's going to take her to meet the school bus, as it's a bit off her usual route. She's horribly messed up, obviously—her mother in the hospital and her father gone AWOL. She wanted to stay home but I didn't see any useful purpose in that, and neither did Yitzy."

"Poor, poor little kid," Yael said with genuine feeling. She knew what it was to be abandoned by parents.

"Yitzy has been in touch with his other siblings. None of them has heard from Dad. They all want to rush over and be with Mum. For now only the Israeli contingent is gathering; the ones who live overseas were told to stay put and wait for updates."

"Gosh," Yael said. She was still sitting in bed, not sure what she should be doing.

"So look," Nena said. "You're still employed here, so may I suggest you clean the house or whatever you usually do. I'll keep in touch and tell you if things change."

"Sure," Yael said, thinking of only one thing: having unfettered access to the safe without having to worry about being caught. She waited until Nena had left, then got up, showered, dressed, and davened. Then she took a yogurt from the fridge and ate it standing up at the kitchen counter. Then, unable to control herself another moment, she went to the bookcase and swung it open. Now, with the combination in front of her on her phone, she tried to open it.

It didn't open.

She stared at the note on her phone and at the safe, the latter accusingly. How dare it not work! But even as she blamed it, she knew she hadn't seen the numbers totally clearly and there was a margin for error. But even with a margin for error, there were only so many variations there could be. And she intended to try them all.

It didn't take long. Only four variations later, and she was in. The safe clicked and swung open under her hand. She sat there, marveling at her own genius at being able to get the combination. She stared into the safe.

It contained *a lot* of passports. Far more than a family of three needed. Ten in all.

Puzzled, she picked out all ten and looked at them. None of them were for Esther Brief or Yonina Brief. In fact, none of them were for Yehuda Brief either.

Although they all carried his photograph.

Some had him with a beard, some without. In some photos he had a moustache, in others without. Some had him with blond hair, in some photos he had dark hair, in some photos he was bald. Every single one was of Yehuda Brief, yet none carried his name. There were ten different identities. Some were Israeli passports. Others were US passports, one was a UK passport. One was Swiss. One Russian. One was, to Yael's shock, an Egyptian passport full of Arabic writing.

What game is he playing? Yael thought. *Ten different passports? Different countries?* She put the passports back in the safe but not before pulling out another folder of documents.

This folder had a zipper with a padlock on it. A padlock with a combination. She stared at it for a few seconds, then looked back at her phone for the safe combination. She was just about to try it, when her phone rang, jolting her in shock.

She swiped it on.

It was the guy from the spy shop in Talpiot. Wanting his camera back.

"Like *now*, please," he said insistently. "Or I won't be responsible for my actions."

Yael looked at her watch. It was barely nine in the morning.

"Gosh," she said, "you certainly take 'in the morning' seriously. I just got out of bed." Not strictly true but a little literary license in such circumstances never went amiss.

"*Now*," he repeated, unimpressed. "I don't care if you're in your pj's."

Oh no, Yael thought. "Okay, I'm coming now. I don't have a car and I live in Ezras Torah so it'll take me a while."

He hung up. Obviously not interested.

Yael used the excuse of distance and public transport to its max, quickly trying all the combinations she could think of for the padlock on the folder, but none worked. Annoyed, she realized she'd have to give it another go on another occasion. In the meantime, she'd try and figure out what Yehuda Brief could possibly want so many identities for.

Closing the safe, twirling the combination to lock it, and closing the bookcase only took a second. Yael put the camera into her handbag, looked around the apartment to make sure it had no traces of her recent nefarious activities, and left for Talpiot.

On the bus, she thought and thought about Yehuda Brief. In her experience, the only kind of people who were required to hide their identity were in general up to no good. But what kind of up to no good? That was the question.

In the spy shop, the salesman took the camera back and examined it carefully, as if just by lending it to Yael for one night, it had somehow acquired some kind of nasty fungal infection. He tested it.

"Hm… Seems to be all right," he said, sounding almost disappointed. He glared at Yael. She looked innocently back at him.

"I hope you didn't use it for anything illegal," he pressed.

"Nope," she said.

"Okay, well… That's it then. Thanks." He seemed at a bit of a loss, as Yael had fulfilled all the criteria of the borrowing, as if he hadn't expected her to. The expected drama had never materialized.

"Thanks!" she said, smiling brightly. "Bye!"

She left, aware of him staring out the door.

Find another spy shop for next time, she told herself. She could never go back there.

Yael realized, on the bus back to Ezras Torah, that all thoughts of a quick return to London had been pushed out of her mind by the discovery in the safe. She wasn't going anywhere until she had worked out what was going on, and what, if anything, this had to do with her father.

Her phone rang. It was Nena.

"How's your mother-in-law? And any sign of your father-in-law?" Yael asked at once.

"My mother-in-law is okay—ish. She's lost a bit of functionality down one side and her speech is a little slurred, but she'll have rehab and they reckon she'll get it back. As to my father-in-law, no sign. I don't get it." There was a pause. "Yael, I can hear engine noises. It doesn't sound much like you're in the house cleaning."

"Um…no. I had an errand to run," Yael said.

"You mean you're off on some jaunt doing your own thing because, well, when the cat's away and all that?"

"The cat's away?" Yael repeated, trying to sound lighthearted. "What a way to talk about your poor, sick mother-in-law, Nena!"

"You know exactly what I mean, Yael Reed!" Nena refused to be distracted.

"Can I visit your mother-in-law?" Yael asked, changing the subject.

Nena sighed. "I'm not sure. Yitzy's siblings, the Israeli ones anyway, are holding a bedside vigil. We're taking turns. I'm not sure the hired help turning up will go down well."

Yael was secretly delighted at this. More time to explore the contents of the safe.

"Oh dear," she said, trying valiantly to sound upset.

"Yonina wants to sleep at home tonight," Nena said. "It seems your spaghetti is nicer than mine. Or maybe it's more fat laden. I'm trying to cut down on the calories where that child is concerned. I gather you aren't."

"Um… I wasn't hired to make her lose weight," Yael said defensively.

"Fair enough. Well, can she sleep at home tonight? Or will you disappear at midnight in a puff of smoke on some jaunt or other? To be honest, it would suit me if she did; my apartment is tiny. Also if she's with you, I can go to the hospital."

"Yes, sure." In truth Yael didn't want Yonina around. Having the apartment to herself would have been ideal, but she could hardly refuse, as she *was* employed to look after the child.

"Okay, I'll send a message to the school that she should come straight home," Nena said in relief.

Yael looked at her watch. She still had a few hours until Yonina showed up. She could achieve a lot in those few hours if she set her mind to it.

"You'd better do at least *some* cleaning," Nena said as a parting shot before disconnecting the call. "You wouldn't want to get fired for laziness and insubordination."

Back in the apartment, Yael whizzed around with a cloth for about two minutes. She spent a little longer on the bathroom and kitchen. The entire cleanup took seven minutes. Feeling a little embarrassed, but unrepentant, she went back to the safe.

Holding the padlocked folder in her hand, she tried the combinations again. Maybe she'd made a mistake of one digit in one of them. Easy enough to do, and she had been in a massive rush before.

And it worked. On the fifth attempt this time, the padlock fell off and the folder lay open in her hands.

CHAPTER 23

IN THE FOLDER there was a single sheet of paper. It was printed in Hebrew, which wasn't Yael's hottest subject in school, and she always managed to make a large block of Hebrew type go straight over her head rather than struggle to decipher it. But now as she stared at it, close, printed Hebrew type, neatly paragraphed, bullet-pointed in parts, she realized this was a document she was just going to have to work through.

But it would take her ages and ages plus some kind of translation aid, and she wasn't sure she had that kind of time. Or a dictionary. She'd have to look around the apartment.

It would be really useful if she could photocopy it; then she could decipher it at her leisure. Staring at it, wondering where to find a photocopier, she thought of taking a photo of it on her phone. But then what? Never mind, she had to do it, and worry about what to do next afterward.

The photo was taken and safely stored on her phone. She returned the document to its wallet, whirred the combination around to lock it, and put everything back in its place in the safe. Once it was closed and the bookcase concealed it, she breathed a sigh of relief. She didn't need to look in that safe again; all she needed to do now was find out what the document said.

As penance for her disreputable activities, she took up the duster and the floor mop and did a more thorough clean of the apartment than the five-minute whiz around she'd done before. At least, if someone did go around swiping fingers over surfaces looking for dust, he or she was less likely to find any.

Not a moment too soon. Almost as she put the floor mop away and surveyed the clean apartment, there was a ring on the doorbell. Yael went to open it, and Yonina came in, looking around her.

"Where's Daddy?" she asked at once.

"No idea," Yael answered truthfully. "And anyway, he's never home at this hour. Why would you expect him to be home at three o'clock?"

Yonina stared at her, trying to assess this line of questioning.

"Sometimes," she said slowly, as if she was talking to someone of limited intelligence, "when Daddy goes away for a few days, or even more, on business, he comes back at funny times. He doesn't keep office hours when he's been away, you know." Her gaze told Yael she thought this was patently obvious and only an idiot wouldn't have worked this out for themselves.

"Ah," Yael said, deciding discretion was the better part of valor in this case. No point in mentioning that however often her father went away on business, it wasn't normal behavior to go away when you'd just dropped your wife at the hospital suffering from a stroke. The child was better off living in a fantasy world where her father could do no wrong. Yael, however, had other ideas about her employer—not such charitable ones.

"So," Yael said, "how was it staying with Nena? She's a friend of mine, you know, not just your sister-in-law."

"If she's a friend of yours," Yonina said, making a face, "maybe you can tell her to stop making me healthy food and give me what I like. She was planning to make me a chicken salad for heaven's sake! How is anyone supposed to eat that rabbit food?"

Yael privately thought chicken salad sounded delicious and she could just do justice to one now, but she held her tongue and made the appropriate face back. Then, in deference to her friend, she said loyally, "She's only thinking of your welfare. That food is very healthy and if you ate it more often, instead of all that pasta and cheese, you might lose weight."

"That's what Nena said." Yonina pouted. "And no doubt I'd lose weight because I'd be starving to death."

Privately Yael wondered what the ratio of chicken to salad veggies would be, and based on her limited knowledge of Nena's budget, she reckoned, not very high.

"Can I have my supper now, please?" Yonina begged.

"At ten past three?"

Yonina made a dramatic impression of a famine-afflicted child, clutching her stomach, looking desperate, and panting. It was a creditable performance.

Yael got the message.

"But if you eat supper now, you'll be starving by seven!" she reasoned.

Yonina bounced up and down excitedly. "Then I'll eat another supper, silly!" she said, slapping her hand onto her forehead.

Yes, that would work, Yael thought, once more reminding herself that she was not there to be Yonina's nutritionist.

Once replete with spaghetti, ketchup, and shredded cheese, Yonina collapsed onto the sofa to do her homework.

"When you learn Ivrit as a second language, does your teacher teach it to you only in Hebrew, or does she speak English most of the time?" Yael asked casually, as she cleaned up the dishes.

"Our school is an American school, but most of our lessons are in Ivrit," Yonina replied, not looking up from her workbook. "They want us to be bilingual, you see."

"Right," Yael said, and washed a few more dishes before asking the next question, so it wouldn't seem related.

"Does your father have a photocopier or a computer printer in his study?"

This time Yonina looked up.

"Oh, you can't go in there," she insisted.

"Why not?"

"Daddy has very important things in there. None of us is allowed to go in there, not even Mummy. Daddy even cleans up in there himself. He won't let you go in there to clean, let alone to use the photocopier."

"Oh, okay," Yael said casually, wiping the counters and the kitchen table. She was thinking she'd either try to get in there anyway, or she'd find a place in the area that had a photocopier or printer, preferably both. She just needed time alone to do that, but now that Yonina was home, she couldn't just go out and leave the child on her own.

As if mind reading, Yonina said, "Just down the block there's a small store that does that sort of thing."

"Oh, good. I'll go there."

What could be in his study that's so…important…that even his wife isn't allowed to go in?

A little later, the phone rang in the apartment. Yonina ran to answer it.

"Oh, hello, Nena. Yes, I want to visit Mummy, how is she? … Yeah, I'd like to go now… Okay, I'll be ready."

Yonina looked at Yael. "Nena's picking me up and we're going to the hospital to visit Mummy."

"How is she?"

"Better, I think. She's starting to talk again. I'll let you know when I get back."

"You'd better sleep at Nena's tonight," Yael said, "as I may not be around to babysit." She thought that would cover every eventuality.

There was no mention of Yael going to visit her employer, so she presumed it would not be the done thing to ask. Anyway, she certainly didn't want to visit the hospital now. Yael was elated. She had the opportunity she needed to get out of the apartment and get that photo of the document printed out.

Once Yonina and Nena had gone, Yael wasted no time. Slinging on a coat, as it was raining again, she ran out and soon found the little store, which was no more than a kiosk, but had a printer and a photocopier. The guy who printed the document for her couldn't help but glance at it as he handed it over, and said to her in English, "Are you sure you should be printing out this document?"

"I don't know, why, what's it about?" Yael said innocently.

"I'm not reading it all, but at the top it says Sherut HaBitachon HaKlali. That's the security ministry. Basically, it's Israel's internal security, rather like your British MI5 or the American FBI. What are you doing with a document of Shabak, exactly?"

CHAPTER 24

Yael had never heard the term "Shabak" before, but she presumed it was the shortened version of Sherut HaBitachon. Either way, it was the Israeli secret service and Yehuda Brief had a document relating to it in his safe. Under lock, key, and password. Admittedly the password hadn't needed too much cracking, but she presumed he assumed no one would figure out the combination to the safe in the first place. He had reckoned without the brilliance of the supersleuth Yael Reed, obviously!

"I could tell you, but I'd have to kill you," was what Yael thought of replying to the kiosk guy, when he asked what she was doing with such a document, but she wasn't sure that would go down too well in Israel. She tapped the side of her nose and nodded at him, and he seemed to accept that. He had more customers and wasn't really bothered by her, so she took her leave and went back to the apartment.

She sat and thought about what she had in her hand for quite a while. Trying to decipher it was way over her pay grade in Hebrew. She tried a word or two, and gave up. She thought of asking Nena, but quickly shut that idea down. If Yehuda Brief had some kind of dealings with the Israeli secret service, no doubt he wouldn't want Nena to know about it.

After much more deliberation, and pacing around the apartment clutching at her curly mop of hair in anguish, Yael decided to call Colin and Leora. Before she'd left for Israel she'd set up a cheap way of calling the UK from her phone, so now was the time to use it.

"I could probably decipher it," Colin said, after she'd explained the whole story. "But Leora is fluent in Hebrew, much better than I am. Something about the way they teach Hebrew in American schools. But Yael...for heaven's sake. What are you getting yourself into *now*? It sounds very much to me as if Yehuda Brief is not the arch-criminal you thought he was, but a perfectly legitimate member of society who happens to work for Shabak. Which is admittedly not the usual run-of-the-mill occupation of a *frum* Israeli man, but hey, each to their own."

"It does explain a lot of things," Yael mused. "His secrecy about his safe and his office, and why no one is allowed in there. The multiple passports he has in his safe, under different names. He even has an Egyptian one, Colin."

"So, I ask again, Yael Reed, what on earth are you getting into? I would strongly advise against you mixing in with the Israeli secret service. They're not known for playing nice, exactly."

"I just have this feeling that what happened to my father is tied up with Yehuda Brief. Maybe Shabak had him killed in that hit-and-run! I've always suspected it wasn't an accident. I just have to find out, Colin. Please can you translate this document if I send it to you?"

"Okay, but don't e-mail it," Colin said firmly. "E-mails can be intercepted and aren't as secure as faxes. I know fax is an obsolete technology, but in several cases fax can be much more secure than any other method."

"Um, I don't have a fax machine," Yael said desperately. "And if I go back to that kiosk guy, he'll really get suspicious."

"I'm sure Brief has one in his study," Colin said. "No self-respecting spy is without a fax machine to transmit documents securely. Not that I know much about spies," he admitted.

"I'll try and get in there," Yael said. "I'll call you when I'm ready to transmit it."

The study was, of course, locked. But it was just a normal door lock, not a super-secure one such as found on front doors. Yael looked around the apartment for a key but didn't find one; she presumed it was on Brief's belt or in his wallet or pocket. As to picking locks, Leora had taught her a thing or two, and Yael never went anywhere without her trusty set of lock picks and tumblers. These had caused her some consternation and worry that they'd be asked about at airport security. As they weren't actually weapons, nor did they even look like weapons, they were allowed through without question, much to her great relief.

She got her kit out and started work on the door. It was a breeze. Yehuda Brief had obviously not considered an inside job when securing his study. The outer door to the apartment was like Fort Knox, and there were metal bars on all the windows, but inside the apartment itself, he hadn't thought to secure his study beyond what was normal—that is, to keep it locked from his wife and daughter, and any hired help.

Said hired help was in his study in two minutes flat.

Looking around, Yael saw a fax machine. She wasn't really interested in exploring the rest of this secret room. Not now, not yet. Soon.

She called Colin. "I'm in."

"How...?"

"I picked the lock."

"You picked the lock?" he asked in alarm.

"I learned from the best. Leora taught me how, remember?"

"Now that you mention it, I do recall a bit of foolishness a while back. Oh well, you're in, I won't ask too many questions. Fax me the document. Here's the number. I'm waiting by the machine so no one else picks it up."

Yael had never used a fax before ("*Sooo* last century!"), but it made sense to use it for this purpose. The first time she put the document in the wrong way around, so it came through blank, but the second time she got it right, and within moments it was done. Colin was holding the document in his hand. He looked at it briefly.

"My Hebrew obviously isn't as good as I thought it was," he confessed. "I'll get Leora on the job. She reads Hebrew newspapers for fun, amazing woman that she is. I'll be in touch once I've had this translated. Now go and behave yourself for a while, if that's even remotely possible for you to do."

"For a short while it is." Yael grinned at the phone.

"Yael," Colin said, "I'm not joking here. The Israeli secret service is not to be taken lightly. They're not clueless like some of our British police are, me and Leora excluded, of course. And Nesbit and Jim. You know what I mean, I'm sure. Please don't go barging into something thinking you can charm your way out of it. You may not be as lucky as you've been in the past."

Yael was far from being of the opinion that her previous successes had been merely due to luck, but she realized that Colin was deadly serious, and it got through to her.

"Colin," she said in what she hoped was a reassuring tone, "I hear you, I do. I'll be careful. I really will. Relax. I'm a big girl and can look after myself."

She broke off the connection before she got any more mollycoddling from him, but she was pretty sure she'd achieved her goal and made him feel much better.

Back in London, Colin looked at his disconnected phone, then at Peter, his chief second-in-command. The look on Colin's face told Peter all he needed to know.

"Yael Reed again?" Peter asked, rolling his eyes. "That girl needs a permanent bodyguard to stop her from getting into trouble. And yet she does seem to get what she wants in the end."

"She's playing around with the Shin Bet this time, Peter," Colin said in a worried tone, "and I'm not sure she has any idea what she's getting herself into. Do we have any associates in Israel who we can recruit to keep an eye on her before she really gets into inextricable hot water?"

CHAPTER 25

YAEL, OBLIVIOUS TO all the goings-on behind her back in London, waited impatiently for the document she'd sent to be translated and faxed back. "Hurry up, Colin!" she said to herself and the silent fax machine. She was too nervous to remain in the study a second longer than necessary.

Colin, meanwhile, had the document translated by Leora within a minute or two, but she had said to him, "I'm not sure you should tell Yael what it says. Knowing her, as we both do, it's like lighting a fuse on a rocket and expecting it not to take off skyward."

Colin looked at the translated document doubtfully. "I see what you mean. Trouble is I don't know how to go about avoiding telling her."

"Doctor it?" Leora suggested darkly.

Colin thought for a moment. "We could be asking for trouble. This document is a pathway to the truth."

"The truth could really cost her dearly, Colin," Leora said worriedly. "It might even cost Yael her life."

"I know all of this," Colin replied slowly. "But I keep coming back to the same thought, over and over again. She needs this; she has the right to it. We can't protect Yael against everything. If we don't allow her this, she'll only find out some other way, and it might be even less safe for her. I think we should send the document back as it is, and make sure we have someone on the ground over there monitoring her."

"Do you have anyone?" Leora asked anxiously. "I'd never forgive myself if sending this fax ended up in Yael's death."

"It's not sending this fax, it's what she does with it," Colin reminded her. "And as I said, at least this way we can monitor things. Yes, I have Doron Yair. He's our best man in the field in the Middle East. I'll call him right now and fill him in. You send that fax."

"I can't, I just can't!" Leora said, and walked away, shaking her head and waving her arms in a dismissive gesture.

Even as Colin pressed "send" on the fax, his own fingers trembled. He felt like he was signing someone's death warrant. And yet he knew he had to do it.

Then he called Doron Yair.

Yael snatched the fax out of the machine and ran out of the study. Closing the door, she used the same tumbler-and-pick system to tip the lock shut as she'd used to open it. Stuffing the piece of paper into her bag, she ran out of the apartment building. She saw it was pouring, and turned to run in again.

And almost ran straight into Yehuda Brief, who was at the door, fiddling with his key. He had a distracted, tense expression on his face. Yael presumed hers wasn't much better. She had such a shock seeing him that she barely gathered her thoughts together in time to say, "Oh, hello, Mr. Brief!" What she almost said was, "What are *you* doing back?" which might not have gone down so well, as it was his apartment, after all.

"Hello, Miss Rifkind. Where have you been in this rain without a coat?"

Yael laughed shrilly. "Yes, silly me, hey? As you can see, I didn't get too far before realizing, so I came back to get my coat. How's Mrs. Brief?"

They both walked into the apartment at this point, and Brief left the door judiciously ajar. He looked so distracted that he barely heard her question. He was going straight for his study. Yael panicked. What if she hadn't left it the way he had?

He suddenly seemed to register that she'd asked him something. He turned at the door to his study and said, "What?"

"I asked how your wife is," Yael repeated nervously.

At first he almost seemed vague, as if he was casting around for an answer to something that should have been obvious to a loving husband. Then he gathered himself and, smiling a little, said, "She's improving. Starting to talk again." Then obviously deciding that attack was the best form of defense, he added, "Have you been to visit her?"

Putting her chin up defiantly, Yael said, "It was made very clear to me that it wasn't my place to visit her."

His eyebrows arched to match her chin. "Oh? By whom?"

Yael realized that her employer didn't really know her relationship with Nena. He might have had a vague idea that Nena knew *of* "Tamara"; after all, she'd said she might know of someone suitable. But that they were close friends from way back in school might have set up a red flag in Brief's mind, which might have meant that he'd do some more investigating into his new employee—the last thing Yael wanted. He'd find out her real name, and from that it wouldn't take a genius, especially if he worked for Shabak, to work out who her father was.

"Just a feeling I was left with. I'm not family. I guess your wife is too sick to want to see me. All she wants to see is her husband and children." Yael couldn't help heavily accenting the word "husband," and at least Brief had the good grace to look somewhat embarrassed. He cleared his throat and made for the study door again.

"Can I make you a cup of coffee, sir?" Yael asked in what she hoped was a subservient voice. He paused with his hand on the door handle and looked at her as if he'd never seen her before.

"A cup of coffee?" he repeated in a puzzled tone.

"Yes, I just thought you looked as if you could do with one," Yael said artlessly.

"Thanks. Yes. You can bring it into my study. I'll leave the door unlocked. I have some things to do there, then I'm shortly leaving Jerusalem for a while."

"Oh? Going somewhere nice?" Yael couldn't help herself.

"I'm going to Eilat, actually. Just for a couple of days."

"Eilat?" Yael said slowly. "Going on holiday while your wife is in hospital? I suppose you've been very busy and stressed..."

Brief looked at her, irritated. "Not a holiday, I can assure you. Eilat may be a resort, but it's not only that. It has industry and offices, and I have a couple of meetings down there. Now let me get on. I take my coffee black, strong, and with two Sucrazits, please."

He opened his study door with his key, which Yael noticed was attached to a bunch he wore at his waist. *Like a jailor*, she thought. At least the door appeared untampered with. She just *had* to see his first reaction to the room, she was that terrified. So she followed him in.

"Decaf or caffeinated?" she asked unnecessarily. She just needed an excuse to be in there.

He was at his desk looking at a pile of papers on it. She hadn't disturbed anything; she'd been too nervous. All she'd done was use the fax machine. Was there any way of him knowing she'd used it? Faxes were so obsolete that the techie Yael had no idea.

But then she found out.

The fax whirred and a sheet of paper spat out. Luckily for Yael, it shot out so energetically that it landed on the floor and not on his fax table, which was next to his desk.

She bent down to it. On it was the heading "Clearing History."

It was the history of all the ingoing and outgoing faxes. Her UK number to Colin was clearly at the top.

"Caffeinated of course," he said, irritated, rifling through the papers on his desk. "What's that fax?"

"It's just the history clearing," she said casually, although she fought to stop her voice from shaking and her hands from trembling as she held the paper.

"Oh, okay, just chuck that in the recycling bin," he said. "And bring me that coffee, stat. I think you're right. I could do with it. I've got so much work to do before I leave for Eilat that it's ridiculous."

"Yes, sir," she said, and left the room holding the paper.

In the kitchen, Yael crumpled the history into a tight ball, and then, rethinking, smoothed it out and tore it into tiny shreds before putting it in the recycling box. Then she leaned against the door until she stopped shaking like the proverbial leaf in a rainstorm.

She put the kettle on and prepared the coffee. While it was heating up, she took the translated document out of her bag and looked at it. Her eyes widened as she read.

According to the document, there was no way Brief was going to Eilat. That was just a story he had spun her to throw her off the scent.

The letter, from Shabak, directed him to go somewhere else entirely.

It contained an itinerary stating he had been booked onto a flight to Cairo. Cairo, Egypt. First thing in the morning.

And Yael was going to follow Yehuda Brief to Egypt and find some answers.

CHAPTER 26

COLIN HAD ASKED Ho Kai Ming to keep checking the airlines out of Israel to see if Yael would book a flight to Egypt. As Leora had said, once she'd read the document, and knew where Yehuda Brief was going, it was only a matter of time before she followed him.

"She might not fly, Colin," Ho Kai said, checking the online flight databases as he spoke. "It's only a five-hour bus ride and probably a lot cheaper."

"Yes, but Brief is flying direct," Colin pointed out, "which will get him there in an hour or less. There's no way, knowing Yael, that she'd not follow him in the fastest way possible. To be six hours or so behind him is like not bothering at all, to that young lady."

"I wonder where she'll get the money," Ho Kai mused.

"I'm sure she won't be flying business class like Brief is. Shabak pays for his comfort. She'll travel in the baggage hold if she has to, to keep up with him."

Ho Kai wasn't known for his sense of humor and looked alarmed.

"I was kidding!" Colin was quick to reassure the Asian techie. "But I'm sure she'll find a cheapish flight. Buses aren't that cheap either, long distance."

"Ah, it's just come up!" Ho Kai exclaimed, pointing with his cursor. "She's taking a one-way flight to Cairo tomorrow morning. She's on the same flight as Brief. Only she has a seat at the back of the plane and he's right up in front."

"That's a bit risky, isn't it?" Colin said.

"Doesn't Yael Reed live on risk?" Ho Kai replied.

"I must get Doron Yair on that flight too," Colin said. "See to it, Ho Kai, stat."

As Ho Kai's fingers flew across the keyboard, he commented, "It's not that cheap," pointing out the price to Colin.

"I can only presume she has some money stashed away from somewhere. Maybe her current job paid her enough, although she's only been there five minutes, so I don't see how," Colin said.

"The one-way part of it is worrying me," Ho Kai said. "Why didn't she organize her return journey, a way out?"

"I suppose she's got no idea how long she's going to be there, and she can always come back to Jerusalem by bus. She's probably thinking that the return journey won't be so pressurized, time-wise."

Colin had it spot-on. These were exactly Yael's reckonings when booking the flight to Cairo. It cost her an arm and a leg as far as her savings were concerned, and she worried about her credit card being refused, but it went through. She had no idea how she'd make the repayments, but decided she'd worry about that later.

The issue of being recognized by Yehuda Brief didn't worry her. She'd been undercover before and had gotten away with it without being recognized even by people who knew her well. Brief had barely looked at her full in the face.

Yael never went anywhere without some disguises in her suitcase. This time she'd brought the bright red nylon wig and the green contact lenses she'd used in the Disappeareds case. Wearing that, along with a pull-on beanie and some fake spectacles, her own mother wouldn't recognize her, she thought.

She pulled herself back on that. Her own mother wouldn't recognize her no matter what she wore, because her own mother didn't want anything to do with her. And now she was going on the trail of her father, who, according to her mother, wasn't worth knowing either. Of course, the likelihood was that Alan Katz was dead, killed in that hit-and-run by accident or design—that was what she needed to find out. Then she could finally close the chapter on her unfortunate parentage and move on with her life.

She didn't want to take check-in baggage, so she rammed some essentials into a large backpack. She hid it under her duvet and went about some evening duties. Brief had locked himself in his study again, doing whatever Shabak operatives did, she presumed. The door to the apartment had been left ajar, but Yael still felt insecure. However, this was soon remedied; at about 10 p.m., Brief emerged from his study, with a wheelie case on a long carry handle, and announced he was going to sleep in a hotel by the airport as he had a business meeting there before his flight and the businessman wouldn't come as far as Jerusalem.

"And it's not right anyway for us to be alone in this apartment overnight," he said. "You lock all the doors and go to sleep. In the morning, I'll get Nena, my daughter-in-law (as if Yael didn't know who Nena was!), to contact you and update you as to your status. If my wife is going to be in the hospital for quite some time, as looks likely at the moment, I don't see the need for your continued employment. If things change and she's allowed out tomorrow or the next day, obviously you'll still be needed, very much so."

Uh-oh, Yael thought. *I don't really want to hope Esther requires an extended hospital stay, but…*

Brief was fiddling with his wallet. "You haven't been paid anything since you've come here," he went on, "and since it's most likely your employment will be terminated as of tomorrow, I want to pay you now, plus some compensation for the short notice." He handed her a wad of notes. "I hope this is okay. You've actually been very good, Tamara Rifkind, especially with Yonina. She adores you, and will be devastated that you've gone. I was even considering keeping you on just for her sake. But you were employed for my wife, and a nine-year-old doesn't really need a full-time nanny."

No, Yael thought, *she just needs her parents, poor little lamb.*

"So who will be here for Yonina, sir?" she asked.

"I have a regular babysitter we used in the past. I'll contact her on my way to the airport. Yonina quite likes her, I think. Not as much as she likes you. I don't think her talent in voices when reading stories is quite as good, but she cooks what Yonina likes to eat, at least."

That child's diet needs seriously taking in hand, Yael thought. But she said nothing on that score. She looked at the wad of cash in her hand.

The payoff was generous and would even cover her flight to Cairo with cash to spare. "Thank you so much for the money, sir," Yael said with genuine enthusiasm and gratitude.

Brief nodded, then looked a little stressed as he glanced at his watch. "Very good. Well, if I don't see you again, thank you very much for everything. I must go now."

Yael wasn't sure if she wanted him never to see her again or not. Only time would tell on that score. She certainly wanted him not to *know* it was her, if he saw her on the plane or in Egypt.

Once Brief had left the apartment, Yael bolted all the locks gratefully, feeling instantly safer. She had a plan, she had a backpack, and she had cash. She was all set to go to Cairo.

She used some of the extra cash to book herself a ride to the airport in a *sheirut* in the small hours. She made herself something to eat, and some extra food for the journey, and lay down on the couch in the living room to sleep for a couple of hours. She didn't trust herself to go to her bedroom to sleep; she thought she might not wake up in time.

In the end she needn't have worried about not waking up, because she didn't even manage to fall asleep. Her adrenaline and tension were so high. She got up in the dark and set about making herself unrecognizable.

Looking at the finished product in the bathroom mirror, she was satisfied. The redhead with bright green eyes that looked back at her wasn't Yael Reed. Nor was it Tamara Rifkind. Her flight ticket was under her real name, but she hoped that Yehuda Brief wouldn't suspect, or even look, that he was being accompanied to Cairo by his wife's caregiver.

Yael finished off her look with red-framed spectacles that gave her a cute but geeky appearance. She applied bright red lipstick that both clashed with her hair and enhanced her overall unrecognizability.

Picking up her backpack, she went out of the apartment to catch the *sheirut*. She planned to call Nena when it was a civilized hour, and tell her that she had been told by her father-in-law that her services were no longer required.

She wouldn't tell Nena where she was going.

CHAPTER 27

"WAKE UP! WE'RE at the airport!"
Someone was shaking her. Yael wasn't even aware she'd fallen asleep in the *sheirut*, although it made sense as she hadn't slept all night. People were getting off, and the driver was busy unceremoniously throwing everyone's luggage out of the van onto the pavement. Some less well-packed suitcases burst open, but he made no attempt to help them repack. Items lay strewn all over. Yael was once again grateful she had no check-in baggage; indeed her overstuffed backpack had proved a comfortable cushion between her head and the window.

Glancing in the *sheirut*'s window for reflection, she checked that her wig and glasses were on straight. Yup, she looked nothing like herself. So if she should bump into Brief, she was safe. She did offer to help one or two people repack their bags, but they seemed to take it as a threat to their personal belongings, as if she'd surreptitiously make off with some valuables, so after two rejected offers, she left them to it. The driver had taken everyone's money and zoomed off. Yael thought he was rude and unpleasant, but the

144 Foundling

other passengers just shrugged and said, "You get what you pay for," or words to that effect.

She went through the usual check-in procedures. When the security officer asked her why she was going to Egypt, she was momentarily at a loss, but then said, "I just wanna see it!" He accepted that, and she was through.

She wandered around duty-free, looking to see if she could spy Brief. She had no intention of buying anything, but then she thought about the fact that she was going to a non-Jewish country and she hadn't packed enough food. So she went to a *mehadrin* takeout place and bought some food to tide her over. It was there that she saw Brief, sitting at a table, eating some breakfast, while studying his usual pile of important papers, making comments and marks in the margin with a pen.

Ho Kai had said something to Colin back in the UK that had never rung more true than at that moment. He'd said, "Doesn't Yael Reed live on risk?" Yael could have skirted around Brief, avoided him like the plague, kept her head down—in case, despite her disguise, a sharp-eyed Shabak operative would recognize her.

But she did none of these things. On the contrary, she decided that if she was going to be following Brief around in Cairo, maybe she'd better try out her disguise to the maximum.

She walked right up to where he was sitting, and, using one of the many voices she'd used to such good effect on Yonina, said in a broad South African accent, "Excuse me, is this restaurant kosher?"

Of course Brief looked up at her. His expression didn't show any sign of recognition, even though she was quaking inside.

"All the restaurants in the airport are kosher," he said, and looked back at his sheaf of papers.

"Ah understand that," Yael maintained. "Ah'm asking if it's, lahk, *really* kosher. You look lahk a *frum* man so ah thought ah'd ask."

Looking vaguely irritated, Brief indicated the *teudat hechsher* that stated "*Mehadrin min hamehadrin*" in brown on a pale yellow background.

"Yes," he said.

"Only ah'm going to Cahro and ah don't think there's any kosher food there," she said, really taking chances. This made Brief look up with interest.

"Cairo? I'm going there too. I can tell you, you won't find much in the way of kosher food there. Fruit and veg—and even that isn't anything remotely as nice as the Israeli produce. You probably won't find any Jews except for other tourists, and those are thin on the ground at the moment. I won't be there for long so it's okay. How long are you going for? And dare I ask why you're going? It's hardly the same as it was before the Arab Spring." Brief was looking right at Yael and he didn't recognize her. She was triumphant.

Yael tossed her red hair in a most un-Tamara-Rifkind-like gesture. "Ah take mah chances where ah can," she said. "Ah'm not scared of danger." That was about the only area where Yael and this new persona merged. The addiction to danger.

She didn't answer the question as to how long she was going for. She honestly didn't know herself.

"You can survive on fruit and vegetables, open a can of tuna and a can of sweetcorn," Brief said. "Those two things have always been my mainstay when I've been traveling away from Jewish areas. Try and get the cans with a ring pull, save having to use a can opener. But it's a dangerous place for a young lady on her own." To his credit, he did look worried.

"Oh, ah'm very self-sufficient," Yael said blithely. "Ah do a lot of solo traveling."

Brief looked somewhat reassured at this piece of information. "Ah, good." He turned back to his papers, signaling the conversation over.

Yael spent a bit more money on food at this second *mehadrin* place. After that was gone, she reckoned, she'd survive any way she could. After a little more thought, she stocked up on some crunchy protein bars. Those were transportable and required no refrigeration. Walking away from where Brief sat, she found herself grinning. Not only had he not recognized her, he'd been fooled by her voice too. What a mistress of disguise Yael Reed, supersleuth, was!

The flight was called, and the two of them walked to the plane together, along with a whole lot of obviously Arab passengers, Yael following Brief just because they were two Jews. *How incongruous is that?* she thought to herself, grinning secretly.

"Where are you sitting?" she asked him.

"I travel business class," he said. "I'd be flying first class if there was any, but this is a small plane, so there isn't. More's the pity. I prefer first to business, but what can I do." He had an "oy, how we suffer!" tone to his voice that annoyed Yael. Some people were so out of touch, they had no idea how ordinary people lived, she thought.

"Oh, posh!" she said in a mocking tone, sticking to her South African accent. "Ah've never flown anything but steerage. Can't afford those kahnd of prahces." *Considering I've only ever flown once in my entire life and this will be the second time…*

"My work pays for it," Brief said. "I assure you, I don't. They want to ensure I arrive fresh and rested so I can get on with my job." He stopped, as if annoyed with himself for being so defensive about his indulgences.

"Oh? What work is that? I must applah for a job!" A little high-pitched laugh.

A slight pause. "International trade," Brief said. "I doubt you'd get a job. It's very male oriented."

Yael bridled at this. "Then it's about tahm that changed isn't it?" she challenged. "Tell me what company you work for and I'm going to applah!"

Brief didn't answer. He didn't need to. Their paths diverged at that point, as he went down the passageway to the business class entrance, and she went down the economy entrance passage. The set of Brief's shoulders, and the way he shook them a little in release, made Yael smile. He looked relieved to be shot of her.

In your dreams you're shot of me, she thought. *You're going to be seeing a lot more of this particular South African tourist yet! Ah'm going to be dogging your worst nightmares!*

CHAPTER 28

ON THE FLIGHT, alone in her seat, Yael's nerve gave way and she sat there wondering what on earth she had got herself into. Basically echoing what Colin and Leora had thought, and the entire sensible civilized world would be thinking if they knew what she was up to.

When Yael's spirits were at their all-time low, as was the case on this short plane ride, one little thought, niggling, annoying, and persistent, always came up to bite her. To remind her that it hadn't gone away and never, ever would.

You think what you're doing will help your shidduch resume?

Most of the time, Yael barely gave much thought to getting married. She couldn't think of any young man alive who would willingly and happily settle down with someone like her, and as she had no intention of changing her personality or behavior to fit the required mold, that was that.

Doomed to remain forever single, but a free spirit to do whatever she wanted, when she wanted, and would be beholden to no one. Ever. That sounded wonderful at times, as she pictured herself flying around the world, solving impossible cases, making a name for herself as *the* detective to contact if you wanted to get things done. She would be as world famous as Sherlock Holmes, Poirot, and Miss Marple all rolled into one.

She liked that image and clung onto it during the dark times. But then the dark times resurfaced and reminded her of what it might be like when she was no longer twenty-one and fancy-free, but forty-one—or even the unimaginably old age of *fifty-one*!—and wrinkling around the edges, arthritis setting in around her knees, and no one to make her feel better when she felt lonely and unloved.

I'll just have to get cats, she thought. I'll be the weird cat lady down the street everybody talks about. *I suppose I could get a big, old, loveable dog*, like Leah Brodie's Ashmedai who she'd encountered in the Disappeareds case, who was meant to be a guard dog, but was as malleable and wimpy as an old dishrag. *I could just about manage a dog like that*, Yael thought.

Now, sitting on that plane Egypt bound, these thoughts overwhelmed her. She turned her face up to the ceiling and, to her annoyance, found great, fat tears rolling out from under her eyelids. She took off her red glasses to dab at them, but they fell faster than she could cope with.

There's supposed to be someone out there for everyone, she thought. *But is there really? Is there really someone for a person as wacky and eccentric and different as me?*

It wasn't often that self-pity overcame Yael Reed. She hated it in others, and all the more so in herself. But now it washed over her like a tsunami and she couldn't stop it. The flight attendant came over to her, looking concerned.

"Are you okay?" she asked the young girl.

Furious with herself, Yael scrubbed at the tears with her sleeve. Well, what were sleeves for anyway?

"I'm fine," she said. "Thanks."

"We're landing in a few minutes. Buckle up and get prepared," said the flight attendant kindly.

By the time the plane bumped gently to earth in Cairo, Yael was composed and calm, her glasses firmly back in place. She'd had her tsunami of pity and it was over. Who wanted to get married anyway? What a bother, having to kowtow to someone else for the rest of your life! She'd stick to a big, soppy dog and a houseful of cats.

She kept Brief well in sight as she went through customs. Like her, he had no check-in baggage, and once through passport control, he just walked straight out of the airport.

Taking her courage in both hands, she walked up to him.

"Ah wonder if ah might be *chutzpahdik* and ask to share a taxi with you into town?" she said. "Ah don't have much money and…"

He looked at her, irritated. "That depends where you need to be. I'm going to the Cairo Marriott Hotel. It's on 16 Saraya El Gezira. In the Zamalek district. Do you know it?"

Yael practically fainted with excitement. "Well, don't that beat all! Ah'm going to the same place! What a coincidence!"

To say that Brief looked marginally disappointed at this news would be an understatement. He looked as if someone had told him he'd lost all his money. He glared at Yael.

"Well, come on, then. It makes sense to share a cab. Although how you managed to afford such an expensive hotel if you don't have enough money for the cab, I'll never know."

Yael got into the cab with Brief. He sat shotgun, next to the driver, and she sat demurely (if Yael Reed could ever be called demure!) in the backseat.

She chatted on.

"Ah never said ah'm staying at that particular hotel," she said.

"Of course it's much too expensive for me. Ah'm staying at a hostel round the corner from it."

"Ah," Brief said.

Yael didn't have the faintest idea if such a hostel existed. All she knew was she wanted to keep Brief within her sights, and would find somewhere cheap to stay to achieve her goals.

Brief regarded their chat as over. Yael was okay with that, and amused herself by looking out the window at the sights and sounds of Egypt.

The highway along which the taxi traveled at breakneck speed could have been anywhere in Israel, although of course Yael hadn't seen much of Israel except for her trips to and from the airport, which looked quite similar to the highway she was zooming along now. She clung to the seats, the door, anything that gave her some degree of security as the taxi driver swerved around other drivers, honking his horn continuously, and yelling at them through his open driver's window.

Brief seemed oblivious to the pandemonium outside. He was doing something no doubt very important on his phone all the while. Yael thought if she even looked at her phone while the car was going at this speed, let alone do anything on it, she'd throw up.

The weather was totally different there, too, from the rainy cool of Jerusalem. In Cairo it was at least ten degrees warmer, sunny, and steamily humid. The car had no air conditioner, and, despite the windows being wide open, Yael began to drip. She divested herself of her coat. Then her jacket. She was wiping the back of her neck with her jacket when the taxi screeched to a halt outside a very smart hotel. The immediate surroundings looked seedy, though, and Yael's heart sank at the thought of finding accommodation one street away from the smart hotel.

She got out her purse to pay her share of the taxi fare, but Brief waved it away. "No need. Good-bye." He was obviously keen to be rid of her.

As she'd thought previously, *In your dreams.*

Brief paid the cab driver, who zoomed off in a cloud of dust, leaving the two of them on the sidewalk looking at each other.

"I'm going in. Nice to have met you," he said.

Yael waved cheerily. "Ah'm off to find a hostel," she said.

"You mean you have nothing booked?" Brief asked her, alarmed.

"Ah told you, ah take mah chances," she said.

"It's not safe!" he protested. "The streets around here are riddled with crime. A young woman on her own is asking for trouble." Yael watched Brief battle with his conscience. He obviously wanted her to leave as quickly as possible, but by the same token he wanted to be able to sleep at night.

"Look." Brief sighed. "I'm a *very* busy man. But I can't have you wandering around Cairo trying to find lodgings. I'll see if the hotel has a cheap room somewhere, the bottom of their price range, and let's see what you can afford. I'm sure I can help you out a bit if it's still too much…"

Yes! Yael thought, but kept her expression neutral.

"Oh, ah'll be okay… Don't trouble yourself…" She made as if to walk off down the garbage-strewn streets toward the slums.

"No. I wouldn't hear of it. Come inside. I'll make it my business to see you're okay," Brief said firmly. "We'll find you a cheap room; I'm sure it won't be luxurious. These hotels only look nice in the lobby areas. I've got one of the better rooms. So yours will be basic, but a whole lot better than what you'll find out there." He waved in the general direction of the city.

"Oh, okay, if you're sure," Yael said with as much reluctance as she could muster without looking ridiculous.

And followed Brief into the hotel, rather like she'd followed Miss Colton down the school corridor seven years earlier, doing a little happy dance behind him, that he thankfully couldn't see.

CHAPTER 29

"So what's the latest?" Colin asked Doron.

"Ehh, you won't believe me if I tell you," the operative said with a bemused smile that Colin could hear even over three thousand miles and a somewhat unclear connection. "That girl would make an amazing addition to the Israeli security services. I think we should get her recruited ASAP."

"Well, tell me anyway!" Colin said impatiently. Leora was listening in on speaker and they exchanged glances at that moment.

"Before I tell you, I must ask you this: How did she get through security in disguise? She looks nothing like her passport photo in that red wig, contacts, and red glasses."

"I wondered the same thing. She called me to explain. She was well behind Brief going through security, so she slipped off her wig and glasses until she got through security, then went into the ladies' bathroom to put them on again. But I read about someone who tested the system by traveling for six months with a photograph of his dog in his passport, and no one noticed!"

"Not on El Al though?" Doron laughed.

Foundling 155

"No, just some less observant airlines. Anyway, tell me what's doing with her now."

"Okay, here's the latest. Not only has she managed to follow Brief incognito, she's managed to chat to him, share a taxi from the airport, and now he's found her a cheap room in his hotel."

"What?" Colin said, looking at his wife, whose jaw had similarly hit the floor. "How did she manage that? Don't tell me. She's in disguise and she fooled him totally. She's done that before in a school."

"Yes," Leora said, "but in the school, no one knew her real persona. Here, she's been in Brief's *employ* for the past few days!"

"Well, whatever it is, she's pulled it off," Doron said. "She's quite the master at this. As I say, a useful asset to Shabak, I'd suggest."

"Are you keeping her under close scrutiny?" Colin asked. "I'd really like to keep that girl safe if at all possible. "

"Not an easy task with someone like Yael Reed," Doron confessed. "But I'll try and rise to the challenge."

He disconnected the call to London, and turned to the next person waiting at the desk.

"Yes, sir, can I help you? You're booked in to room 507? I have your reservation right here, just fill in the details for me, please, and let me swipe your credit card…"

Doron Yair was twenty-six years old, dark, handsome, and looked Sephardi even though he wasn't, so was well placed to pass as an Egyptian hotel worker. How he managed to get the undercover job was another matter, but Shabak, and Colin's connections to it, had far-reaching tentacles, even in the Arab world.

Colin had looked into Yehuda Brief and he had come up clean. He was a legitimate member of the Shin Bet, although he'd never admit it to anyone he knew. In his own community in Ezras Torah, Brief was a businessman; no one knew quite what he did, but he gave generously to charities, attended the local shuls regularly, so no one asked too many questions. "A businessman" had so many meanings, and people were willing to accept him on face value.

So if he was clean, what had happened to Alan Katz? Doron had quite a task ahead of him: keeping Yael safe, if at all possible—a task and a half in itself—and trying to help unobtrusively in whatever she was trying to find out at the same time.

Yael wondered what was wrong with her room at first. It looked fine to her. And had been almost unbelievably reasonable in price. She had a strong suspicion Brief had something to do with the reasonableness, but beggars couldn't be choosers and she really needed this room. He was right; she must have been nuts to think she could go off on her own in this alien city looking for a hostel.

Having looked more closely at the room, Yael could see its shortcomings: furniture that fell apart when she opened drawers and closets; a single, dingy mirror that swung precariously off its hook on the wall; nasty-looking multi-legged critters residing in the cramped bathroom; and a panoramic view of a building site outside her dirty window. The bed, too, creaked ominously when she sat on it, and the sheets looked none too clean. She pulled the bedding open nervously, hoping no more awful critters would be lurking there, but thankfully, there was nothing else organic under the covers.

Thinking for only a moment, she unpacked her spare clothing, but kept any valuables in her knapsack. The room had no fridge of course, and it had a rusty, noisy AC unit that didn't promise much in the way of cooling. She worried about her food going off but there wasn't much she could do.

Hm...maybe...

She took the elevator down to the ground floor and went to

the front desk. The young man behind it maintained an impassive expression when he saw her approach.

"Can I help?" he asked her.

"Yes," Yael said, pulled out her stash of perishable food from her knapsack. "I wonder if you have a fridge I could keep this in until I need it?"

He took the package, noted the *mehadrin* hechsher, but only smiled inwardly. He didn't want her to guess who had sent him to watch her, or who he really was.

Putting on an Arabic accent he nodded and said, "Yes, miss, I can put this in the fridge for you. I'll label it. What room number are you?" Even though he knew exactly.

When that was settled, Yael made for the door. Doron was alarmed.

"Miss, are you going out?" he called after her.

"Yes, going to explore," she said. Yehuda Brief had not appeared since he'd sorted out a room for her, so she decided to start following him the next day. Today was just for her to take a look around.

"Not safe, not safe for missies on their own," Doron said in his overdone Arabic accent, but Yael didn't notice.

She waved an "I don't care!" arm behind her and walked out the hotel, slinging her knapsack over her shoulder as she went.

Doron wasted no time in getting a stand-in for the hotel desk, and within moments, he was following her down the street at a discreet distance, so even if she turned around, suspicious, she wouldn't spot him.

Yael quickly realized that what everyone had been warning her about wasn't a fantasy. After she'd been hassled and approached a few times with "Can I practice with you my English, please?" and "Please you come to my family's restaurant to experience authentic Egyptian cuisine!" she felt uncomfortable and harassed.

She made one stop into a mini market to buy some canned tuna and sweetcorn, making sure both kinds had ring-pull openers. She also bought some disposables to eat it in, and plastic cutlery, and bottled drinks.

There was a rather sweet and friendly girl behind the counter who actually spoke English quite well, and made Yael feel welcome. Her name was Jana. They chatted for a while. Yael told her about the hassles she'd been subjected to in the street. The girl frowned.

"Oh, you must never accept their invitation to experience authentic Egyptian cuisine!" she warned Yael. "They'll give you a free Coke or Sprite, then slam you with overpriced goods once you're in their store. Next time, pretend you don't speak English, and then they won't try that one with you."

"How come you speak such good English?" Yael asked, impressed.

"I went to college in London," Jana said.

"I'll be honest with you," Yael said. "I'm lost here, and I need someone who knows the language. Would you have any time to go around with me? I'll pay you of course, as long as it's not too much. I don't have much money."

"I have to work in this shop," Jana said, "but I have time usually in the mornings when my brother works here instead of me. I could be your guide then. You mean as a tourist? Show you the sights?"

"Um, not really. More as an interpreter," Yael said. "I'm a private investigator, but I can't do much investigating if I don't speak the language."

"A private investigator? How exciting! I'd love to help you! I'm sure we can work out a reasonable fee that would be okay for both of us!" Jana looked thrilled. "Shall I come to your hotel tomorrow morning?"

They arranged a time, and Yael left the shop. She was tired after the journey and the stress of being undercover, so decided to go straight back to the hotel, eat her meager supper (after retrieving her food from the hotel refrigerator to supplement the tuna and sweetcorn), and go to bed early. Jana would be there early the next morning and she reckoned an exciting day awaited. She wanted to follow Yehuda Brief.

If she noticed that a different hotel worker was at the front desk and got her food for her, it didn't trouble her unduly. Doron Yair had barely made a mark on her subconscious. One hotel worker was very much like another to her.

She'd definitely made a mark on his subconscious, though. He'd followed her, overheard her conversation with Jana, and had already transmitted it back to Colin and Leora in London.

Colin sounded worried. "Find out who this Jana is," he instructed Doron, "and if Yael is safe going out with her."

CHAPTER 30

"I'LL NEVER COMPLAIN about my bed at home again," Yael grumbled at 2 a.m. as she tossed and turned on the uncomfortable mattress that seemed determined to poke her all over her body. She was sure she'd be bruised black and blue by morning. She'd had the light on and off, she'd taken two showers and even soaked in the tiny, unattractive tub, just to try and ease herself into sleep. She'd never felt the bed in her own rented apartment in London was up to much, but it was heaven compared to this. How was anyone supposed to sleep on such a lumpy, bumpy mattress?

The story of the "Princess and the Pea" kept coming back to her, but she was no princess, and it was no tiny pea that was causing her such discomfort under ten perfectly good mattresses. This was one paper-thin, dirt-cheap affair with broken springs, if there were any springs in it at all; she rather suspected it was just a thin piece of foam, laid on a rough, lumpy wooden base.

At two forty-five she got out of bed for about the fifth time to turn the mattress over, thinking maybe it would be less lumpy on the less used side. It didn't look much better on the underside, possibly more stained than the upper side, but she patted it down, trying to get it more even…when she felt a lump in the middle of the mattress that had nothing to do with the cheap foam it was made of.

She felt it again. It was a small, oblong lump, hard and unyielding, and it was not part of the bed.

Puzzled, she looked at the mattress, turning it this way and that. Yael was wide awake now, all thoughts of sleep forgotten. After looking at it in the dim hotel light for a while, she got out her phone, which had a flashlight on it. This gave her a much clearer view.

By the bright light of the flashlight she saw it.

A small slit in the mattress. Yael slipped in her hand and retrieved the object. It was a USB flash drive.

Yael sat down on the mattress and looked at the flash drive. Who would hide one in a mattress in a hotel in Cairo? After only hesitating a moment, she got out her laptop from her backpack, switched it on, waited impatiently for it to boot up, and then inserted the drive and clicked on the files.

She could barely believe her eyes. It was all in some kind of code. Handwritten but totally illegible, and in no alphabet that Yael had ever seen before. She thought she could have recognized Greek, Russian, Arabic, the Indian languages, but this was like none of those. It was numeric, and letters mixed up. She stared at it for a while, then gave up. She put the laptop in her knapsack. She had used a code guy before, in the Disappeareds case. Jimmy had known someone. She'd maybe e-mail him a few files from the drive for him to look at.

Not for one moment did Yael consider putting the drive back into the mattress, in case whoever had put it there might assume it would still be there when he or she came back. That was not in her radar.

She put the sheet back on and lay down. Thinking about the drive hurt her head. She gave up and eventually fell asleep.

She awoke to a knock on her bedroom door. The sun was blazing through the paper-thin curtains and it was already so hot that she'd thrown off her covers in the night.

"Who is it?" Yael called nervously from her bed.

"It's Jana. You said we should meet at nine and it's already half past. I've been waiting downstairs. The desk clerk gave me your room number and said it was okay to come and check you were okay."

"Oh my… Is it really nine thirty?" Yael jumped out of bed and was halfway to the door before she stopped in her tracks.

Yael realized that Jana had only ever seen her in her disguise. And right now she was plain old Yael Reed, curly hair and all. She hastened to pull on the wig, and put on the green contacts before she opened the door.

"I'm so sorry!" Yael blustered, letting the girl in. "I couldn't sleep until really late and then I slept in, obviously… It'll take me a while to get ready. I'm so sorry!"

"No problem," Jana said. "Shall I go and order breakfast for us downstairs while I'm waiting?"

Yael paused in her rushing around to think that one through. "Um, I don't know."

How much of her heritage should she reveal to this Arab girl? Had she already guessed that she was Jewish?

"I'm a vegan," Yael said at last. "Is there just fruit and vegetables, maybe?" *I hope she doesn't remember that I bought tuna from her yesterday…*

"I'm vegetarian myself," Jana said. "And I'm sure there is. I'll go check and meet you downstairs."

After she closed the door, Yael realized the girl had assumed

Yael would pay for her breakfast. Which at hotel prices wouldn't come cheap. *It's a good thing Brief gave me a bonus wad of cash when we parted*, she thought. *I'm going to need it!*

Yael stuffed some of her stash of food into her mouth before she went downstairs, in case there was nothing she could eat. She put some protein bars in her knapsack, and left the rest in her closet. The perishable food from the night before was almost gone; there wasn't enough to make it worth putting back in the hotel fridge. Oh well, she still had her cans of tuna and sweetcorn.

The hotel dining room catered well to tourists and there were all kinds of salads and fruit, as well as things Yael couldn't eat. She took a plate with some whole fruit and tomatoes and whatever else she thought was non-problematic and joined Jana at a table.

As Yael ate her fruit, she looked around and saw Yehuda Brief. He was drinking coffee and talking on his phone at another table. He looked extremely agitated. She watched him go to the hotel desk, which was right next to the breakfast room. She saw him talking to the guy behind the desk and waving his hands around. He started shouting.

"What's going on there?" Jana asked, gesturing to the desk. "That man seems to be making an awful fuss."

"I have no idea," Yael said honestly.

"Do you know him?" she asked.

This gave Yael pause. If she admitted knowing him well, it was akin to admitting she was Jewish, and she didn't yet trust Jana enough for her to know that.

"Vaguely," she admitted at last, waving a hand to illustrate how vague.

This vagueness was soon to be called into question because Brief was coming over, aiming straight for her table, and his face looked like a thundercloud. Yael looked behind her, hopefully, to see if there could possibly be someone else he was looking at, but no luck. It was her.

"The desk man gave you the wrong room," he said.

Yael didn't quite know what to make of that. After a pause, as he continued to look at her angrily, she just said, "Oh?"

Brief looked at her, then at her companion. Then, as if realizing how he must be coming across, his whole demeanor changed.

"Yes," he said with a charming smile that made Yael feel sick to her stomach. "When I said a cheap room, I didn't mean quite *that* cheap. It's the worst room in the whole hotel. You deserve better than that."

"Ah can't afford better than that," she said, remembering her South African accent last minute.

Brief flushed, looked awkward, then said, "It's all arranged. You're to move to a much nicer room, with decent furniture. Same cost. Nothing more. Go to the desk and he'll tell you what room, and you can move right across."

He smiled at her again and stormed off, leaving the two girls sitting there gobsmacked.

"I thought you said you didn't know him," Jana said.

Yael didn't quite know how to answer. But what she was thinking was, *How does Brief know what my room is like? And why is he so adamant that I leave it?*

CHAPTER 31

"I SAID, I THOUGHT you didn't know him," Jana repeated. Yael looked at her, as if seeing her for the first time.

The girl had a hard, penetrating gaze that almost frightened Yael. Not being one to be easily intimidated, though, Yael said brightly, "I met him on the plane and asked to share a taxi with him. Then I said I was going to stay in a hostel and his conscience got the better of him and he arranged me a room in this hotel. He said it wasn't safe for a single girl to stay in a hostel in Cairo."

"He's right," Jana said. "You'd have been very stupid to have stayed in a hostel on your own." She was still looking at Yael very hard. "You spoke differently when you spoke to him than how you're speaking now," she said.

Oops, Yael thought.

"I was playing with accents. I pretended to be South African when I first spoke to him, so I had to keep being South African with him, that's all," she said. It was as honest as she was willing to be with Jana at this stage.

It seemed to work. After another hard stare, the girl relaxed and laughed. "That was a pretty convincing South African accent, actually."

Phew, Yael thought.

"So where are we going today?" Jana asked, finishing her breakfast.

"I'd like to see the sights of Cairo a little bit," Yael said cautiously, "but I'd really like to know what that man is up to. How do you fancy helping me be a PI and let's follow him?"

Jana looked keen at this prospect. It was certainly more exciting than just traipsing around the same boring old tourist sites.

"He's still at the desk," Jana said. "Still angry by the look of him."

"Let's go and try to eavesdrop," Yael said.

They pretended to be deeply fascinated by a rotating display of postcards close to the desk and listened intently to what Brief was saying.

"Are you sure that was the room you gave her?" he said. "How can you have been so stupid? That was the room I specially asked you not to give her and you go and give it to her!"

"I'm so sorry, sir," Doron Yair said.

"Never mind. As long as you give her another room and don't charge her any extra," Brief said, slightly mollified.

"Well, that was our cheapest room, so any other room will cost more," Doron said. "But as you say, it's our mistake, so we won't charge any more for another room of a similar standard."

At this point, Brief finally noticed the two girls. Clearing his throat he said to Doron, "I want her to have a *nicer* room, not another room of a similar standard, do you understand? That room was little better than a slum."

Yael could contain herself no longer. Putting on her red glasses she said to Brief, moving back into her South African accent, "Have you stayed in that room then? How do you know what it's lahk?"

Brief looked across at her, startled. "I haven't, no. I only stay in the premium suites. But I've heard reports."

"Ah, okay," Yael said, and took her glasses off again.

"So are you moving your stuff out soon?" he asked her.

"Is there a rush?" she asked innocently.

"Well, I'm sure the hotel will need to turn the room around for the next guest."

"You mean there's someone else who wants to stay in that slum, as you call it?" Yael asked, wide-eyed.

"We do require guests to vacate by eleven in the morning," Doron said, coming to Brief's rescue.

"Ah'll be out of there sooner than that, if you just tell me which room to move mah stuff into, which you haven't yet done," Yael said.

Doron handed her a new room key. "Lower floor, nicer view, much better furniture," he said.

And no doubt, no flash drive inside the mattress, Yael thought.

She told Jana she'd be ten minutes. Jana said she'd amuse herself in the lobby. Yael needed twenty seconds to pack her stuff, as most of it was already in her knapsack, and nine minutes forty seconds to take another look at that mattress.

She had a good feel around, inside the lumpy foam block, but there was nothing else there. What she wanted to do was render the mattress unnoticeable that it had been interfered with, but her skills at sewing up blocks of foam were nonexistent—even if she'd had a sewing kit, which she didn't. So she put the mattress back in such a way that the small slit was in the furthest corner, and it would take quite a lot of scrabbling around and turning the mattress to find the slit again. She couldn't do any more, so she tidied up as best she could and went downstairs.

"Ah've vacated the room," she said loudly enough for Brief to hear.

"The new room will be ready in a couple of hours," Doron told her. "They're just cleaning it."

"That's okay, ah don't need it at the moment."

As Yael suspected, Brief suddenly had a very important reason to go upstairs. Yael saw that Jana was happily occupied in the hotel shop, so she left her at it, and, watching Brief take the elevator, she took the stairs, racing up them as fast as she could. Arriving breathless on her floor just before he emerged from the elevator, she hid in the staircase until she saw him go into the room she had just vacated.

She went quietly to the door and listened. She heard scuffling, and Brief talking loudly to himself. He sounded very angry. More scuffling, then he was on his phone.

"It's not there!" he said.

Silence as he listened, then, "I don't know. Any number of people could've used the room. I can't believe it's her. She's just a flighty young girl... Yes, I'm sure it's not there. I've practically ripped the mattress open. Someone must have come in after he left it in there and taken it out. One of the others, I'm guessing. You'll just have to pick up some of the usual suspects, and lean on them until they squeal. We need to get it back. ASAP."

Yael heard Brief stomping back toward the door, so she ducked back into the stairwell at double time. He stormed out of the bedroom, and she peeked out of a crack in the fire door and saw his face.

He did *not* look like a happy camper.

He stomped back to the elevator, stabbing the button with his finger so many times it almost shrieked in protest.

Once he was in the elevator, Yael hotfooted it down the stairs, almost tripping a couple of times, but was there, calmly examining the postcards, by the time Brief came to the desk.

"I'm going out," he said. "Your superiors will be hearing about this mess-up."

He thumped off toward the door. Jana was just emerging from the shop, empty-handed but curiously looking at Yael, who jerked her head. *We're following him. Come on.*

Flighty young girl, am I? Yael thought as they followed Brief at a safe distance down the crowded Cairo streets. *We'll see who's flighty and who isn't…who has the flash drive and who doesn't. Eh? Eh?*

CHAPTER 32

THEY WERE FOLLOWING Brief down the road at a discreet distance. All Yael could think about was the flash drive in her bag and how she hadn't gotten around to e-mailing Jimmy any of the files yet. She was impatient to know what secrets the drive held.

By the set of Brief's shoulders as he walked swiftly along, he looked angry and impatient. His was not the relaxed amble of someone confident that he knew what he was doing. The upside of his obvious bad mood was that he was so wrapped up in his own bubble of whatever was bothering him that he didn't turn around and check if anyone was following him.

After ducking into doorways and hiding behind pillars for a while, the two young women realized that they didn't have to be quite so cloak and dagger. Soon, Yael, who was used to living on the edge, sauntered quite openly a few meters behind him. Jana, who wasn't used to this, was more nervous, but followed Yael's lead. Her obvious advantage was that Brief had never met her and would probably not remember her from the postcard display at the hotel.

Foundling

Yael was only worried about one thing: if Brief took some form of transport other than a bus. At the moment he was walking as fast as he could, along the main street, but if he decided to take a cab, they'd lose him for sure.

Suddenly he veered off the main street and onto a side street that took him down to the banks of the Nile. Yael had never seen the Nile before, so had to force herself not to get sidetracked by its beauty and busy trade going on, with boats and traders vying for space on the banks.

Oh no, Yael thought, *he's going to get on a riverboat.*

And so he was. Brief strode up to a jetty, gave the man in charge something (money or a card, Yael couldn't tell), and boarded the boat before she could blink.

"What shall we do?" she asked Jana desperately. "I can't lose him."

Jana pulled something out of her bag. "Easy-peasy," she said with a grin. She showed the man on the jetty the whatever it was, said something in Arabic, and he waved them both onto the boat.

When they were seated, as far away from Yehuda Brief as they could be while still keeping him in their sights, Yael whispered to Jana, "What was that? What did you say?"

"It's a travel card. I told him to take two passages off my one card, as you were a tourist and didn't have one."

"Wow, thanks," Yael said gratefully.

The riverboat steamed smoothly along. Brief seemed to be permanently on his phone. When he did take a break, he stared out at the passing river traffic with a hard, irritated gaze. Even this beautiful voyage didn't relax him one iota. Yael was trying to both watch her quarry, and enjoy the experience, at the same time. Jana seemed oblivious to her surroundings. She was obviously a seasoned traveler on this form of transport and the novelty had long worn off.

The boat stopped and started at several points, but Brief remained deeply involved in his phone, and ignored all the stations.

Jana whispered, "He's taking quite a long ride. I hope my travel card has enough credit."

Yael felt a little twitchy at this. She was totally dependent on her newfound acquaintance's travel card and had little funds of her own.

Just as Yael was almost beginning to relax and enjoy the ride, Brief made movements that led her to believe he was finally preparing to disembark.

"He's getting off," she whispered to Jana, who looked relieved.

"We still have to get back, though," Jana whispered in return. "I don't know if my card will cope…"

"Can you put some more credit on it?" Yael asked. "I'll pay." This last part was said with a lot more confidence than she felt.

"Yes," Jana said, as Brief stood up, gathered his belongings, and made for the door, just as the boat shuddered to a halt at another jetty. He showed his card to someone on the jetty and walked off. Jana did the same, gesticulating at Yael and saying something in Arabic. Yael thought she heard the Arabic for "two," *athnan*, confirmed because she signaled "two" with her fingers. He nodded and they disembarked, following Brief.

"Well, at least that," Jana said. "I'll probably have to put some more money on to get us back."

Yael waved that concern away as if she had endless funds, while panicking inside. She hoped transportation in Cairo was relatively cheap.

This part of Cairo was obviously not intended for touristy eyes. It was shabby, run-down, smelled disgusting, and there were no smart hotels or palm trees to soften the grime and degradation of the area. It reminded Yael of the seedier parts of London—full of graffiti and peeling paint—but supplemented with barefoot children, feral cats, and rats that ran straight over her shoes, making her bite her tongue to stop herself from screaming aloud.

"Why don't the cats keep the rat population down?" she hissed at Jana.

"Have you seen the size of the rats?" Jana hissed back. "It's more a case of the rats keeping the cat population down around here."

It was true. It was hard to say which of the two species was bigger, but it was a no-brainer as to which looked fiercer. The cats looked rather like those in Egyptian wall paintings—thin, with long, pointy ears—and the rats looked better fed.

Brief seemed unfazed by both rodent and feline. He certainly seemed to know his way around Cairo. Without pausing to check his phone or look around, he strode along purposefully. Then, suddenly, he was at his destination. He stopped at a door and knocked.

The two girls ducked into a doorway this time. Peering out, they saw the door open, Brief go in, and the door close.

Now what?

Jana looked at Yael with raised eyebrows. Yael thought for a split second, then went up to the house in question. She was careful as she sidled along. There was a window facing the street and it was that window that drew her attention. It had one of those gauzy blinds she could see through if she was up close. The window was open to let in the hot, steamy air.

"Be my lookout," she said to Jana. "I'm going to try and see in."

Jana nodded. The street was relatively deserted, aside from the cats and rats, but there was traffic noise coming from the next street along so it wasn't safe to assume the street would stay that quiet.

Flattening herself against the wall by the window, Yael slid along until she could see in.

Yehuda Brief stood there, gesticulating angrily at someone.

"What do you mean it's gone?" the other guy said. "It was meant for your eyes only."

"Some idiot gave the room to a tourist, but I don't think she took it," Brief said. "I can only assume *they* got their hands on it before she took the room."

"How do you know it wasn't her?" said the guy.

"Look, I've been in this business long enough to pick them out. It's not her. Besides, she's South African."

"Ah," he said, as if being South African explained everything. "I'll have to make another copy of it and try and destroy that one remotely," the guy went on.

"You can do that?" Brief asked, sounding impressed.

"Only when they access the files on a connected computer," the other man said. "Once they do that I can make sure that whatever's on it is instantly destroyed."

"That's great," Brief said. "Get on it."

"Why did you come all the way here instead of just phone?" the guy said.

"I wanted to give you this," Brief said, "and I didn't dare send it by any other means." He handed the guy something that Yael couldn't see.

The guy looked at it and nodded. "Good," he said. "This will help a lot."

"Make sure what's on this is on the new copy," Brief instructed.

The guy nodded. "Sure. I'm on it. Next time let's find a better place to make the drop. Still, it doesn't really matter who has it. As soon as they connect it—boom!—it's gone."

Outside, Yael thought of the flash drive in her bag; how on earth was she going to get it to Jimmy now?

CHAPTER 33

"Get out of the way!" Jana hissed. "The police are coming!" Jana herself looked totally panicked. As if the police were not friends of hers in the least.

Two policemen were coming along the street, on foot, and Brief was apparently drawing his conversation with the other guy to a close and getting ready to leave the building. This was not a good combination, with the girls caught in the middle. Yael was so glad she'd heard about the remote "detonation" of the flash drive if she connected it to the Internet again. As long as she didn't connect it, the data on it was safe. How she was going to get it to Jimmy for decoding was another matter.

By the time the police caught up with them, the two girls were ambling innocently along the street. Yael, who was good at pretending, was anxious that Jana was not, and would give the game away. She could almost feel the other girl trembling and shaking at her side. With a sudden move, she tucked her arm inside Jana's and held her tightly in a close friendship gesture. This helped to stop the Egyptian girl from shaking, and kept her walking at the same pace as Yael. It also prevented her from turning her head to see where the police were up to, which was a clear giveaway of suspicious behavior.

The two policemen didn't seem interested in the girls and passed them. Yael breathed more easily once they were out of sight and earshot.

Where's Brief? Has he left that house yet? she thought, stopping with a jolt. As Jana was firmly attached to her, this almost sent the two girls flat on their faces on the pavement.

"Hey!" Jana said. "You could have warned me!"

"Sorry. I'm not sure what it was that the Israeli gave the guy in there, or what its significance was," Yael said.

"So…?"

"So, I'm going to try and find out," Yael said airily.

"You're crazy!" Jana replied. "You're going back there?"

"Being a PI isn't about keeping myself nice and safe and cozy by the fireside, you know," Yael said, with a confidence she didn't feel. "It's about putting myself out there, taking risks, that sort of thing."

"You're totally nuts," Jana said. "I'm not sure I want to be your guide anymore. I'm scared."

This brought Yael up short. She stopped and looked at Jana. Her face was pinched and frightened looking. Yael felt a stab of pity.

"You don't have to if you don't want to," she said with a martyred air. "I'm sure I can find my way back to the hotel somehow… eventually…"

Jana sighed deeply. "Emotional blackmail isn't a nice ploy. But it works. I couldn't live with myself if I just left you here."

Yael grinned triumphantly. "I'll do all the dangerous bits," she tried reassuring the other girl. "You can hide somewhere very safe while I do. I just need you to get me back in one piece afterward."

Jana had no intention of doing anything else other than hiding in the most secure hollow in any wall or doorway she could find.

"You'd better come out," she warned Yael. "You owe me money for the boat trip!"

Jana said it with a light-hearted smile, but Yael saw something glint in her eyes that made her wonder whether indeed she was making a joke of it or not.

They made their way back to the building where Yael had witnessed the exchange between Brief and the other guy. Jana ducked into an alleyway and signaled to Yael that she wasn't coming out. Yael made an "okay" gesture and went back to her position at the side of the window and peeked in. The guy was still in the room, but Brief was nowhere to be seen. Watching, Yael saw the guy open up a laptop and switch it on. Waiting for it to boot up seemed to take forever; it was obviously not the most up-to-date model. Yael struggled to get a glimpse of whatever it was that Brief had handed him; there were various bits and pieces of clutter on the table and she didn't know which it was.

And then she did. Because when the laptop had booted, the guy took something off the table and looked at it for a while. It was another flash drive.

He put it down again. Then he started typing speedily on the laptop without the flash drive in place. The way he sat back at the end of it, clasping his hands behind his head, leaning back with a self-satisfied smile, led Yael to one possible conclusion. The guy had set up the remote-destruction program for the flash drive she held in her bag.

Then he inserted his flash drive and looked at it. Yael tried to see what was on the screen, but it was too far and the font too small. He typed on his computer for a while, then he pulled out the flash drive and laid it back on the desk.

Then, he got up and left the room.

The window was open to the hot day. Yael took her chance. She climbed through the open window like a monkey, grabbed the flash drive, and slipped out again. The whole maneuver took less than ten seconds.

"Let's go!" she said to Jana, who was still cowering in the alleyway. She herself raced down the street, not waiting for Jana to confirm she was following. After a few seconds Yael thought this wasn't very public spirited of her, considering the girl was her guide and all, so she looked around and Jana was racing to catch up. There was no sign of anyone emerging from the house, so the guy obviously hadn't come back and found his flash drive missing yet.

Yael didn't want to think about what would happen when he did notice. Hopefully she'd be far enough away by then for him not to find her.

The two girls ran like greased lightning down the dirty streets. "I don't know why I'm taking the lead!" panted Yael at one point. "I have absolutely no idea where I'm going!"

"Turn left here," Jana panted back. "We need to get back to the river."

"We're going back on the boat?" Yael gasped.

Jana just grunted her reply; she was too out of breath by then.

And there was the river, glinting brown in the sunshine. Brown, polluted, but it was the Nile nonetheless. The noise of traders and boats and people filled the air. The two girls saw the riverboat just docking as they approached.

"We'll make it if we hurry!" called Jana.

They charged down to the jetty and Jana slammed her travel card into the hand of the guy who was taking tickets and money. "*Athnan!*" she cried.

He swiped her card and said something back to her.

Foundling

"Not enough credit," she translated to Yael.

Yael didn't hesitate. She pulled out her purse and paid up for both of them in cash. They boarded the boat and collapsed into seats.

For the first mile or so of travel, the girls were too winded even to talk to one another. They just gasped for air and waited for their heartbeats to slow down. Once they were breathing normally again, Jana said, "So did you see what it was?"

"Better than that." Yael grinned. And patted her bag. Jana stared at her, the bag, and back at Yael.

"Tell me you didn't. Please, no."

Yael grinned smugly but said nothing.

"You're crazy. You've made yourself a target, you realize that?" Jana looked terrified out of her wits.

"How can I be a target when no one has any idea who took it?" Yael said.

"You have no idea," Jana said, looking around her as if unspecified baddies were going to leap on her at any moment. "This is a very cruel city. People find out things. Don't ask me how. I don't think I can be seen with you anymore; it's not safe for me. Give me my money for today and we'll part ways."

Yael looked at Jana to see if she meant it.

Yes, she did.

With a sigh, Yael took some money out of her bag and handed it over.

"You get out two stops from now. The hotel will be a short walk from there; you can ask someone for directions. I'm getting off here." Jana stood up and slung her bag over her shoulder.

"You're serious, aren't you?" Yael asked, feeling the beginnings of genuine panic. Had she really gone too far this time?

"Yes. I'm sorry. I thought it would be exciting to be a private investigator instead of a tour guide, but I can't take the risks you take. Good-bye."

The boat docked and the girl was gone.

Yael sat there stunned, clutching her bag with its two precious yet unknown flash drives.

Then a voice interrupted her blank mind, bringing it sharply back into focus.

"Ah. The South African lady. What are you doing on this riverboat, may I inquire?"

She looked up into the hard and curious stare of Yehuda Brief.

CHAPTER 34

YAEL PUT ON her red glasses as if to see who exactly had spoken to her. It was actually to get her head into role. She peered up at Brief and made an "oh, so it's *you*!" face, even though she had known all along, by just his voice. She was trying to get her heart out of her boots as she beamed up at him.

"Hah there! What am ah doing on this riverboat? Well, do ah have to have permission to travel on it or something? Ah heard that to go on the Nahl was one of the best ways. And it is!"

Brief frowned at her chutzpah, then gathered himself together. "I was due to return to Jerusalem tomorrow," he told her. "But circumstances have changed cases and I'm staying a little longer…to sort something out. How long do you plan to stay?"

Circumstances, like the missing flash drive—now two *missing flash drives, only he may not know about the second one yet*, Yael thought as she gave Brief a winning smile.

"Ah'm having *such* fun, perhaps ah'll also stay on a bit longer," she said. "Ah never knew Egypt could be so…exciting!"

She was hamming up the flighty personality to the max, as it just went to confirm in Brief's mind that she was far too unintelligent to have ever taken the flash drive.

He didn't look impressed. "Can you afford the room though?" he asked. "I've helped out with the cost, but this isn't a free ride where you stay on as long as you like on my tab, you know."

Yael considered this. "You're correct," she said at last. "Ah've been imposing on your good nature for way too long. Ah'll move out this evening and get a hostel downtown."

Brief looked alarmed. "No, that's not safe. Look, how about you stay in your room until I leave? I don't think it'll be more than another night, though."

"That's really nahce of you." Yael grinned. For a split second she thought Brief recognized her, but then he turned away and went to sit down in another part of the boat.

Yael was a little nervous about missing her stop. So she made sure to get off when Brief did, and to follow him a little way behind, so he wouldn't know that she had no idea how to get back to the hotel.

In a way, she was very grateful that he'd turned up on her boat or she might have drifted down the river and ended up who knows where. Yael's geography wasn't too great, but wasn't Egypt close to Africa? Sudan—that was it. She'd just drift on and on into Sudan.

Anyway, she was off the boat, thankfully on dry land, and following Brief back to the hotel. She had two flash drives in her bag. Life was sweet, even though she had no idea what she was going to do with them.

At the hotel, Doron had been having a fit not knowing where Yael was. His job had been to keep an eye on her, to keep her safe, but she was as slippery as ten eels in a sack.

He'd called Colin earlier in desperation. "I have no idea where she is!" he'd said, "so I can't follow her! She just disappeared suddenly, with that Arab girl."

"Did you find out about her? The Arab girl, I mean?" Colin had asked.

"Yes. She doesn't seem to have any hidden agenda. I think she's genuine."

"At least that," Colin had said, breathing a sigh of relief.

Doron's face, when he saw Yael come in shortly after Brief, was a study in relief, but he had to compose himself quickly, as a desk clerk in a hotel wasn't meant to exhibit emotions of any sort at the sight of returning guests.

"My new room now?" Yael asked him brightly.

"Yes. Lower floor, nicer furniture and view. Same money. Someone is looking out for you," he said with a smile.

Yael nodded and took herself up to her new quarters. Wow. It even had a small fridge. And it was empty, not full of overpriced mini-bar drinks and snacks. She could put her tuna and sweetcorn in it, and any cold drinks. The bed was bouncier and didn't feel like it was about to break underneath her when she sat on it. The cupboard doors weren't hanging off their hinges and there was, luxury of luxuries, a full-length mirror inside one of the wardrobe doors!

It was a big step up from the last room, and she flung herself on the bouncy mattress in an attitude of bliss. Nothing cut into her. There was unlikely to be yet another flash drive inside of this mattress. She got up and went over to the window. No river view, but a nice street view. She unpacked, opened cans of corn and tuna, and ate a simple supper out of paper bowls.

Then she took out the two flash drives and looked at them. Not that looking at them would give her any insight into what was on them, but she was just considering what to do. However tempting it was to slip the new one into her laptop, she was petrified it would self-destruct like the guy had said the other one would.

With a sigh, she called Colin.

"I'm really sorry to bother you…" she began.

"Yael!" he interrupted. "Where have you been all day? We've been so worried!"

"I've been following Yehuda Brief," she said, puzzled. "Why didn't you phone me if you were so worried?" She looked at her phone. "No missed calls from anyone."

Colin realized he'd given too much away. He sighed. "I'll be honest with you, Yael," he said. "I'd given someone the job of looking out for you. This person said they couldn't find you today." By using "they" he was keeping things gender neutral.

"I thought you might have," Yael said. "You're much too much of a control freak to let me off the leash completely. And that's you *and* Leora included."

Colin laughed.

"So who's watching me?" She paused. "Don't tell me it's Jana. If it is, she's done a terrible job because she dumped me mid River Nile."

"No, not Jana. You came upon her by yourself. That would have been too contrived, if we'd set that up. It's the desk clerk at the hotel."

"Desk clerk? Which one? They change shift every five minutes!"

"He's on duty now. His name is Doron Yair and he's Israeli."

"Oh." Yael didn't quite know what to make of this unwanted guardian angel in her life. She didn't like being monitored and "kept safe." It went against all her free-spirited nature. But a small part of her found comfort in it.

She told Colin then about the flash drives and what had happened in the house Brief had been to.

"I listened and watched outside," said Yael. "They're set to self-destruct if they're connected to the Internet in any way. So how can I get the files to you or Jimmy?"

"Give them to Doron," Colin said. "He can get them to the UK by courier or someone taking them personally."

Yael suddenly felt a huge protective surge about the flash drives she'd gone to such efforts to obtain.

"You sure you can trust this Doron guy?" she said doubtfully.

"Yael," Colin said with a sigh, "he's one of us. Give. Him. The. Flash. Drives."

"I'd rather not do it downstairs at the desk," she stalled. "Brief might spot me handing them over."

"Oh, for heaven's sake. I'm sure you can find a way. Now go and give them to him. You've done a great job in Cairo. Better than any operative of MI5. Now, get back to Israel."

"But I haven't found…" Yael was going to say "out about my father yet!" but she was talking to a dial tone.

CHAPTER 35

YAEL WENT DOWNSTAIRS to the desk. She had no idea which desk clerk was on duty, so she asked one of the other staff for his name. The woman looked doubtful.

"He new here," she said. "I no know name."

Yael went up to the desk and said quietly to the young man behind it, "Look, no messing. Are you Doron Yair?"

The flash in his eyes told her she was right. "I presume Colin told you," he said. She nodded.

"Colin told me to give you these flash drives. They have to go back to London ASAP. Overnight courier if possible. And get them to him physically, not by Internet. They're programmed to self-destruct if they're connected."

"Okay, I'll get them to him, as they are, no worries. He's spoken to me about them already."

Yael felt a gut wrench when she handed them over, like she was parting from something very precious. But somehow, at the same time, she knew they'd be in safe hands.

Turning away from the desk, she wondered what to do about

supper. She was beginning to long for a place where there was easy access to kosher food. Israel, or back home to London, maybe? But how could she leave without finding out about her father?

"Do you want dinner?" a passing waitress asked her. "Just serving now in dining room."

Yael thought she'd look and see if any fresh fruits and veggies were available. She made up a paper napkin full of non-problematic produce and stuffed it in her knapsack for later. The hotel didn't seem to mind what the guests secreted from the dining room, as long as it wasn't on hotel plates. She went upstairs and surveyed her stash of food. She still had a few protein bars and bottled drinks. Time to go shopping.

She went back down to the lobby and made her way to the hotel entrance. It was growing dark, but the humidity still made the air feel like soup. It was November for heaven's sake! She kept reminding herself that at this time of year London was dreary, dark, cold, and wet. *No wonder the Brits spend their time seeking out winter sun; we're starved of it!* Yael thought.

She'd hardly taken two steps outside the hotel into the noisy, muggy night before she was grabbed from behind by two strong arms and a female voice hissed in her ear, "Keep walking. Don't act suspicious. I have a knife."

Yael's blood ran cold. She recognized the voice at once.

It was Jana.

"Jana, what on earth are you *doing*?" Yael said, trying to keep calm as the two of them frog-marched along the street.

"What am I doing?" Jana repeated. "I'm looking after numero uno, that's what I'm doing. I saw you have money. You were happy to pay me for my time, and to pay for the riverboat when I ran out of credit. I think there's more where that came from and I want some of it."

Yael had never been so shocked. She'd almost thought of the Arab girl as a friend.

"So you're robbing me? In the street?"

"That's vulgar and unladylike," Jana said. "No, I'm not a common street thief. Let's just call it a sensible business transaction."

Yael screeched to a halt and turned to face Jana. "A what? And where's your knife? Show it to me."

Jana sighed. "Okay, I lied about the knife."

Yael couldn't help laughing. "Oh dear. I'm shaking in my boots. Not."

Jana's eyes narrowed. "You think I'm joking about this? I may not have a knife but I have something that can hurt you a lot deeper." She pointed to her mouth.

"You're going to bite me?"

"Stupid. No. I mean, you give me money, lots of money, or I'll tell that Jew in the hotel everything you've been up to."

Yael was shocked. She hadn't thought of Jana blackmailing her. Somehow the camaraderie of their association had seemed like two friends on an adventure, but obviously Jana hadn't felt the same about it. She was in it for what she could get out of it, end of story.

"I don't have much money, really," she protested.

"Oh, yes you do. All Jews have lots of money. All Israelis have lots of money. My brother told me. He said to get as much money as possible from the Jews."

"Okay, you win," Yael said. "Come back to my hotel. I'll get you the money."

The girl smirked. "There, you see? I knew you'd see sense."

The two girls did an about-face. "How did you know I'd be going out anyway?" Yael asked conversationally as they walked back toward the hotel.

"I didn't," Jana said. "I was coming in to see you when you

came out. I was taken by surprise as much as you were that we bumped into each other."

"I see." Yael's mind was whirling, thinking of a way out of this. The last thing she wanted was Brief knowing who she really was and what she'd been doing in Egypt.

A thought came to her.

"Give me a moment," she said to the girl. "I'm expecting some cash in an envelope. I just need to see if any packages came for me."

She saw greed gleaming in the other girl's eyes as she nodded. "I'm watching you," Jana said, "so don't think you can sneak off and escape."

"I have no intention of doing that," Yael said honestly.

The girl stood back a little as Yael approached the desk where Doron stood.

"Isn't that the girl who…?" he asked.

Yael spoke in a low voice. "Yes, and she's trying to blackmail me by threatening to tell Yehuda Brief what I've been doing. Now, give me the key to my old room, please. I presume no one is using that dump?"

"No, no one is using 'that dump,' as you so eloquently put it. Here's the key. Do you want me to call the cops?"

"No, not yet. Thanks. Oh, when is Brief checking out?"

"First thing in the morning, he said. He didn't sound too happy, but he said he had to."

"I'm not surprised he's unhappy, as he has no idea what's happened to the flash drives." Then, Yael raised her voice and said loudly, "Oh, so the package is already in my room? Splendid. Thanks."

She turned away from the desk and walked over to Jana.

"You're in luck. The package was delivered just now while I was out, and it's in my room. Come up and I'll give you some money."

They had the elevator to themselves. As it ascended, Jana asked, "How much money?"

"Whatever it is, it's a one-off payment," Yael said. "I'm not having you holding this over me forever."

"Oh, absolutely," Jana said glibly.

They got to "the dump," which was, conveniently for Yael's purpose, situated at the very end of a long corridor, with no immediate neighbors. Yael opened the door.

"It's not much, but it's home," she said with a smile. "After you."

Jana stepped inside.

And Yael shut the door and locked it.

"Hey!" the girl shouted. "Let me out!"

"Not tonight, sorry," Yael said through the door. "So you might as well make yourself comfortable. There's no telephone and the bed's a bit lumpy, but hey, beggars, or should I say blackmailers, can't be choosers. You'll be released in the morning after you've had a good night's sleep. Good night, sleep tight, don't let the bedbugs bite—which in this case is a distinct possibility."

Jana was still banging fruitlessly on the door as Yael walked away. There was no one to hear her.

Downstairs, Yael said to Doron, "I locked her in that room. Here's the key. Let her out in the morning once Brief is on the plane and out of the country. Can you get me on another flight back to Israel, not the same one? I think I've seen enough of Egypt. I expect Colin will let me know when the flash drives have been decoded?"

"I expect so. They're already en route to London. My work will be done here tomorrow too." Doron paused as Yael made her way to the hotel entrance. "Where are you going at this time of night?"

"Where I was going before Jana jumped me. To get some food. I hope there are still some shops open."

"I can arrange some kosher food for you," Doron said. "Go to your room and it'll be delivered to you in half an hour. I'll book you on a flight. And make sure Jana can't find you, or Brief. Imagine her thinking she could blackmail you!"

CHAPTER 36

TRUE TO HIS word, Doron sent Yael a heated prepackaged airline meal of strictly kosher food up to her new room.

It was meat and potatoes and some unidentifiable vegetable, but it was bliss. There was some weird sliced something or other for appetizer, she couldn't tell if it was fish or meat so she left it, as she didn't care for fish, and a blob of cake for dessert. That, together with the fruit and vegetables she had impounded from the hotel dining room, made a more than satisfactory meal.

"I'll never complain about airline food again!" Yael sighed rapturously as she ate. She wondered where the desk clerk had obtained this food, then realized it was probably one of his own stash. So Doron was observant; he didn't look it. She guessed he couldn't be seen looking Jewish in his line of work.

Finishing the meal, Yael was surprised to hear the phone ring in her room; not her cell, but the hotel phone. She hoped it wasn't Jana, having found out where she really was.

But thankfully it wasn't; it was Colin.

Foundling **193**

"Now listen to me, Yael Reed, and don't deviate from my instructions. Do you hear me?"

"Yes," Yael said meekly. She was quite shocked by Colin's tone of voice. He sounded as if he was at the end of his tether.

"I've booked you on a nine o'clock flight tomorrow morning to Ben Gurion; that means you have to be at the airport at seven. I've organized you transportation that leaves your hotel at six. I cannot do anything from here if you miss your ride and your flight. Your ticket will be waiting for you downstairs at the desk, along with an envelope containing one thousand dollars, and a thousand shekels too. That should be enough for your expenses, plus to get somewhere to stay back in Israel temporarily. After that, I'd like you to come back to England; you can't be wandering the world on someone else's *cheshbon* forever."

"A thousand dollars and a thousand shekels?" Yael was stunned. "From you?"

"Who else is destined to spend his life bailing you out from impossible situations, Yael?"

"Oh." She sounded so crestfallen that Colin laughed.

"Don't sound so miserable," he said soothingly. "Despite your refusal to listen to reason and behave sensibly, you get things done, although heavens knows how, with the risk-taking you do on a daily basis."

"Well, thank you," Yael said, flattered, "but I can't be that great. I came here to find out about my father and am going back none the wiser. All I did was follow Yehuda Brief around and get nowhere. Oh, and almost got mugged by Jana. Who knows what might have happened if I did have money on me. I'm still very upset about her treachery." She sniffed.

"Oh, don't be," Colin said. "You acted very cleverly locking her in the room, by the way; it was a masterstroke. From what Doron told me when we spoke a few minutes ago, Jana's just acting as she's been preprogrammed to do by years of upbringing in that corrupt society. I don't think we could've expected much more of her. In fact, when you locked her in that room, *that* was a language she understood. Only normally it would be followed by her father or brother coming in and beating her. So Doron says, and he knows these things."

Yael made a noise that indicated disgust at this. "Well, thanks for everything as usual, Colin. One of these days I'll actually behave as if I'm grateful. I'd better go to bed early if I'm to be downstairs at six," she said.

"Brief's flight is at four tomorrow morning, so he'll be long gone before you come downstairs. I'll tell Doron to let Jana out at seven, once he's sure you're on the transportation and well out of the way."

"What is the transportation? Do you happen to know what's been arranged?" she asked curiously. She'd seen enough donkey carts and the like around to be suspicious.

"A private taxi. Not a *sheirut*. And don't worry, we've vetted the driver and he's okay. At the Israeli end of things, though, you're on your own."

"Wow, thanks so much!"

Colin said good-bye and disconnected the call. He spoke to Ho Kai and told him to get ready to decode some flash drives that were on their way over. "Pull an all-nighter," he ordered Ho Kai. "We need to know what's on those files."

YAEL PACKED HER FEW BELONGINGS, checking around to make sure she didn't leave anything behind. Somehow she felt this was a place she didn't want to come back to.

"*Yetzias Mitzrayim,*" she told herself as she closed her suitcase. "On a much smaller scale, of course."

She got ready for bed. While she was lying there, she thought about her father. Maybe the clues would be on those flash drives, she thought as sleep overtook her like a tsunami.

Yael liked to think of herself as one of those rare people who could always wake up when she needed to. In truth, after a bad night, she sometimes slept in, as had happened more than once recently, but when it was important enough, she knew she could emulate the hero of a thriller she once read about a man who had an "alarm clock in his head" and all he needed to do was set it and he would wake up at that time; he didn't even own a watch. She'd thought that a little on the fanciful side, but allowed for literary license to be believable. She herself definitely did need a watch, but she never needed to set an alarm.

She awoke at five on the dot. She got herself ready and davened, then ate one of her protein bars for breakfast, and drank some of her bottled drink. She was set. Again making sure she hadn't left anything in her room, she went downstairs to wait for the taxi.

The lobby was quiet. She went over to the desk, where a smiling lady was on duty.

"You have something for me?" she asked and gave her room number.

"Yes, I have this package," said the lady and handed it over. Yael peeked inside. It was an airline ticket and a bulky envelope. The cash. She tucked it into her bag.

"Oh, the other desk clerk left you something else too," the lady said and handed Yael another frozen airline meal. "Don't ask me why; I'm just passing it on," she said. "The clerk said you can ask the flight attendant to heat it up for you, that it's double wrapped, whatever that has to do with it."

Yael accepted it with thanks and tucked it in her backpack. It could come in very handy. She was unlikely to get kosher food on the flight.

❦ ❧

HO KAI HAD RECEIVED THE flash drives. He made doubly, triply sure the computer he was working on was disconnected from the Internet before he inserted them into the USB drives. He was working on two non-connected computers simultaneously, sitting on a wheeled chair, and whizzing from one to the other. It wasn't going to be an easy job, but he could do it!

It was in the early hours in the UK, almost the time that Yael in Egypt got up to get ready to leave for the airport, that he finally deciphered the files on the first flash drive. And stared.

Among other things, it was clearly stated that there was a Jewish agent working in the Egyptian government. It didn't name him. Maybe that name would be on the second drive, which was proving harder to decode. Ho Kai copied the decoded files onto another flash drive, which he put in his pocket. His eyes were closing. He reckoned he'd work better if he took an hour's nap. The office was used to all-nighters and provided a small side room with a bed for tired workers to grab forty winks. Ho Kai took the second drive out of the second laptop and pocketed it, too, but left the decoded one in the first laptop.

Shortly after that, another sleepy all-nighter came along to work on the computer, yawning and rubbing his eyes. Saw it wasn't connected to the Internet, and connected it. He was surprised to see the screen go white for a while, then black, before returning to normal. There was also a faint fizzing noise coming from the USB drive, but as this worker hadn't personally inserted anything into the USB drive, he didn't take any notice.

He shrugged, and carried on with his work.

※ ※

YAEL WENT TO SIT NEAR the door of the hotel so she could see the taxi when it drew up. She smiled as she thought of Israel. She couldn't wait to get back there, even if she had nowhere to stay once she did.

It was with a great sense of shock and horror that she witnessed what happened next.

It was the guy from the building she had spied on when she'd been following Brief. The one who'd set the flash drives to self-destruct. The one from whose house she'd stolen the second flash drive. He was outside the hotel, with a suitcase, flagging down a taxi, and she clearly heard him tell the driver, as he climbed in, "The airport, please!"

CHAPTER 37

MAYBE IT WASN'T him? Maybe he just looked like the guy in the building she'd spied on? Yael had to hope that was the case. Even if it was him, who said he was going to the same destination she was? That was highly unlikely; just because he was going to the airport didn't mean he was going to Israel.

Her taxi arrived and she got in, still shaking a little, but slowly managing to persuade herself that this guy wasn't going to be a problem to her. If he was going to Israel, so what? He had no idea who Yael was and what she looked like, and hopefully no idea that she'd taken the flash drive. All she needed to do was brazen it out like she'd done before. She wasn't wearing her disguise at the moment because she didn't see the point, but she had it in her backpack and could easily slip it on if needed.

It soon became clear to Yael that vetting a taxi driver for security purposes didn't mean that Shabak had vetted him for his driving skills. She found herself clinging onto any protrusion that she could find in the back of the car, and doing so for dear life, as the driver twisted in and out of traffic lanes and blasted everyone with his horn along the way.

"I get you to airport very fast!" he called back to her triumphantly.

"Maybe not quite so fast!" Yael responded. "There's plenty of time!" But for him this was a drag race and he wasn't going to give up on it just because his passenger was terrified.

She breathed a huge sigh of relief when the taxi screeched to a halt outside the airport, flinging its lone passenger forward. But she was there, and she was alive. Just about.

The driver said her ride had been paid for and Yael was disinclined to give him a tip after the experience she'd just undergone. So she thanked him and, gathering in her stuff, went into the airport to look for the Air Sinai desk to check in. She went through security and then approached the desk.

She saw the guy from earlier, at once, right there at the desk. He had a big suitcase that he needed to go in the hold, and a small black wheeled cabin luggage that he seemed overly protective of, although that could have just been Yael's sense of intense suspicion about him. She stood as close behind him as she dared, to hear where he was going, and her heart sank when she discovered he was going to Tel Aviv.

Just to compound matters, he wasn't flying business class; he'd be in the same cabin as she was. Yael would have to make sure she wasn't sitting anywhere near him, she decided. If she was, she'd ask someone to change with her.

He finished his dealings at the desk and walked briskly off, wheeling his small black case. It was her turn.

"I've got no check-in luggage," Yael told the woman behind the counter as her passport and ticket was inspected and her boarding pass issued. "Can you tell me the name of the passenger you just dealt with?"

The check-in woman looked suspiciously at her. "I'm sorry, miss. We cannot give out that information."

Yael blushed. "No, of course not, sorry. But maybe at least can you ensure I'm not sitting near him. Is that possible?"

"Yes, I can do that. As it happens, you're sitting several rows behind him. He asked for a bulkhead seat, for more leg room. You don't get that privilege, I'm afraid."

"Well, I'm short and he's tall, so fair's fair." Yael tried a weak smile, while hiding her relief.

"Here's your boarding pass. Boarding is in thirty minutes. Have a pleasant flight."

Yael spotted the guy in duty-free. He was examining a display of expensive Scotch whiskies. She hovered a little. He made his choice and paid for it, then strode off to the gate.

Obviously not buying perfume for a lady, Yael thought uncharitably. He didn't even glance at the fragrances display. Just whisky for himself. She liked him less and less.

They called their flight and Yael made sure she was several people behind him in line but yet close enough to hear if anything useful came up. Like him being called by his name. But he was just handed his half of the boarding pass and told to have a pleasant flight.

Yael had to pass him as she made her way to her seat. That was nerve-wracking. But he was already deep in a newspaper (in English, she noted with interest), and took no notice. She made a mental note of his seat number, although what use it would be to her during this extremely short flight, she had no idea. She reached her seat, which, thankfully, was an aisle seat. A free spirit like Yael didn't like being trapped, even between two innocent passengers on a plane. This way she could get in and out as she pleased.

Less pleasing, however, was the very large woman sitting in the

Foundling **201**

middle seat, which meant that Yael had only half a seat to herself. Yael tried accommodating her by squishing herself as far away as she could, but it wasn't easy. She smiled sweetly at the woman.

The woman had a king-sized bag of Doritos in front of her and offered it to Yael. Yael was hungry, and noticed a hechsher on it. Soon the two of them were companionably sharing the bag, munching in concert. They chatted about this and that as the plane took to the skies. Every now and then Yael felt a compulsion to check and see if the guy was still in his seat, but she knew she was being ridiculous. It wasn't as if he could go anywhere.

The woman had put away the remains of the bag of chips (which wasn't much), and was now snoring loudly. The woman on the other side of her kept shooting her dirty looks, as if the larger woman would stop snoring just by dint of the sharp glances. She looked over at Yael.

"I'm trying to watch the movie," she complained.

"Put your headphones on," Yael suggested.

"They ruin my hairdo," the woman said and turned away from her.

Yael rolled her eyes and opened her book, trying to ignore the racket coming from the next seat.

About twenty minutes into the flight, the plane took a sharp swerve to the right, which sent everyone falling about in their seats and items rolling around the aisles. The flight attendant too, was almost thrown off her feet, seemed unprepared, and looked anxious. Someone tapped her and asked her what had happened.

"I don't know," she said. "I'll try and find out." She went forward to the cockpit. Yael couldn't see what was happening because she was in the back of economy and the cockpit was forward of business class.

After a few moments the flight attendant returned, white-faced. She faced the economy passengers and spoke in a shaking voice.

"Please stay in your seats and make sure your seat belts are securely fastened. On no account try and go to the front of the plane. There is a security issue. We are dealing with it as best we can. I will update you when I can."

Yael looked at the flight attendant's face. She had never seen anyone look as petrified. Something was very, very wrong. Before she obeyed the command she had been given, she just had to know. She got out of her seat, and, ignoring the flight attendant's pleas to sit down, she moved a few paces down to look at the bulkhead seat.

The guy was still sitting there. He looked as shocked as the rest of the passengers.

So it wasn't him.

CHAPTER 38

"P LEASE GO BACK to your seat!" the flight attendant ordered Yael. Her voice was shaking. It was obviously not a routine problem.

"What's happened?" Yael asked. Everyone around her looked interestedly at the flight attendant for her reply.

"Nothing to worry about. Just a security issue. Sit down and fasten your seat belt, please."

Yael sighed, realizing she wasn't going to get any information. She went to her seat. The plane was banking and rocking quite sharply at this point. There was no turbulence. The cabin crew was all holding on to seat backs, and all looked similarly white-faced, while trying to maintain a calm outward appearance. And failing miserably, Yael noted grimly.

Looking around her, all the passengers were sitting tightly in their seats, with matching expressions of fear. One passenger said audibly to his wife, "I told you we shouldn't have booked Air Sinai. Look at all the problems this airline has had recently."

To which his wife said, "So which airline would you suggest?

They're all as security lax as each other. The whole world is one big risk at the moment."

El Al, Yael thought. But she wasn't sure if El Al flew to Egypt or not, so she kept quiet. Her question was answered a moment later by the husband in question.

"We should have flown El Al. I *told* you we should have."

The wife sniffed. "I didn't want to fly with an *Israeli* airline." She made it sound like the biggest insult she could manage.

"I get that," he said, "but at least this wouldn't be happening!" Several other passengers nodded their agreement.

Why hadn't *she* been booked on El Al, Yael wondered. She was willing to bet that Yehuda Brief was busy living it up in business or first class on El Al. Why was she on this rubbish Air Sinai plane that was now rocking and banking and causing all the cabin staff to look as if their last day had come? Had Colin or Doron or whoever had paid for this flight cheaped out on her or was there another reason? Yael's thought processes weren't working too well, which was understandable given the circumstances. She clung onto her armrests and tried to get her brain into gear.

She had, she vaguely recalled, insisted that she be booked onto a flight that wasn't the same one as Brief's. Was it she who had asked it, or Colin who had offered it? Either way, as the saying goes, be careful what you wish for; you might just get it.

Yael couldn't imagine there were that many El Al flights from Cairo to Tel Aviv, so if she was to avoid being on the same plane as Brief, and be well out of the way of Jana, the timing of her flight was crucial, and there may not have been a great deal of choice of airlines.

Either way, she was stuck on this one. And…well, what exactly *was* happening to it?

She didn't have to wait long to find out.

The cockpit door opened. First out was the pilot. That was comforting, to see him standing there in his smart uniform. Until she noticed two things about him. Firstly that his face looked as if it had gone ten rounds with the world heavyweight boxing champion of the day. Secondly, behind him, menacingly, stood a gunman, and the pilot's hands were behind his back. Then the copilot, similarly bruised and battered, with his hands behind his back, and another gunman behind him. Both gunmen had their weapons jammed into the smalls of the pilots' backs.

Yael's mouth opened of its own volition and the words burst out without her controlling them. "So who's flying this plane, exactly?"

As soon as the words emerged, she wished with all her heart she could take them back. It drew the attention of the gunmen to her seat. To her. The lead gunman, the one controlling the pilot, shoved his hostage in front of him until they stood right by her. Yael tried to look brave and nonchalant, but she had a feeling she wasn't doing a great job.

The gunman wore a balaclava ski mask, out of which black eyes glittered malevolently. He glared at Yael. In a mocking tone he mimicked her, while rocking his head from side to side.

"So who's flying this plane exactly?" His eyes narrowed. She shrank away. "Stupid child. You never heard of autopilot?"

Despite Yael finding a youthful appearance an advantage at times, if it was one thing that got her riled up, it was being called a child. Glaring right back at him she said, "Of course I have. But autopilot wouldn't have caused the plane to rock and swerve the way it did." Admittedly, now, with no one flying the plane at all, apparently, it was flying smoothly.

He stuck his face at hers again and growled, "That was during...the transition of control. Got it?" In other words, there'd been a fight, the pilots had been beaten up, and the gunmen had taken over.

The gunman's accent was thick and foreign. Arabic. Yael decided discretion was the better part of valor and she kept her mouth shut before he decided she was an expendable nuisance.

Giving her one last glare, he turned away from her, still holding the pilot in front of him, and faced the rest of the terrified passengers.

"This plane is now under the control of Al Khilafah. The Caliphate, to you infidels," he snapped, and there was a collective intake of horrified breath at the dreaded words. "We are flying this plane to Tehran."

The man who had expressed a wish to fly El Al exhaled the word "Daesh…"

The gunman immediately turned toward the sound. "Who used this insulting term for us?"

The man wisely kept quiet. But the large beads of sweat popping out on his brow threatened to give him away.

"We have been told to cut out the tongues of anyone who uses that name for us!" the gunman growled in the general direction of the man. "So I suggest if you want to keep yours in your mouth where it belongs, you guard it in the future!"

The man tried to make himself as small as possible, and kept his mouth firmly closed. However, he looked bug-eyed and terrified. Thankfully the gunman wasn't in a surgical mood at that particular moment, and, grabbing his hostage, turned back toward the cockpit. The copilot and the other gunman were already standing there. Before he reached it, he turned around once more to the cabin.

"You will all stay in your seats. Anyone attempting to storm the cockpit or do anything stupid will be shot immediately. The flight is not long. If you need the bathroom, you can wait." The cockpit door opened, both gunmen shoved their hostages through the door, and the door closed with a bang.

At first there was stunned silence in the cabin. After a while, a low murmuring of voices. No one, however, moved or got up. Not even Yael; her gutsy risk-taking went only so far, and she certainly didn't intend to lead a rebellion against the terrorists holding the pilot and copilot hostage.

And then, after several minutes, someone did get up.

It was the guy who had spoken to Brief. The one from whom she'd taken the flash drive.

He stood up, faced the back of the economy cabin, and made some hand gestures to tell them all to be quiet.

Everyone was silent, watching him. Wondering what he was going to do. No one was more interested than Yael.

CHAPTER 39

BRIEFLY, YAEL HAD wondered why the guy standing in front of everyone now had taken so long to get up and take control. She didn't have long to wait to find out. Once she realized why, it was so obvious that she felt dumb for even wondering.

He wasn't going to stand up in front of everyone and announce things in a loud voice. The terrorists in the cockpit would overhear. So he'd used the intervening few minutes (which seemed like hours) to write messages on sheets of paper using thick black marker pen. He obviously had a stash of paper in his briefcase because he showed them one after the other to the passengers, and there were about five messages.

The first one read, *Everyone, remain calm. I'm a secret service agent.*

Yael was not surprised by this, even though everyone else in the cabin seemed to be. After all, if he'd been dealing with Brief, who worked for Shabak, it made sense. Everyone else was riveted to this man, watching his every move as if he was a famous politician or actor.

He held up another sheet of paper. *The main thing is, we're flying to Tehran. We would only be endangering ourselves if we tried to stop that from happening.*

Everyone nodded. Then another piece: *However, once we're on the ground we can storm the cockpit and overpower the two terrorists. There are only two of them, after all, and dozens of us. So anyone with any army or special ops training on board? Make himself known to me quietly, please. I'm in seat 45C.*

Everyone looked around at everyone else. Some people definitely exhibited somewhat of a smug air. Yael presumed these were the guys with military training.

Does anyone have a weapon? read the next piece of paper. *Yes, I know you aren't supposed to, but circumstances alter cases. Did anyone manage to smuggle one on board—besides the terrorists, that is?*

A couple of guys tentatively raised their hands. Looking around themselves sheepishly.

Yael was gobsmacked. She hadn't really thought of how the terrorists had managed to smuggle their weaponry on board, let alone the passengers. She'd heard of guns being made of material that didn't trigger security when searched for. She'd also heard that El Al knew about this and knew what to look for. Once again, she wished she hadn't flown this airline instead of the Israeli one with its top-notch security.

The guy with the sheets of paper held up one last one. *Be ready. We can do this.*

The passengers who'd admitted to having weapons nodded and smirked at each other. The other passengers tried to look brave and up for anything.

The flight attendant, white-faced, came around with bottles of water and packets of nuts. Yael examined the nuts packet, saw a hechsher on it, and decided to eat it. With what was going on, she didn't know where her next meal would be coming from. She'd already been fantasizing about getting a big falafel back in Jerusalem, dripping with techinah and oozing with salads, and now she had to make do with a packet of nuts. Well, to be fair, more than one. The flight attendant was dishing them out generously. Yael amassed four packets, and put three in her bag. Each of the passengers was allowed two full five-hundred-milliliter bottles of water as well.

There was some activity at the cockpit door. The flimsy piece of plastic rattled and buckled forward, showing that someone was pushing against it from the other side. The guy with the sheets of paper sat down quickly, and from what Yael could see, he'd tucked the paper well out of sight.

She wasn't sure where he'd hidden the sheets, but by now, she had a certain warm feeling toward him that transcended what had happened in Cairo. There, she'd seen him as an opponent, someone who was deliberately sabotaging her attempts to find out what was on the flash drives—and therefore, she hoped, what had happened to her father. Now, however, he had taken on a rosier hue: that of a kind of hero whom she hoped would lead the resistance against these two terrorists. However feisty Yael was, she was no superhero, leading the people in its struggle.

The cockpit door burst open. The two gunmen stood there, guns pointing directly at the passengers. No sign of the pilot or co-pilot. Yael shivered in fear. What had happened to them? Autopilot was one thing, but the plane had to be landed at some point, be it in Tehran or anywhere else. Yael wasn't sure that autopilot covered landings. She found herself gripping her seat arms so tightly that her hands hurt.

Almost by themselves, her lips started moving in prayer. She sent up heartfelt words to Heaven for salvation from this horrible situation.

"We will be landing soon," the lead gunman said, waving his gun menacingly from side to side, encompassing all the passengers. As his gun passed over them, each side shrank back. Yael found herself doing the same thing, and thinking how pointless and yet instinctive it was to do this. It reminded her of being a passenger in that helter-skelter taxi, where she found herself instinctively shrinking and drawing up her feet to avoid a side collision even though her presence inside the taxi wouldn't make the slightest difference to the likelihood of such a crash.

"You will all remain in your seats. No one is to get up, no matter what. Is that clear?" The last phrase was growled, and passengers on all sides of Yael nodded in terror. For some reason, Yael couldn't bring herself to nod, too, and stared stubbornly at the gunman without reacting. Just her luck. He noticed that she wasn't following the rest of the sheep in the meek nod. He came over to her seat, gun pointing directly at her forehead.

"What is it with you, girl?" he growled at her. "You want to be a hero, huh? *Huh?*" Leaning forward, invading her personal space. His breath, even through the balaclava, smelled of garlic and onions, and Yael almost gagged. His personal hygiene left a lot to be desired—although, Yael thought, that would apply to most people on the flight, what with all the terrifying events going on.

Despite her fear, she held firm and stared him out. Said nothing, but didn't shrink.

"Maybe a bullet in the leg would make you a bit more compliant, huh?" he threatened, pointing the gun at her knee. This did terrify Yael. To be incapacitated wasn't on her agenda. She decided there was being stoic, and there was being plain stupid. So she shook her head, and did a creditable performance of being petrified—which wasn't that difficult.

Her subservience mollified the gunman and he moved the gun

away from her leg. With one last glare at her now dramatically shrinking form, he turned to the rest of the economy cabin.

"In case you are wondering how this plane will land," he said, "the pilot is now in a state of total obedience. He will do exactly as we say, and land the plane where we want. So stay buckled up. Once we land, we will inform you of developments."

Yael couldn't help wondering what had happened to the pilot to enable that state of "total obedience." Actually, she decided, she'd rather not know. She presumed it hadn't been pleasant.

Outside, the ground was starting to come up to meet them. It was still a long way off, but there was no doubt about it. The plane was on the descent.

The woman next to Yael hadn't budged or said a word during this whole episode. She was like a frozen lump of terror.

Yael peered over this lump out of the window. Below, she could see spires and pointy towers of mosques and other tall buildings.

Tehran. They really were going to land in Tehran.

CHAPTER 40

"COLIN," DORON SAID, and his voice was shaking.

"Yes, I know," Colin said. "Out of all the flights and all the airlines flying out of Cairo, I had to book Yael on that one." He was running his hands through his hair in a despairing gesture as he spoke. Leora, at his side, was white-faced and grim. A hijacked plane was not good news in anyone's language.

"What are we going to do?" Colin asked his man on the ground. This was way above what he was used to handling. He was used to foreign agents operating on his behalf in local skirmishes or terrorist incidents like this one.

"Yehuda Brief is safely back in Israel," Doron said slowly, thinking hard. "He has to be told who the South African lady really is. Yael thought Brief was the enemy, but in fact he's on her side and deserves to know. So he can help."

Colin was unsure. "He won't be very happy that he's been followed around, had his flash drives stolen, and made to seem like an idiot," he pointed out.

"He's a big boy, he'll get over it," Doron retorted unsympathetically.

"He has to know the truth in order to help Yael."

"Okay. Get on it, pronto. We need help for those guys in the plane. And not only Yael Reed."

BACK IN HIS APARTMENT IN Jerusalem, Yehuda Brief was sulking. His mission to Cairo had not been a success. Two flash drives missing. He'd only just heard about the second one from his contact who'd told him about it while waiting for his own flight to Israel. That plane should have landed by now. Brief paced around, irritated and impatient, waiting to hear from him.

Esther, home now from the hospital after her stroke, which had thankfully proven to be minor, but feeling weak and needy, watched him from the couch and wondered when it was ever going to be her turn to take priority in his life. Never, she presumed. If she was married to a Shabak operative, she could expect little else. Luckily the money he was making at least partly made up for his unsupportiveness. It had enabled her to hire another caregiver, who was, at this moment, in the kitchen, preparing dinner for all of them.

This girl was an expert cook, but no good with kids. Esther fondly remembered the last girl, Tamara Rifkind. She couldn't cook to save her life, but Yonina had loved her. And now Yonina had been shunted from pillar to post while her mother was in the hospital, staying with Yitzy and Nena, where there was no room for her and Nena wasn't prepared to make her pasta and cheese all the time either. If that hadn't been traumatic enough, she was then dumped on a friend of the family who had eight kids and was forced to share a room with four of them. For an only child used to her own space, that was akin to torture.

Yonina had reverted to bad behavior, tantrums, and refusing to eat anything, even her beloved pasta. You'd think, with this hunger strike in progress, that the pudgy child would have lost some weight, but Yonina's hunger strike was only for show. She had plenty of food stashed away in hiding places and stuffed her face desperately when no one could see, crying all the while. She missed Tamara too; she'd been fun and different and wacky. This new girl concentrated almost entirely on her mother and she, Yonina, came a very poor second.

Yonina couldn't understand why Tamara had left, and couldn't help taking it personally. The atmosphere in the Brief house was not a pleasant one, and Yehuda Brief looked for every and any excuse to get out.

So when he got the phone call, he snatched the phone up hastily, hoping whoever it was would suggest a meeting somewhere. Anywhere.

When he heard it was Doron Yair, he was puzzled at first. Brief had very little to do with him; just about knew he worked as an Israeli ear to the ground for the British police and MI5. As he listened, and his jaw slowly descended floorward, he realized he'd been duped by the South African lady. As a Shabak operative, it wasn't a good career move to be deceived by such a young girl. Let alone one who had worked in his house—he should have recognized her in seconds! He'd have to go back to spy school and work on his observational skills, that much was clear.

Then Doron hit him with the big guns. The plane on which Yael Reed (as he now knew Tamara Rifkind was called) was flying had been hijacked and was, at this very moment, sitting on the tarmac at the Tehran airport.

"Are you sure she's actually called Yael Reed?" Brief demanded. "Maybe that's just another of her alter egos." The name sounded vaguely familiar to him but it was just out of his grasp; where had he heard that name before...?

"No, this is her real name. Well, as real as she gets. Her surname was picked up from her foster parents; she doesn't really know her real last name. In fact her reason for following you around was to try and trace what happened to her father."

"Why would I know what happened to her father?" Brief demanded.

"I don't know exactly," Doron said. "Something to do with a hit-and-run that you know something about..."

"A hit-and...oh, wait." Brief reached behind him for a chair and sat down, shaking.

Doron waited.

"Never mind," Brief said, his brain racing. "What flight did you say had been hijacked?"

"Air Sinai out of Cairo at nine this morning. I forget the flight number. Aiming for Tel Aviv, but it's in Tehran. The police and special forces are surrounding the aircraft, but this is Tehran we're talking about, so you can guess how invested they are in rescuing the passengers. They're more interested in rescuing the terrorists and giving them a hero's welcome, I should think."

"Did you say nine this morning, out of Cairo?" Brief repeated, feeling faint.

"Yes, why?"

"Oh, nothing. Thanks for the info. I'll be in touch."

He hung up, leaving Doron staring at his phone in a puzzled manner. What a strange conversation they'd just had. One thing was for sure. Yehuda Brief knew a whole lot more about something than he was letting on. Trouble was, Doron had no idea what.

Brief shut himself in his study and locked the door. He went to a hidden panel under his desk and brought it up. From there he switched on a button that said "soundproofing." A buzzing sound ensued. It was not strictly soundproofing, but it produced speakers of white noise that flooded the door area with sound. There was no way he was going to have prying ears at the door during the conversations that would follow.

He made a phone call.

"Shalom, Ari? Hi, this is Yehuda Brief... Oh, you've heard about the Air Sinai flight? I wanted to know if... Oh, he *is* on it. That's what I feared. There's someone else of interest on that plane. A young woman called Yael Reed. I can't tell you at this stage why she's of interest, you're just going to have to take my word for it. I want your best undercover Arab lookalike operatives in Tehran right there, right now... Good, thought you would have.... They're already there, surrounding the plane? Why aren't they storming the plane right this minute? ... Biding their time, you say? Well, let's hope he has his own plan of action from inside."

He disconnected that call and sat thinking for a while. Yael Reed. So close...

Then he remembered. The girl whose flight from London to Israel he'd canceled. Had she managed to slip through the net? He thought he'd covered all the bases, but somehow she was there, and just to add insult to injury, she was on the same plane as his colleague.

This was too much. Brief slammed his fist down on the table. What was this girl, a wisp of smoke, that she could constantly elude and fool him?

He tried calling his man on the plane. He reckoned that since they'd landed, he'd have his phone switched on.

It was a long shot, and it didn't pay off. The phone went straight to voice mail. Either the terrorists had confiscated all the cell phones on board, or something bad had happened to the passengers. Best-case scenario, his colleague couldn't use his phone for his own personal reasons.

He left a message. "There's a young woman on the plane, Yael Reed. If you can, make yourself known to her. But be careful. She has some kind of agenda; I don't as yet know what it is, but she's probably the one who took the flash drives."

CHAPTER 41

BRIEF PACED HIS office, which was no mean feat as it was a very small room. He felt like a caged tiger in a space far too small for it. Breaking free of the restriction of the study, he unlocked his door and burst out into the living room, where his wife and daughter sat nervously. They had heard him pacing, they'd heard what sounded like a prisoner trying to break free of shackles. Esther sat frozen, wondering if he was smashing his study into pieces. She looked behind him through the open door when he came out, but could see no sign of damage, much to her relief.

"I want Tamara back." Yonina pouted. "She was nice and loved me. She read me stories in voices. I hate this new babysitter. She makes me eat vegetables!"

"Vegetables are good for you, dear," her mother ventured weakly. "But I do agree, Tamara was nice to you."

"I don't like vegetables! I won't be made to eat things I hate! Tamara made me pasta and cheese and ketchup every day!" Yonina protested. "It was yum!"

"How did we find Tamara Rifkind?" Brief suddenly rounded

on his wife and asked insistently. "She didn't just appear out of the ether, I presume?"

"No, dear," Esther said. She could feel a headache coming on and wondered if this conversation was good for her health. She could feel her heart pounding alarmingly in her chest. "No, Nena suggested her to me."

"Nena? As in Yitzy's Nena?" Brief growled.

"How many other Nenas do you know?" Esther quavered.

In a second, Brief was back in his study, door locked, and on the phone with his daughter-in-law.

ONE THING NENA BRIEF HAD never signed up for was family feuds or conflict.

She was slowly getting her head around the shocking fact that her father-in-law was a Shabak operative. She'd always just assumed he was a businessman involved in much foreign travel, but this was mind-blowing. She wanted to ask Yitzy why he'd never told her, but she knew what his answer would be: that it was all far too top secret to talk about, even among close family members.

Nena knew that Yehuda Brief, too, was getting his head around the fact that Tamara Rifkind was the same girl whose flight to Israel he'd attempted to cancel. Apparently this girl, whom he knew now was Yael Reed, had nevertheless managed to slip into the country; not only that, she'd gained employment with his family! It was the most outrageous breach of his own personal security that he'd ever encountered.

He was blustering and shouting at his daughter-in-law about family values and loyalties, and she just capitulated on all counts and admitted everything—except the reason for Yael wanting this trip and why she had chosen the Briefs to work for. Nena saw no reason to reveal that.

Nena took the shouting meekly and tried telling herself that she was doing it for Yael, but she was really annoyed that things were turning out this way.

"So where's Yael now?" she asked. It was a relief to voice her real name.

"She's on that Air Sinai plane that's been hijacked by Daesh," her father-in-law told her.

Everyone knew about the hijacked plane. It was top news on all media and everyone in the street was talking about it because there were several Israeli passengers on board. One was rumored, on the streets of Israel, to be a Shabak operative. Which was comforting but alarming all at once, because if Daesh discovered his identity, which they were likely to do, it meant he was a highly prized target.

Nena gasped when she heard this. All her annoyance at Yael dissipated at once, and she felt horrified for her friend.

Brief, his anger somewhat spent, calmed down and said, "We're doing whatever we can to get everyone safely off the plane."

"Yes, but they're in Tehran!" Nena said agitatedly. "This isn't Entebbe!"

Brief felt his irritation levels rise again. "I'm aware this isn't Uganda," he said, trying to keep his voice level. "But we're doing our best. I'll keep you informed. In the meantime, Nena, do us a favor and don't go blabbing to your friends about Yael being on this plane." Nena had been anticipating calling Rosie or Shuli and doing just that, but not now.

He hung up the call. Nena collapsed into a chair and sobbed her heart out. *Yael, Yael, Yael! Why did you continually get yourself into these scrapes!* She could only see this situation turning out badly. They were in the hands of one of the worst enemies of Israel, and on their home turf too.

The Yehuda Brief who emerged from his study after the call was a different man from the wild bull who'd been thundering around a few minutes earlier. He still looked white-faced, but calm and rational, and even managed a smile at his wife and daughter.

"Are you okay, dear?" Esther managed. She still had that headache, although it was easing now that her husband was calmer, but she still feared his flare-ups. Yonina just looked disgruntled.

"All getting sorted, no worries," he said. "And yes, Yonina, Miss Rifkind was certainly quite an unusual nanny. Yes, indeed."

Yonina beamed. "So can we get her back, Daddy?"

THE WORLD'S MEDIA HAD ITS attention focused on the plane; it was hailed as a second Entebbe by the headline writers. Everyone watched and waited to see what demands the terrorists would make.

To conserve fuel, the plane's engines had been turned off. This meant that the air-conditioning on board was no longer functioning. Luckily, however, the weather in Tehran had taken a turn for the worse, if one gauged it by British weather standards. But this meant it was cold, windy, and damp outside, with occasional flurries of rain. Perfect, as it meant that the temperatures on board could be kept the right side of unbearable.

However, as the plane was sealed shut, and no windows could be opened for ventilation, there was only so much air on board for the passengers to breathe. So despite the coolness of the weather outside, on board, the temperature was rising slowly but steadily.

The guy in 45C seemed to be the only one on the plane who

was keeping his cool. Once the plane was on the ground, and before the terrorists showed themselves outside the cockpit again, he, without a sound, had moved around the cabin, garnering all the active soldiers and people who could fight, and issuing them with instructions. He was like the best general in a field operation, ordering his troops silently but effectively, and everyone understood exactly what to do. They all sat in their seats like coiled springs, waiting for the order to strike.

CHAPTER 42

"Get them out of there!" Brief bellowed down the phone at person or persons unknown. "You're wasting time!"

He was once again locked in his study, his wife and daughter doing a good cowering act on the sofa outside. The study wasn't totally soundproof even though he'd done his best to make it so, and they could hear him yelling and ranting.

"I'll have you fired if this isn't sorted!" he yelled.

Esther heard that and wondered, not for the first time, what exact position her husband held in Shabak. It had been a huge concession for her to know he worked for them at all; many wives spent their whole married lives in blissful ignorance as to what their husbands did until after retirement, or sometimes not even then. Brief had entrusted her with that knowledge, but no details. To hear him threaten to fire someone meant that he had to be in a position where he could do such a thing. She couldn't help being impressed, even though she had no idea what was going on.

MEANWHILE, DORON YAIR HAD INSTRUCTIONS of his own to follow. He was already dark skinned and dark haired, but just in case that wasn't enough, he was accentuating these attributes at the bathroom sink, while at the same time booking a flight to Tehran as early as he could possibly find one. The flight was only two hours and forty-four minutes from Cairo, so he was hoping to be there before it was too late.

MEANWHILE, ON THE TARMAC AT the Tehran airport…

The temperature on the plane was getting unbearable, even though outside the window, rain whipped by wind lashed the plane and the tarmac was shiny with oil and water. People were taking off jackets and any clothing they could decently get rid of. The woman next to Yael seemed particularly uncomfortable. The woman, who had told Yael her name was Sonia, squirmed and sweated profusely on her seat, forcing Yael into an ever more tight corner of her own.

"Can't we open a window?" Sonia finally burst out loudly, looking longingly at the rainswept tarmac outside.

Yael laughed a little, but to her surprise, the guy in 45C stood up when he heard her and turned around.

"Actually, she isn't being so ridiculous," he said. "Aside from the obvious opening of the cabin doors and emergency exits, there are two openable windows in the cockpit. But once we do that, we're literally opening the floodgates from outside. Right now we're a sealed unit and no one can get out, but also no one can get in. It's a waiting game. It won't be much longer."

"Maybe the terrorists have the windows open in the cockpit and are enjoying fresh air while we suffocate in here," someone said, sounding in obvious distress.

"That's entirely possible," the guy in 45C said to the distressed person. "But the feeling of suffocation in that case would be largely psychological. The cockpit door to the cabin is not sealed. Air can escape underneath and round the edges. Just calm down, breathe slowly, and imagine that lovely, fresh, cold air from outside coming in through the leaks in the cockpit door, and you'll feel better. It's mind over matter." He sat down.

"It's unbearable! Whatever you say about mind over matter and fresh air coming under the cockpit door, I can't stand it!" Sonia gasped, and stood up, throwing caution to the nonexistent wind, flinging her arms around like a windmill trying to create some airflow, her arms hitting Yael and the woman on the other side more than once. Yael kept quiet and just tried to make herself as small as possible to avoid the blows, but the woman in the window seat wasn't having any of this treatment.

"Sit down and stop hitting me!" she yelled.

"I'm not hitting you; I'm trying to get some air on me!" Sonia yelled back.

"You are so hitting me!" the woman responded, and hit her back.

Everyone around Yael's seat gasped. A fracas was developing. There was no space, hardly any air left in the cabin, and they chose now to start a fight.

The guy in 45C stood up and came over to Yael's row. "Stop it!" he hissed at them.

They took no notice. They were just beginning and Yael was getting pummeled. The guy looked at her for the first time.

"Come and sit in my row," he told her urgently. "It's not safe here."

"Oh, I'm just a bit bruised and battered," Yael said, trying to laugh it off. "I've had worse."

"I said, come and sit in my row, it's not safe here," he repeated, and there was something about his tone of voice that brooked no argument.

Yael got the message. With the ridiculousness of the fight between the two women, the terrorists were bound to hear eventually. In a situation like this, nothing was normal.

She got up and moved out of her seat, receiving a few more blows. With a few silent "ow, ow's," she went to row 45.

The window seat was empty, so Yael sat there. 45C sat in the aisle seat, and there was one woman between them. Yael looked out the window and rested her head against the damp coolness of it. Outside, the tarmac seemed deserted. Was no one out there to rescue them?

"Ignore the fight," the guy in 45C whispered to Yael and the other woman in their row. "This is not going to end well."

At the same time as saying this, the guy was sending silent signals to the other armed Israelis on board. Something was going down, and it was going to happen pretty soon.

"It really is hot," Yael commented, fanning herself with her hand.

The guy in 45C leaned over and spoke to the two in his row quietly but intensely.

"Look, every plane as an APU, auxiliary power unit. It's fuel driven, like the main engines. It could control the electrics including air, while we're on the ground. The pilots have access to it and can switch it on at any moment they choose."

Yael gaped at him. She was thinking of the two women back there, whose fighting had subsided somewhat out of sheer heat exhaustion.

"I know this is hard," he went on, "but it's for the greater good of this situation. Basically the terrorists don't know about the APU, just as you don't. We're literally sweating them out, like we'd smoke out an unwanted wasps' nest."

"It has its risks, though," Yael said. "It's so hot in here, some people might get seriously ill."

"It's a chance we'll have to take," the guy said with a shrug.

A second later, a risk Yael hadn't anticipated manifested itself. Sonia thundered down the aisle past her, and started banging on the cockpit door.

"Open up! We're dying of heatstroke back here! I bet you have the cockpit windows open and you're sitting there enjoying the fresh air!"

The guy in 45C got up at once and intercepted her. "Are you crazy? Do you want to get us all killed?"

She batted him away as if he was a fly, and continued pounding on the door.

It had a result. Maybe not quite the one she had hoped for.

The cockpit door opened, a terrorist looked out, saw her, and fired his gun. It was deafening. Sonia, screaming, fell to the ground, clutching her lower leg, which was bleeding heavily. She lay on the floor and continued screaming, clutching the wound. The flight attendant made as if to come toward her to help, but the terrorist gave her a look and she kept back, shaking in fear.

Everyone joined in screaming. They screamed and screamed. It was bedlam.

The terrorist glared at the cabin full of shrieking, sweating passengers.

"Shut up!" he yelled, and everyone went instantly silent, terrified to share Sonia's fate.

The terrorist didn't look too great himself, from the little they could see of him behind his mask, which was sodden with sweat. There was no rush of fresh air from the cockpit either, so it seemed like the pilots either hadn't chosen to open those openable windows, or weren't in a position to do so.

"Anyone else want to play stupid games?" he threatened. "They'll end up the same."

The cockpit door slammed shut.

CHAPTER 43

THE GUY IN 45C had kind of taken control of the passenger side of the plane. No one had appointed him "captain," no one had asked him to be in charge, and yet, no one questioned his leadership qualities either. Even the passengers who looked like they were tougher than he was, big, brawny men who'd confessed to having sneaked a gun on board just like he had, were looking to him for direction. He'd intimated to everyone that they could turn on their cell phones, but to keep them out of sight and on silent. They could send messages to their loved ones telling them they were okay, but nothing else.

He himself sent various messages on his cell, and received some in return. He read the messages quickly, responded, and put his phone away.

He took charge of Sonia's care without actually doing it. A look here, a pointed hand there, and the cabin crew ran to do his bidding. They weren't equipped to handle major injuries like a bullet to the leg, but they could do a patch-up job in the meantime, while waiting for developments.

Sonia was not a brave patient. She lay on the floor taking up the entire aisle in front of the cockpit door, and wailed continuously. 45C's warnings to her to keep quiet, that it could result in the terrorist coming out again and finishing her off, weren't heeded. The other passengers sat silent and petrified, willing her to be quiet. 45C went over to the flight attendant and said something quietly to her and she nodded. She opened one of the overhead lockers; it contained equipment that the crew needed, and took out a medical kit that seemed to have nothing to do with the bandages she'd already applied to Sonia's leg. It contained meds.

As Yael watched, the flight attendant took out a syringe, filled it with something from a small vial, and injected Sonia. Yael was rather surprised at the injection site; not the arm or leg as she would have supposed, but right into her neck. Sonia screamed once, and then, to everyone's surprise, went silent and slack. She was out cold. 45C nodded his satisfaction at this outcome and sat down again.

Yael looked at him. While she was relieved that the awful wailing had stopped, and knew his motivation was to prevent the terrorists from going berserk with their guns out of irritation, she wondered what his next move was. And he didn't seem inclined to share that information with anyone, let alone a young girl sitting in a nearby window seat. But then he surprised her, by turning in her direction.

"I think you know Doron Yair," he said.

Yael's eyes widened in shock. "Yes," she said, unwilling to impart any other information, as yet unsure who she was dealing with. In her mind, all kinds of dots were beginning to join up, not the least of them the fact that if he knew that she knew Doron, it was highly probable that he knew she was the one who'd stolen the flash drives. Which was not a comfortable situation for her to be in.

45C realized Yael's caution and nodded his acceptance of it. With a flick of his eyelids and a jerk of his hand, he intimated to the passenger sitting between them that she should switch seats with Yael.

Yael was very reluctant to do so for all kinds of reasons—fear, trepidation, modesty—in equal measures. She shook her head. The other passenger was already standing, preparing to do the switch.

"Stop being so difficult, girl," 45C growled at her. "Sit here and I'll explain everything. Circumstances alter cases, and here we have a circumstance that alters everything."

The switch was done, but Yael sat as far away from 45C as she could manage in the next seat.

He leaned in a little, while keeping out of her personal space.

"You know that Doron is an operative who works for your London friends, Colin and Leora. He's their foreign agent working in Israel. And as such, he's now working with me."

This made sense to Yael, even while other dots were wildly racing around her mind, trying to connect.

"Well," went on 45C, "he's standing outside this plane at this very moment, dressed as, and looking for all the world like, a local Iranian security guy. But he's been communicating with me on my cell phone and he's given me the numbers of the terrorists' cells."

Yael was puzzled. "So what, you're going to call them and say hi?" she asked sarcastically.

45C's eyes flickered with annoyance. "I see you've got guts," he said. "Only to be expected, I suppose, for someone who managed to steal those flash drives from me."

She recoiled at this, wondering what he would do next, but he shrugged. "No big deal. Water under the bridge, under the circumstances. No, I'm not going to call the terrorists to say hi. But Doron and I have a way to intercept their calls and texts and find out what their next moves are."

"Ah," Yael said, impressed. "So what is their next move, exactly?"

"Usual boring stuff. Asking for Daesh prisoners in Israel and other countries to be released in return for the plane and its passengers. Heavy negotiations going on at the moment." He looked at his cell briefly as if to confirm this, then put it away.

"I hope they don't agree to that," Yael said bravely. "I wouldn't want to spend the rest of my life thinking I owed my continued existence to the fact that several ISIS members had been freed to commit more terrorist acts."

45C looked at Yael with renewed interest. "You certainly are a spirited young lady."

She nodded briefly in acknowledgment of this truth about herself. "So, what? We're just going to sit here while they negotiate? It could take days. The passengers are about to pass out, looking at some of them."

"Plans are afoot. You don't need to know everything at this point." He paused. "So why *did* you take my flash drives?"

Yael flushed and looked away. "Sorry about that. I thought they might help me in my inquiries. I'm a private investigator, you see."

His eyebrows rose. "I know that. Obviously, if I know you're connected to Colin and Leora Sommers. Question is, what are you investigating that makes my flash drives of such interest?"

She was just about to answer, when the cockpit door opened. One of the terrorists, still wearing his sweat-soaked ski mask, stepped out and almost fell over the supine and unconscious form of Sonia.

"Is she dead?" he asked with only a mild curiosity as to the answer.

The flight attendant shook her head and said something to him in Arabic that seemed to satisfy him as he nodded.

"You all sit there like the good apes that you are," the terrorist growled at the passengers in the cabin. "And no harm will come to you. Now you..." He glared at the flight attendant. "Bring us food and drink! Knock on the cockpit door when you have it ready. Now!"

She ran back to the galley to do his bidding. He said, "We will soon have our demands met, and then you can all go free."

The cockpit door slammed again. 45C said to Yael, "I think he has other plans for us and not plans that include us going free. Which is why we can't just sit. Things are about to happen outside this plane, so be prepared."

"Okay," Yael said.

"So," he said, "you were about to tell me about your investigation. And why my flash drives were of such interest."

"Well, in truth I have no idea if the flash drives contain anything of interest," Yael said. "They're being decoded in London even as we speak. But my investigation is about finding out what happened to my father. I think he was in a hit-and-run, supposedly killed. But there's so much mystery and secrecy around that accident. He doesn't seem to have a burial place, at least not one that I can find. Everything points to some kind of conspiracy."

"A hit-and-run, you say?" 45C said with mild curiosity. "And how old might you be? You look around twelve but I presume you're older."

"I'm twenty-one," Yael said, unoffended.

At this, 45C's mild curiosity changed to a sharp new interest.

"And where were you brought up?"

"I was left by my parents outside a hospital in England," she said. "I've traced my mother, not that she wants to have anything to do with me, but she won't tell me what happened to my father. I've kind of traced his movements to Israel. I worked for Yehuda Brief for a while, I think you know him."

He said, "Not only spirited, but resourceful." There was a pause. Then he said, "I think I may have answers for you."

Foundling 235

CHAPTER 44

"Answers?" Yael repeated.

"Of course, I might be wrong and it could be someone else entirely. I don't know your father's name. Do you?"

She sat up straight at this and turned to face 45C. "I think so..."

At that moment, the cabin doors rattled from outside. Everyone's head swiveled to look.

There were ladders leaning against the fuselage. And men climbing them.

"Someone's trying to get in!" one of the passengers shouted.

At the noise and vibrations, the cockpit doors burst open. The two gunmen leaped out and began shooting at the cabin doors. It was pandemonium. All the passengers started shrieking and ducking down in their seats.

All except the ones under the command of 45C, who, at a signal from him, jumped up and took action.

It was all over in seconds. Some bullets from the two terrorists ricocheted off the doors and caused some injuries to passengers, but thankfully nothing serious. The two gunmen lay dead on the floor and the hijacking was over. It had been all about waiting for the right moment. Storming the plane had only been a diversion to what had been planned inside; they'd needed the gunmen to come out, and be totally distracted, for the command to act, to be given by 45C. And so it came to pass.

When the screaming died down, 45C looked around briefly and ordered the flight attendant to attend to the injured—at least the ones he noticed in his quick glance. Then he gave the order to open the airplane doors.

It was not all quite over yet because the forces from outside were not all friendly; they were local Iranian security guys and uninterested in the well-being of the foreign passengers, particularly the Jewish ones. But Doron Yair and others secretly undercover from Israel had that under control too. They were not going to stand any nonsense from hostile forces toward their own people, and a few well-placed threats, plus the even better-placed eyes of the world's media trained on this incident (orchestrated by the Israelis, too, to ensure nothing untoward happened while the world's back was turned) ensured the Iranians were on their best behavior. The undercover Israelis, and the telephoto lenses of the cameramen focused on the plane, made sure of that.

Doron and his gang yelled commands. Ambulances outside appeared and started lifting the injured off the plane. There was no way the Israeli undercover guys were going to allow their own people to go off in an Iranian ambulance; they had their own ready and waiting, emblazoned with fake Iranian symbols so they wouldn't be attacked in the streets of Tehran, but carrying an almost imperceptible Israeli symbol somewhere too. They weren't going to take them to the local hospitals either.

It was then that 45C noticed Yael Reed had taken a bullet.

It was to her left shoulder, and it was bleeding profusely. She lay unconscious, curled in her seat, and had almost been passed over in the general chaos of getting more seriously wounded passengers off the plane.

"Get her help, quick!" 45C barked. "She's bleeding out!"

Someone rushed forward and applied pressure to Yael's wound, then lifted her arm high so the blood would flow back to her body. It was strapped like that, as she was carefully lifted onto a stretcher and off the plane. Onto one of the waiting Israeli ambulances.

"Is that Yael Reed?" Doron asked 45C.

"Yes, I'm afraid so. I should have noticed sooner. I had my back to her. I feel beyond guilty. Take her to the El Al plane we have waiting, you know where that is. We need to fly any wounded Israelis back home. We don't dare treat them here in Iran."

The El Al plane had been kitted out for transporting stretcher cases. Luckily there were only two who weren't walking wounded or just minor injuries. Yael and one of the tough soldier types who'd taken a bullet that had bounced off the cabin door.

"No fatalities at least," Doron reported. "Yael looks bad, but with a transfusion and some patching up, she should be okay."

"I'm coming on the plane with her," 45C said. "I have a conversation to finish off."

If Doron thought this was a bit strange, he didn't show it. Anyway there was so much to do, getting all the Jewish passengers safely off the plane and onto safe transportation back to Israel, that he was happy someone else had taken Yael under his wing.

In the ambulance, a paramedic looked at Yael's shoulder. The bullet had gone clean through but had left a serious wound on her back.

"Do you know if she's a righty or a lefty?" the paramedic asked 45C, who just shook his head.

"I barely know the girl," he said with a shrug. "First time I met her was on the plane."

"Well, for her sake," the paramedic said, first washing, then irrigating, then packing the wound lightly with sterile gauze and wrapping a dressing around her upper arm, "let's hope she's right-handed because she won't be doing much with her left for a while. This is a horrible injury, and the shoulder has so many complex ranges of movement that'll need to be worked on before she gets back full use of it again. She's going to be in physical therapy for quite a while, I'd say."

"Poor kid," 45C said.

"The good news is, she'll live. I'll give her some intramuscular antibiotics now, and once she's in the hospital in Israel they'll probably put her on intravenous, just to make sure she doesn't develop sepsis or some other nasty infection from that wound." He stabbed her with a needle as he spoke, and she didn't stir. She was still deeply unconscious. "There, that'll do it for now."

The ambulance was bombing along some main highway, its lights flashing but no siren. Suddenly it swerved sharply off the road, along what felt like a dirt track. The vehicle lurched violently, then it was on a smooth road again, in total darkness. No street lights or markings of any kind. Wide open country on both sides.

Suddenly, there was the El Al plane, looming phantom-like out of the darkness, its pale fuselage sitting there like a giant, brooding moth, wings outstretched. The cabin doors were open, and other ambulances were already offloading their human cargo into its welcoming belly.

"Come on, let's get her up there," the paramedic said.

Two paramedics carried the stretcher, and 45C tried awkwardly to help. Inching carefully up the retractable stairs, they managed to get Yael on board. Seats had been removed from the cabin to create a bigger space for the stretchers. Doctors were attending the wounded, while talking animatedly on their cell phones to hospitals in Israel, telling them the conditions of the injured.

The paramedic handed over Yael. "Caucasian female, approximately twenty years of age, bullet went straight through her left shoulder, damaging several layers of muscle. I've given her one dose of one-half-milliliter intramuscular antibiotics."

"How long ago?" the doctor asked while examining Yael's wound. "Good job on the packing, by the way. It looks nice and clean."

"Thank you," the paramedic said, pleased. "Just about fifteen, maybe twenty minutes ago."

"Okay. That's enough for now. She can have Novocain if she wakes up and requires pain relief." He recovered the dressing and moved on to the next patient.

The cabin doors closed and they were informed that the plane was taking off without delay. The longer it stayed in Iran, the more danger they were in. Within minutes, it had taken to the skies and was banking around, heading for Tel Aviv.

45C stayed by Yael's stretcher. After about half an hour into the flight, her eyelids fluttered and opened. She looked at him, then moaned in pain and started twisting away from the source of it.

"Oh, my shoulder! What happened?"

"You were shot," he told her. "We're on our way back to Israel. You've been well tended to, and you'll be fine. I'll ask for some pain relief for you." He waved an arm and a paramedic came over and administered an injection that made Yael yelp, but slowly as it took effect, she relaxed.

"That's better," she murmured. "So much better…" She opened a bleary eye. "On the plane, the other plane, we were talking about what happened to my father."

"Yes. And I said I may have answers for you, but that would depend on who he is, of course."

"Well," Yael said. "From my research, which may of course be wrong, I think his name is Alan Katz."

Then the drug took hold in full measure and she drifted. Which was just as well, because 45C sat in front of her, frozen in shock. An ice sculpture. Alan Katz was her father? How could that possibly be? No, impossible. She must be wrong.

CHAPTER 45

"SHE'S OUT," THE paramedic said unnecessarily. "You don't have to sit there the whole flight. Anyway, why *are* you sitting there? What's she to you? A relative?"

"No, no relative," 45C said dully. "Just...look. Is there any way at all I can make some calls while on the plane?"

The paramedic shrugged. "Don't ask me, I'm only a medic. I'm not in charge of communications on board."

45C got up from his seat next to her stretcher, feeling a bit foolish for assuming a paramedic would know how to make a phone call from the plane. He found a member of the cabin crew, and the paramedic saw the two of them in a huddle in the corner discussing the logistics. 45C was waving his hands around urgently, and the paramedic saw sweat trickling down his face.

Then he saw the cabin crew guy nod at 45C, and showed him to a fixed telephone. 45C sat down next to it and started jabbing numbers with a frightening intensity. The paramedic watched him talking on the phone, and saw his face grow white with shock. By the time he came back to Yael's side, he looked as if he might be about to faint.

242 Foundling

"I'm thinking you need me more than this patient does," the paramedic said. "Are you okay?"

"No, I'm not okay," 45C said, slowly sitting down, holding the back of the seat for support. "I need to talk to this girl. But in private, if that's possible."

"She's out," the paramedic said again. But then Yael started to stir and come around. She opened her eyes and looked around her. Saw the paramedic, smiled. Saw 45C and frowned a little.

"You still here?" she said.

"Well," he said in a voice he barely recognized as his own, "I can hardly get off the plane now, can I?"

"True," she said, and smiled again.

"I need to talk to you," he said, "but only if you're okay to talk. You're in pain."

"Not anymore," she slurred. She was so high on Novocain that she was surprised she was still attached to the stretcher, and hadn't started floating up toward the roof of the plane. "In fact, I've never felt better." She sighed. "They should put this stuff in the water supply."

45C looked at the paramedic attending to her, who smiled back and shrugged. "They often get like this on Novocain," he told him. "It's a powerful drug. She has a severe injury."

"Who needs shoulders anyway?" Yael giggled. "Useless appendages."

"I'll leave you to it," the paramedic said, and moved away, giving them privacy.

"Don't get off the plane!" Yael insisted.

45C frowned. "Maybe let's wait till you're more lucid till we have that talk, hey?"

"Lucy?" Yael asked. "Who's Lucy? My name is Yael."

45C looked around and made sure no one was in earshot before

Foundling 243

saying anything else. But by the time he turned back, Yael was out cold again. He gave up. He had to wait until the right moment.

The El Al plane landed smoothly at Ben Gurion Airport. An ambulance had been alerted and was waiting on the tarmac. Yael, and the other patients who needed stretcher care, were carefully moved off the plane, bypassing all passport control lines and security. Someone came on board the ambulance and checked their papers were in order. Yael, waking up briefly at this, said, "This is great! I should do this every time to avoid all those horrible queues! Rent a bullet! Hire a terrorist and avoid the lines!" No one laughed.

When Yael opened her eyes, she was lying in a hospital bed next to a window that overlooked stunning mountain-and-forest scenery. Hadassah Ein Kerem hospital. Her shoulder was throbbing agonizingly, and, despite herself, she moaned aloud in pain.

"Novocain!" she groaned. "It hurts, it hurts, it hurts!"

To her surprise, the guy from 45C appeared at her side in an instant, with a very concerned look on his face.

"I'll ask the nurse for something," he said.

"What are you still doing here?" she asked, twisting her body in an attempt to get away from the pain.

When she wasn't twisting, she was looking at him with an expression that encompassed both anguish and puzzlement in equal measures. She needed pain relief and she needed answers, again both in equal measures.

45C called a nurse, who came quickly. When she saw the agonized figure of Yael on the bed, she hurriedly administered another dose of Novocain.

"You'll soon be feeling much better," she said soothingly. And left them alone together again.

Indeed, as the meds took hold, Yael lay quietly on the bed. 45C waited for her to ask her question again. And she did; even through the delightful fog of medication, her ability to reason wasn't totally absent.

"Why are you still here?" she repeated. "It's a bit weird, you hanging around. Creeping me out."

45C got up and closed the door of her hospital room, came back and sat down.

"You said your father's name is Alan Katz," he said.

"Yes, I said I thought so, why?" she murmured.

"Let me introduce myself." He paused. "I'm…Alan Katz…and I think I could be your father."

Through the fog of the drugs, Yael gawped at him. "But…Alan Katz is dead."

He looked straight at her, and laid two fingers on his wrist. "Nope, there's a pulse. I'm very much alive, last time I checked. Which was right now."

Still struggling through the gunge that had replaced her brain now that the meds had kicked in, Yael said, "But you…how can you be my father?"

"Apparently I can," he said. "Even though I had no idea until a short time ago, that I had achieved fatherhood for twenty-one years and not known about it. It's come as a massive shock to me, I can tell you. So I made some calls on the plane and the facts seem to fit."

"But if you're my father, you must have known about me," Yael said. "You and my mother put my Moses basket in front of the hospital."

"Not me. Only your mother. We'd divorced by then, and it wasn't amicable. All I wanted to do was get away from life itself. Start over, somewhere else. So, to all intents and purposes, I vanished. That hit-and-run, the newspaper reports were faked. It was all faked, to enable me to disappear and start over under a new identity."

Yael struggled to make sense of it all. So that was why there was no burial recorded when she went looking.

"And where's the best place for someone wanting to start over? The Israeli secret service. So I joined Shabak. Well, actually they recruited me at a time I was looking to disappear. Of course I never would've disappeared in the first place if I'd known I was going to become a father."

"So if you'd known, you'd have stayed? Tried to work things out?"

"Not sure about staying with your mother, to be honest," he said. "But I for sure would have wanted to be a father, to get to know you. I had no idea." He paused and looked at Yael.

There she was. All of a sudden, this child of his, who he'd never even known existed, was lying there with a serious injury. She'd been so brave in the face of such trauma and terror. Before that, she'd exhibited such feisty daring, stealing those flash drives from him. Despite his extreme annoyance at the time, now that he knew the perpetrator was his own daughter, he couldn't help feeling a grudging pride in her gutsy behavior—no, not even grudging it, he *was* proud of her.

"I wouldn't have believed it myself, but you are so my little girl," Alan Katz replied. "Every cell in your body is a chip off the old block. Everything about you is me, all over again. I'm shocked beyond belief that you're here now. But you are here and you're my daughter, so yes, I'm your father. You say your name is Yael Reed?"

Yael struggled to sit up and dizziness overcame her. Katz rushed to arrange the pillows behind her head and back so that she could sit semi-reclining.

"You're really my dad?" The word "dad" didn't trip easily off her tongue.

"So it would seem." He smiled. Then a shadow crossed his face, and she saw it, caught it, like seeing a spider on the ceiling that you might not have noticed if it hadn't moved.

"What was that look?" she asked. "You don't look entirely happy that I'm here. Does part of you wish that I'd never appeared?" It was blunt and cruel but she had to know.

"Part of me does," he admitted. "Although part of me couldn't be happier to meet you at last."

"What part of you wishes that I'd never appeared?" Yael asked relentlessly. She was so used to rejection in her life. She wasn't going to allow herself false hope that this man, who apparently was her father, really wanted her around.

He paused. "The part that's been working undercover for all these years," he said, "and now my cover has been blown. And I have to consider the ramifications of that. Do I take on a new identity and go undercover again? And if so, would you come with me? I don't want to lose you again."

CHAPTER 46

"Go with you?" Yael repeated in shock. This was her whole world suddenly turned upside down and inside out all at once. This man by her bed, this total stranger until five minutes ago, was now suggesting that she leave everything familiar and dear to her and disappear with him. No, she couldn't do it! It was so unfair of him to expect it of her!

"I know it's a lot to take in," he said. "I also have to get my head around having a daughter I didn't know existed till just now. I'm not even sure we'll get along."

Yael grasped at this straw like a drowning person. "Yes, exactly!" she said. "We'll probably hate each other's guts, get on each other's nerves, and end up practically killing each other!"

Katz looked at her with undisguised admiration. "Wow, you really don't want to come with me, do you?" he asked with a wry smile.

She blushed. "It's all just too much too soon," she admitted. "I've been on my own for most of my life: self-sufficient, independent. I'm building up a nice practice as a PI. I can't just throw that all in and disappear with you to…where?"

"So look," he said. "If you come with me, we'll both start afresh. Somewhere completely new. Shabak will set us up. You can start working for me."

"I can start working for the Israeli secret service?"

"You certainly have what it takes," her father said with a smile.

"Wow," Yael said. "That's quite some offer."

"So what do you say?"

She looked at him. He had the face of a stranger and yet...and yet...something about him was so familiar, almost dear. When she'd first laid eyes on him, there had been no magical connection—no moment of light bulbs going off above her head, no instant *knowing*. Yet now, how could she *not* have known who he was? He had her eyes. She saw a small curl escaping from the buzz cut just above his ears that spoke of her own unruly mop. So familiar. Her very own father after all these years.

And yet...could she just give up everything she had known and go away with him? More importantly, could she really give up the thing that was most precious of all to her—her independence and freedom? She'd never be able to do what she wanted, when she wanted, if she had her father breathing down her neck—however wonderful a father he might turn out to be.

Mind you, she reasoned with herself internally, she wanted to get married one day, didn't she? She'd have to kowtow to an even stranger stranger than this one. A man who shared no genes with her whatsoever. How on earth could she do that if she didn't even want to be with her father, with whom she shared so much DNA?

Yael realized he was sizing her up just as she was assessing him. And he was waiting for her to give him an answer.

"I need time," she said at last. "To think. Anyway," she said, indicating her shoulder, "I'm just not in any fit state to do much of anything at the moment." Suddenly her awful injury became a source of comfort to her. A reason for delaying what she hoped would not be the inevitable. "I need months of physical therapy," she said smugly.

"They have physical therapists all over the world, you know," Katz responded. Looking at him, Yael saw the sadness in his voice, in his eyes. He already felt the tenuous strands that connected them loosening and drifting away like spiders' webs that you brushed when you walked past them.

"Yes, but…"

He dismissed her protests. "It's okay. I understand. You can't be expected to want to go away with me. Till just now you didn't know I existed. There's an old song that sums up how I have to deal with this, I guess."

He sang it, and his voice was a sweet tenor. He was obviously very musical. Yael smiled.

"You sing so nicely," she said.

"Can you sing?" he asked her curiously. "Your mother is tone-deaf."

"I can hold a tune, I think," she said modestly.

"Sing me something," he said. "Anything. I just want to know if this is something else we share."

Yael had never sung in front of a man before. *But it's my father*, she realized. She started to sing *"Lechah Dodi"* from the Friday night davening. A tune she had learned in seminary and still used when she davened either on her own, or with the other young women in the apartment block.

Katz watched and listened, and she saw tears well up in his eyes. She knew she was singing it well. Often when they sang it together, the other young women would subdue their own voices just so they could listen to Yael's for a few beats.

"That's just beautiful," he said when she stopped. He wiped his eyes. "Unfortunately, with me going undercover as I have done, and living in Egypt for quite a while, I've let my religious observance slip somewhat. You've just reminded me of how things used to be."

"Were you ever happy with my mother?" Yael asked curiously.

"We weren't together very long," he admitted. "I think we realized pretty fast that our marriage had been a mistake."

He hadn't directly answered her question, but from what he said, Yael gathered that the answer was no.

"So, Yael Reed, you've inherited my musical ability as well as so many other traits of mine," he said, smiling. "You sing like an angel. You're feisty and a daredevil. And you are a free spirit, as unwilling to be tied down as a bird is willing to be caged. You need to fly free."

"I'm afraid so." Yael smiled back. "Doesn't sound hopeful on a *shidduch* resume, does it? I can't imagine any man putting up with me."

Katz didn't answer. He wasn't really in a position to discuss her marriage prospects so soon after finding her.

"So," Yael said after a moment's silence, "do you absolutely *have* to go undercover again? I mean to say, who really heard you divulge your real name?"

"Hm," Katz mused. "You could be right. I'll have to speak to my bosses and see what they think. They might be happy to redeploy me in Jerusalem instead of sending me back to Egypt. Would you be okay with living with me here? It's not as bad as disappearing completely."

"It's still not my own life back in London," Yael said. "Although I do love Israel and can envisage myself making a life here." She stopped, and he filled in the gaps.

"But not yet," he said.

"Yes. Not yet. And I'm not really sure I'd ever be happy living with someone who's watching over me, and who would expect me to tell them when I'll be back, and will ask me where I'm going when I go out. That kind of control would drive me nuts."

"And if I promise not to control you at all?" Katz asked sadly.

"Then," Yael said, "what kind of father would you be?"

He nodded. "I hear. We'll both have to think about this. Maybe you could live in Jerusalem, but not with me? Maybe be independent, and just come and visit?"

"I could come and visit from London too," she said.

He paused. "I see you're very unwilling to give anything up for me," he said.

"Well," Yael said, bristling, "let's put it this way. Would you come to London and live there so I can carry on my own life? You seem to want me to give everything up I hold dear, but what are you going to give up for me?"

"That's not how father-daughter relationships work, surely. The father making all the sacrifices? And believe me, Yael Reed, just finding out I have a daughter changes everything for me too. I have responsibilities now. I'm a father. I have a child to consider in everything I do from here on in. That's a sacrifice. A massive one."

"Then," Yael said, "just forget about me, and I'll forget about you. Then both of us entirely selfish human beings can carry on with our own lives as if the other one had never existed. How does that sound?"

CHAPTER 47

Throughout Shabbos, they were like two alley cats, circling warily around each other, each one not wanting to be the first to strike, or the first to turn tail and leave. Hostility and suspicion hung in the air like a bad smell.

At the same time, both of them looked totally, utterly terrified. If Yael decided to go with her father, she'd be giving up so very much. And if not, what would she be losing out on? He obviously thought the same. He wanted his daughter with him, but at the same time he'd lived, how many years, without knowing she existed, and had gotten used to being a loner.

Suddenly, despite the wearing off of the Novocain and the growing pain in her shoulder returning, Yael saw the funny side of this. She laughed aloud.

"What's so funny?" Katz asked, looking put out.

"Can't you see how alike we are?" Yael giggled. "We're almost a mirror image of each other. We're so, so similar and that's what's scaring the living daylights out of the two of us. This is hardly the storybook ending I expected. Foundling girl, rejected by her mother, finally finds her father. He has a glamorous, important job in the Israeli secret service. He asks her to go away with him, and off they go together into the sunset. Instead of which you're, if anything, even more scared of me than I am of you."

Katz said nothing at first, then nodded his acceptance of this scenario and said, "What are we so afraid of, do you think?"

"It's obvious, isn't it? Of change. Of losing our independence which we obviously value beyond family, beyond anything. We're two sides of the same coin, you and I."

Katz sat silently for a while, as Yael moaned slightly at the increasing pain in her shoulder. "More Novocain?" he offered.

"I'm not sure I can have any just yet," she said. "It's too soon. Much as I'd like to spend the next few weeks totally pain-free, that isn't going to happen."

Katz nodded again, and sat quietly a while longer. Then he said with bewilderment, "So, what are we going to do, you and I?"

She moaned a while before responding. "We move forward, talk, decide how we want to handle our raw new relationship in such a way that we don't end up killing each other just to get away from each other."

He looked genuinely horrified at that idea. "Yael! What a thought!"

She didn't smile. "Believe me, there have been times during this search when I absolutely, truthfully hoped that you *had* died in that hit-and-run. It would have solved so many problems for me, don't you see? I'd have known who my father was, who he had been, it would have all been very sad and all that, but I could have moved on with my life as before. Packaged your existence away in a box, and put you in the attic. Gone back to London, everything fine and dandy. Finding you alive and kicking, as it were, has presented me with far more problems than it has solved."

"And as I had no idea I even had a daughter, I'll need much more time even than you to get my head around this whole 'being a father' thing."

"So what now?" Yael asked.

Katz threw up his hands. "No idea. I mean, I said I didn't want to lose you again, but that was a kind of knee-jerk reaction. The thought of having you trailing around with me doesn't appeal."

"To me neither," Yael agreed cheerfully.

"What a pair we are to be sure." He smiled. "Useless father; rebellious, free-spirited daughter."

"Oh dear," Yael said. "What a mess. Why can't this be a storybook reunion instead of this awful muddle?"

"Because this is life, not a storybook," Katz said sadly. "And we are two extremely flawed and self-centered human beings."

They could barely look at each other. They were at an impasse.

Motza'ei Shabbos, there was a knock at the door of the hospital room. Yael was lucky that she'd been allocated a room on her own. She needed the isolation in case of infection, and also for security. This man she could still not bring herself to call either Dad, or by his name, Alan Katz, had waved his hand when she'd been admitted, and a private room had been found for her. She still thought of him as 45C. Less chance of being hurt that way.

He went to the door and opened it. A nurse stood there, holding a package.

"This came for the patient," she said in Hebrew. "I think it's chocolates."

"Ooh, chocolates!" Yael said excitedly. "I wonder who would send those. Maybe Nena?"

Katz thanked the nurse and shut the door. "Who's Nena?" he asked.

"She's Yehuda Brief's daughter-in-law," Yael answered. "One of my closest friends from school. She has her own backstory. You'd be interested in it once you get to know her."

She realized that by saying he'd get to know her friends, she was assuming the father-daughter relationship would continue. So she stopped. Then, changing the subject slightly, she said, "You know, for a while, I thought Yehuda Brief might be my father. Can you imagine that?"

"Heavens no!" Katz said with a little laugh. "You and he are like chalk and cheese."

"Yes, I know!" Yael said. "I don't know what it was, exactly, that was wrong about him being my father. But it just didn't fit, you know?"

"I know," Katz said, looking at his daughter fondly. "As soon as I saw you, I saw myself. A real chip off the old block, as they say, in more ways than one."

Yael grinned. Then she frowned. "I was thinking about those flash drives. What are those all about?"

Katz looked a little uncomfortable. "It's extremely top secret," he said. "But they contain very sensitive information about someone high up in the Egyptian government who might be financing a terrorist group that's working against Israel. There are a lot of people who would kill, literally kill, to have what is on those drives destroyed forever. I can't copy it onto any database because it's so sensitive at this stage."

"I hear you," Yael said. Even though she was as curious as could be, she knew it would be pointless pushing her father any further on this topic. She looked at him to see if he was willing to divulge any more, but his face was closed. Smiling at her lovingly, but closed.

She sighed inwardly and changed the subject. "So, let's have a look at the chocolates," she said, pointing at the box. "Does it have a card with it?"

"Yes." Katz looked at it, without taking it from its sticking place on the package.

"What does it say?"

"It says, 'Get well soon. Love, Mummy.'"

"Huh? 'Love, Mummy'? Are you sure it's for me?"

Katz stared at it a beat longer, then pulled out his phone. Before he dialed he said to her, "We need to get you out of here, and evacuate at least this floor of the hospital. This is not chocolates. I've been stupid thinking they wouldn't figure out who I am by how I behaved on the plane. This could be a bomb, Yael."

"They? Who are 'they'?"

"My enemies. Who have now become your enemies. The enemies of Israel. I've spent years worming my way into the higher echelons of the Egyptian government. They learned to trust me, assume I was one of them. Now they know I'm not, by what happened on the plane. I've given myself away."

"Throw the package out the window!" Yael shrieked. The pain in her shoulder was rising; tension and fear was only making it worse.

"Can't do that, unfortunately," Katz said. "Firstly, it could contain a lot of information my superiors might need. Secondly, I don't want to put the safety of people on the ground at risk. This could explode on impact."

He opened the door and shouted something urgently. A nurse came running. He barked orders at her.

"I want a container. A very secure and impenetrable one. The kind you use for dangerous chemicals. And I want it *now*."

She ran to do his bidding.

He put the package outside Yael's room until the nurse came back. "If it explodes, at least this will contain the worst of the blast," he said, putting the box into the container and sealing the lid. "But we need to evacuate everyone on this floor until the bomb disposal people get here. And something else, Yael."

She knew what he was going to say next. She looked at him with dread and despair. The pain in her shoulder was becoming unbearable again, but it was nothing compared to the pain in her heart.

"This means we don't have a choice about me going undercover again. They've found out who I am. They're going to come after me wherever I go, unless I disappear and take on another new identity. You don't have a choice either; you have to come with me."

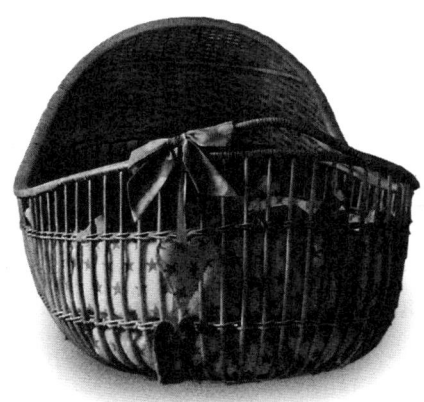

CHAPTER 48

"No, no, no..." Yael murmured. "A bomb? I don't want to go... You go without me. I'll be okay."

"Not going to happen," Katz said dismissively, dialing on his phone as he spoke. "Your safety has been compromised as much as mine has. Leaving you here is condemning you to death. You're my daughter; I'm not letting that happen."

"I'm not well enough to travel," Yael tried again, laying on some extra-effective moans, which were only partly exaggerated. Her pain levels were rising again, and the thought of being carted off on another plane ride was far from appealing.

Katz ignored her. Outside the hospital room, things were happening. She could hear police sirens and ambulances downstairs. They were getting ready to evacuate the hospital.

Then the bomb squad came thudding up the corridor, and took away the container that had the "chocolate box" inside it.

"Maybe now they won't need to evacuate," Yael said hopefully. "After all, they've taken away the package. Seems excessive to me. These are sick people, after all."

"Precautions. But you could be right," Katz said. "Things seem to be scaling down, vis à vis the evacuation, at least. It's a massive job to evacuate an entire hospital, and as you rightly say, once the bomb is off the premises, there may be no need."

"So I can stay?" Yael asked desperately.

"No, I'm afraid not. You and I were the targets of this attack. We have to disappear, whatever happens to the rest of the hospital."

With that, Yael's last shreds of hope disappeared. She turned her face away so Katz wouldn't see the tears rolling down her cheeks.

He was still making endless phone calls, which she barely listened to in her misery and despair, when someone from the bomb squad came into the room. Dressed in protective gear, he pulled off his helmet and face mask to tell Katz that the chocolate box had not been an explosive device. It had been a box of chocolates—laced with airborne anthrax, which would dissipate into the air once the box was opened, and kill everyone within range.

"And sent to you," Katz told Yael grimly, "not even me, although they assumed we were together in this room, so we'd both die a slow, inescapable death once exposed. *Now* do you believe you're in danger?"

Yael kept her face averted but nodded her head. Tears kept rolling.

"We've isolated the chocolates, so they've been made safe," the bomb squad guy said. "Luckily we're trained in hazardous chemicals and biological warfare as well as explosive devices, although this is the first time we've actually encountered active anthrax. You did well to put it in a sealed container. Although, to be honest, if it had been a bomb, that container wouldn't have done much."

Katz shrugged. "It was all that was available at short notice," he said.

"Better than nothing," the bomb squad guy agreed. "Anyway,

no need to evacuate the hospital. The anthrax chocs have been taken away for closer inspection and are safely off the premises."

"I'd rather keep a news lid tightly on this story if possible," Katz said. "If it hits the press, it'll panic people, and then whoever sent this will know it didn't work. Let them think we opened the chocolates and are enjoying the cream ones."

"I prefer truffles myself," Yael said irreverently. In these circumstances, it was a case of, if she didn't laugh she'd cry. And she was crying plenty as it was.

"Look," Katz said. "It won't be so bad. We'll live well, Shabak always makes sure of that. I'll ensure you get your physical therapy and rehab so you're back using your shoulder and pain-free in the shortest possible time."

"But where are we going?" Yael turned to face him for the first time in a while, and let him see the full force of her tears. He looked quite shocked.

"Albuquerque."

"Never heard of it," Yael sounded totally panicked. "Where on earth is Albuquerque?"

"It's the most populous city in New Mexico," he told her.

"New Mexico? What's wrong with the old one?" she said, alarmed.

"Mexico is in Central America. New Mexico is in the southwest of the United States of America. Next to Arizona. It's not instead of the 'Old Mexico,' as you called it; it's as well as." Katz managed a small smile.

She was quiet for a moment or two then asked, "Any Jews?"

"There are Jews pretty well everywhere in America," he replied. "New Mexico has twenty-four thousand Jews. However, I'll be honest with you. Most of the Jewish population are older people who've moved there from interstate. There aren't a lot of young families. But that's good for us. We want to disappear, not be the biggest *machers* in the community. Shabak has already been in touch with Witness Protection Program there and they've found us a nice, small house. It even has a swimming pool."

"Well, whoopee-doo," Yael said without enthusiasm.

"And new identities of course, and new jobs. Maybe not quite on the scale of what we've been doing until now, but Shabak will still be my employer unofficially. And yours too. You've just been recruited."

"I can't wait," Yael said in a dead voice.

"Thing is, of course," Katz said, "that because we're meant to be hiding in plain sight, we can't really take part in much of anything that's going on Jewish-wise. If I start going to shul… Well, I suppose I could, under my new name…"

"Uh-huh," Yael said without interest. She already hated Albuquerque with a passion.

Katz picked up on it and said cheerily, "We'll be fine, you'll see."

Then the nurse came in. It was time for Yael's shot of Novocain. "Can you double it?" Yael asked. "Pretty please?"

"No," the nurse said, firmly administering one dose and walking out.

"Spoilsport!" Yael called after her as she closed the door.

"I'll make plans for us to leave in the morning," Katz said.

"In the morning? I can't walk out of this hospital like this!"

"I think you can," he said firmly. "Your shoulder's been injured, not your legs. They'll strap you up good and proper so your arm doesn't move and hurt you, administer some local anesthetic, leave me with some Novocain to give you, and send us out. No reason why you should lie around here taking up a bed."

"I only got shot yesterday!" Yael protested. "You can hardly accuse me of being a bedblocker!"

"I'm not," Katz said, "but the longer we stay here, the more like sitting ducks we become. They've tried once, and they will try again."

Their eyes locked.

Then Yael sighed. "Okay. Tomorrow we go to Nowhere, New Mexico."

"It's really not that bad," Katz said. "Stunning mountain scenery, high elevation so the climate is pleasant most of the year, despite being so far south. The Rio Grande. Deserts around there are beautiful. And from what I hear, people live well there. We'll be on a much higher standard than if we'd stayed in Israel."

"Please," Yael said, tears welling up again, "don't compare Albuquerque to Israel. I just couldn't bear it."

"I'll miss Israel more than you will," he told her. "I lived here for years before I went undercover in Egypt. You've only been here a few days. We'll be back once things quiet down," he said. "Shabak is hunting for the perps behind all of this, and once they're caught, we'll be able to rejoin civilization. In the meantime, a nice house with a pool. I've never lived in a house with its own pool."

"In the middle of nowhere," Yael finished with a martyred sigh. "In the middle of absolute nowhere."

CHAPTER 49

ALBUQUERQUE!

Yael looked it up and still knew nothing about it. No one she knew had ever been there, no one knew anything about it. But there she was, walking slowly, carefully, out of the hospital, her arm still very much strapped tightly in a sling. Her father at her side.

Her father! Who was he? He was as unknown a quantity to her as Albuquerque. Yael was going with a stranger, to a strange place she'd never heard of. It was the weirdest feeling in the entire world and she absolutely hated everything about it.

A car with blacked-out windows waited for them at the curbside outside the hospital. No problem with parking attendants, apparently; Shabak had taken care of all that.

"We're going straight to the airport," her father told her. "You had a knapsack with you on the plane, so we've transferred that straight to Ben Gurion."

"I might have wanted to pack different things," Yael said, miffed. She was determined to like nothing about this latest unwanted adventure.

"If your things aren't suitable, there's a budget for getting new stuff down there in Albuquerque. Most people go into Witness Protection with nothing but what they're wearing. They often don't have much advanced warning."

"I certainly didn't," Yael sulked.

"True," Katz said as the car slid smoothly away. "But you had a knapsack. A lot of people don't even have that."

Yael looked at him suddenly. She'd been so wrapped up in her own misery that she hadn't really taken into account that he, too, had been ripped away from all that was familiar.

"Like you, for example," she said with sudden insight.

Katz was wearing a small knapsack on his back. Aside from that, he had no luggage at all.

"I travel light," he told her. "Baggage is, well…baggage. Unnecessary."

She indicated the knapsack, which he dismounted from his back as he was leaning uncomfortably against it in the car.

"Toothbrush, spare clothing…" He paused, looking embarrassed. "I haven't put tefillin on for a while, I confess, but in your honor I'm going to start again. So yes, tallis and tefillin are in there, too, looking shamefully pristine."

There was a silence, then Yael ventured, "Why did you stop? Or were you never really that *frum* to begin with?"

Katz cleared his throat. "Did your mother seem *frum* to you?"

"I don't know, to be honest," she said. "I didn't physically meet her; we only spoke on the phone. But she lives in a religious neighborhood, so I presumed she was."

Katz didn't comment on this. There was a long pause, then he said, "Putting my life on the line for Israel on a daily basis seemed enough. I felt I was doing my bit for Him upstairs. Can you understand that, at any level?"

"I think I can," Yael said slowly. "I heard that a lot of Holocaust refugees who found their way to Israel before the war stopped being religious once they lived here. As if being in the country was enough."

"Right," Katz said, turning to her. "And now, you've come into my life after twenty-one years. I'm taking it as a sign."

"From Him upstairs." Yael gave a small smile.

"That I should change my ways, at least try to. I'm starting with putting tefillin on again. See where we go from there."

Yael nodded her approval. "From tiny acorns, mighty oaks do grow," she said.

"*Mussar* from a kid," Katz said with a wry smile. "I guess I had it coming."

"I'm not a kid!" she protested. "But yes, you had it coming. However much I admire you as a Shabak operative, and a hero, I have to look up to you as a Jew if you want to be my father."

Katz gave her a quizzical look. But then he smiled and said, "If I had to be anyone's father, I'd want it to be you."

"Aww, warm and fuzzy time," Yael said with a giggle that ended in a moan, as she had shrugged her shoulders when she giggled and the pain shot up straight into her head.

"You really must learn to keep that shoulder still," Katz said with a concerned expression. "It has to heal."

Yael winced in recognition of this fact. "I vaguely remember saying, 'Who needs shoulders, anyway?'" Yael mused. "Did I really say that?"

"You did. When you were under the influence of Novocain."

"Could do with some more now," she said.

Katz glanced at his watch. "No can do. Another two hours."

"You're kidding. Two hours?"

And then they were at the airport.

Katz carried everything. Yael walked slowly, painfully, every step sending a jarring shock of pain up the side of her body, through her shoulder and into her brain.

"You wouldn't think that walking could hurt your shoulder, would you," she complained.

"We use our whole body when we walk," Katz replied. "Swinging our arms and such. You'll have to learn to walk without moving too much."

"This flight is going to be a nightmare," Yael said. "How are we going?"

"Two flights. El Al to Los Angeles. Then Southwest Airlines to Albuquerque. Nineteen hours in the air."

"You're kidding me. I've never spent longer than a few hours in the air."

"Then you haven't lived," Alan Katz said with a twinkle in his eye. "Come on, I'll buy you a meal before the flight."

He took her to a meaty *mehadrin* fast-food place on the airport concourse. Yael hadn't realized how hungry she was until he brought her the food. Eating one-handed wasn't easy, but Katz helped her cut up her food so she could handle it American style, with just her fork.

"I'm used to eating with just a fork," her father told her. "I guess I've been around Americans for too long to do it the British way any longer."

"Well, I can't use my left hand to cut up my food, so I couldn't even if I wanted to," Yael replied.

"So Dad has his uses, finally." Katz smiled at her.

Then, out of the corner of his eye, he saw someone he didn't want to see.

"There's someone looking out for us here," he told her. "Finish your meal—fast. Or take it with you in a napkin."

Foundling 267

She followed his instructions, wrapping her food in a napkin and walking as fast as her pain would allow her down the concourse toward their departure gate.

"Where are we going?" Yael moaned, as he pushed her through her pain barrier and beyond. Her pain was reaching every part of her body now. She thought she'd faint from the intensity of it.

"We're going to board early. The guy, I know who he is, and he's definitely not our friend. I don't think he saw us, but boy oh boy was he looking. I don't want to hang around there until they announce boarding, it's far too risky."

"Who is he? Ow, ow, ow, it hurts! I can't take it!" Yael moaned.

"Try and hold on till we're on the plane. Then I'll give you some Novocain, early or not."

Her eyes were rolling up, but she forced them to stay steady. Katz reached the gate, flashed some kind of badge that got them right in. The lady at the gate nodded, spoke to someone on her radio, and rushed the pair of them through and onto the plane, closing the gates firmly behind them despite the protests of some other early arrivals who couldn't see why the pair had been given special treatment.

"We're flying first class, courtesy of Shabak," Katz told Yael as she collapsed into a very comfortable armchair. She couldn't have cared less how she was flying, she just needed to sit. Or rather to lie. Katz tilted the chair back for her and she was out.

"I guess you won't be needing the Novocain quite yet, in that case, baby girl," he told her. The fond term of endearment shocked even Katz himself, and he realized—as he spoke urgently on the phone to his superiors about the guy he'd seen looking for him, describing him, so they could track him down and neutralize him—that he was, after all, turning into a father.

CHAPTER 50

Sometime during the long flight, Yael woke up and looked groggily around, overcome by pain. Her father administered a dose of Novocain at that point, hating being the cause of even the briefest moment of pain to her, even while he knew how it would take that pain away. Yael winced as the needle jabbed her, but forced a smile at him and murmured, "Thank you," as the drug took hold.

As she drifted, and her eyes closed, Katz looked down at her with the strangest, most alien feeling in his chest—a feeling he'd never experienced in his entire life, and wasn't even sure he knew how to give a name to it. It hurt, and it felt good, all at the same time, but overall he liked it. It was a feeling of never wanting to let Yael out of his life again, but knowing she was as temporary to him as a bird that had landed on his shoulder.

He'd gently relieved her of the napkin-wrapped remains of her meal as soon as she'd collapsed into her seat upon boarding. Now he unwrapped it, picking out the bits of napkin that had become attached to the meat, and looked at it. Congealed fat sat on the lumps of meat, making it considerably less appealing than it had looked back at the airport. But remembering that restaurant, and the man who had skulked around looking for him, anything was preferable to being there now. So he wiped the fat off the meat as best he could, asked the cabin crew for a double wrap, and to heat it up for Yael when she awoke and was hungry.

Before everyone else had boarded and the plane had taken off, Katz had made several more phone calls, trying to elicit who the guy was and if his superiors had made any progress in catching up with him. His superior told him it was most probably Ibrahim ibn Mustafa, an Egyptian Katz had had several dealings with over the past few years and had always been wary of.

"Did you get him?" Katz had asked. By "get" he didn't mean holding him in a nice, cozy jail cell awaiting questioning. He meant to neutralize him.

"No," his superior had said. "Firstly, he hasn't actually *done* anything. Skulking around isn't a federal offense, even in Israel, last time I checked. And secondly, and probably more significantly, even if we had decided to go all vigilante, the guy is like a puff of smoke. He's vanished into thin air. You sure you saw him? He couldn't have gotten that far into the airport without security clearance. It's not like he's seeing anyone off. Being almost at the gates means he either has to have a flight ticket…"

"…or be working at the airport in some capacity," Katz finished the sentence for him.

"Exactly. Which should be easily checked. Baggage handler being the most likely, or cleaner. But we have checked, and no one with his name has security clearance at Ben Gurion."

"False name?" Katz asked with a sigh that sounded patronizing even though it wasn't meant to be.

"Names mean nothing. But ID numbers do. He doesn't have a

teudat zehut as he's not an Israeli citizen. But he has an *el bitaqa*."

"The Egyptian version of the *teudat zehut* is problematic," Katz commented. "The photos are so poor you could get away with putting your dog's picture in there and no one would notice."

"Either way," his superior said, "he's a slippery customer. We're doing our best. You'll be much better off in Albuquerque for the time being in case he gets really smart at tracking you down here in Israel. That's about the safest place we know, and there are good people on the ground there too."

Then the flight attendant had come over and almost apologetically told Katz it was time to take off and he had to cut off his call. As if he'd been holding up the entire flight. Which, when he checked his watch, he probably had.

Yael slept most of the way to Los Angeles. Katz busied himself with work, and watching her. Watching her was like trying to capture a memory in a glass bottle for posterity. He tried to imprint her facial features on his mind, even as he did so, knowing it was as futile as trying to remember the shape of a snowflake before it melted on his sleeve.

At LAX, Yael awoke as the plane bumped onto the tarmac. She groggily asked for more Novocain, which Katz gave her, but this time he halved the dose.

"Why?" she asked him desperately.

"I'd like to see a little more of you awake," he confessed. "Be able to talk to you. Can you try and cope with a smaller dose? Is the pain not easing at all?"

Yael considered this. "I guess I'm scared to experience the full force of it," she admitted. "It was so bad." She paused and smiled at him. "But you're right. I can't have been much fun being so out of it. I'll try."

Yael walked around the airport during their short transfer,

holding her left arm as tightly as she could in its sling to keep it still. She managed to smile and talk to her father as they looked around the duty-free shops. He bought her a beautiful backpack, and some costume jewelry, a necklace and a bracelet, which was nicer than anything she had ever owned, and she wore them with pride.

"No one has ever bought me anything like this before," she said. "Actually, no one has ever bought me presents. I love it, all of it. Thank you so much."

Katz helped her transfer her belongings from her tatty, old backpack to the new one, and they ceremoniously dropped the old one in a garbage can. "Leaving my old life behind," Yael said, and there was a trace of wistfulness in her voice. He caught her looking back at the garbage can as they walked away, as if she half wanted to run back and retrieve the tatty, old part of her past.

"The new one is so much nicer," he told her.

She nodded. "Not everything new is nicer than the old stuff."

He didn't reply and looked away, pretending to busily examine a display of men's watches.

Yael realized she sounded ungrateful and backtracked. "But this is truly beautiful and I'm very appreciative."

"I've never bought anyone presents either," Katz admitted. "Except myself. Never had anyone to buy for, so you're doing me a favor by allowing me to do it."

"Not even my mother?" she asked curiously. "Surely when you first married, you must have bought her a ring or something?"

Katz thought for a moment, then said, "Yes, I bought her a ring and a necklace, a real one. I never thought of it as buying her a present. I thought of it as something I had to do. Of discharging a duty."

"Hm," Yael said.

"That's what it's like when you're unhappy," he explained. "If you're happy with someone, giving to them is a joy."

She looked up at him.

"Like giving to you," he said, smiling.

Then it was time to board their second flight, Southwest Airlines to Albuquerque. A mere couple of hours in the air, but taking them to their final destination was like closing a door forever.

LA had been warm, even though it was late November. The sun had shone dazzlingly outside the airport windows. Albuquerque, too, was sunny, but there was a chilly desert wind blowing as they left the airport and the temperature hovered around fifteen degrees centigrade. Yael could feel the cold coming on as the sun dipped behind the mountains.

"It's getting dark very early," she commented. "It's barely five o'clock."

"Yup, I think days are short here in the winter," Katz said. "I don't know much more about the place than you do. Oh, look, there's our ride."

The Mexican-looking guy at the wheel did nothing to make Yael feel more comfortable. She felt like the proverbial stranger in a strange land. Even this man at her side, her father, was a stranger to her, although slowly becoming less so with each passing moment.

Yael gritted her teeth against the growing pain in her shoulder, and stepped boldly out to face an uncertain future.

CHAPTER 51

"How far?" Katz asked the driver in an attempt not to speak too good an English in case the Mexican didn't know much of the language. But aside from a strong Spanish accent, his English was perfect.

"Twenny minutes or so, mister," he said. "You'll like the house and the neighborhood. It's real nice over there."

Yael watched the scenery go by. Everywhere the mountains formed the backdrop. The streets were so wide compared to both England and Jerusalem. So much sky. She'd never seen a sunset like the one she was witnessing now. Buildings were low slung and sprawling. No need to crowd, no need to build high. She saw cacti like she'd seen in Israel, only the fruit seemed purple instead of green. Elsewhere the grass was lush and irrigated. But it was the space that drew her attention most. Golders Green was crowded and cramped; so was Jerusalem. This place seemed to have spread out over endless land and made itself comfortable.

Eventually, the car turned into another wide, quiet suburban street with single-story houses on both sides, ranch style. Equally wide driveways separated each house and they each had a front lawn that stretch to the curbside. That was certainly different from Golders Green, and in Jerusalem hardly anyone, at least in her experience, had a house at all, let alone a garden, front or rear. Maybe she was just mixing in the wrong neighborhood, but everywhere she'd looked she'd seen crowded apartment buildings reaching for the skies. If your neighbor coughed, you'd hear it; here, you could scream your lungs out and your nearest neighbor wouldn't hear you.

She wasn't sure if this was a good thing or not.

"Here's the home, I think you'll like it," pronounced the driver, which made Yael instantly want to hate it on sight. How dare he decide what she'd like or not? But despite herself, she found the low-slung, ranch-style house appealing. It was clean and freshly painted, and the garden in front was well tended and had a riot of desert flowers growing in beds and pots. Through the side gate she could see a glimmer of blue in the last rays of the sun. The pool!

Inside, the house was cool and pleasantly welcoming. Yael and her father wandered around picking out which bedroom they each wanted. There were three, and each one was nicer than the last, and each one had a private bathroom attached.

Out back was the pool, glinting as the sky turned from red and gold to navy blue, and stars appeared in their millions against the desert skies. It was surrounded by stone flagging, and a well-tended lawn, and there were comfortable-looking lounge chairs arranged around it.

"It's gorgeous, isn't it, Yael?" her father said, staring out at the mountains behind the house.

"Much as I hate to admit it, it is rather gorgeous," she said reluctantly. "But so is the Amazon, and the Himalayas, and I wouldn't want to live there either." She turned around and went back into the house. She unpacked her suitcase and then joined her father in the open-plan kitchen/living area, where he was looking into the fridge.

"They've stocked us up with some basic stuff," he said, "but we're going to have to go shopping pretty soon."

"Shopping where?" Yael asked. "There's hardly a Kosher Kingdom or Osher Ad downtown, is there?"

"There's a Chabad," Katz said. "I've looked it up. Rabbi Chaim Schneider and his wife Devorah Leah will be our first port of call."

Rabbi Schneider told them on the phone that Trader Joe's was the best place to find kosher products, including meats, chicken, packaged goods, and braided challah. He gave them the address.

They looked at each other.

"Oh," Katz remembered suddenly, "we have a car. It's in the driveway outside and the key is right here. And we're both insured to drive it."

"That's great, only I don't know how to drive," Yael said.

"You can learn while we're here. Great opportunity. Meanwhile, I'll drive us to Trader Joe's. Come on, an adventure!" He paused. "I hope it has GPS. I have no idea how to get around this town."

"My shoulder hurts," Yael said.

Katz looked at her. "Bad enough not to want to come shopping with me?"

He looked so crestfallen that she couldn't admit what she was really feeling; that she felt like hiding away in her room like a wounded animal and pretending the world could just go away. She managed a small smile.

"No, not that bad," Yael confessed. "I'll come. I've never been to a Trader Joe's."

The car they were allocated was medium sized by American standards and yet neither of them had ever been in such a comfortable vehicle. There seemed to be holders and cubbyholes for all their bits and pieces, and they sat back in the utmost comfort in the soft seats. After the minimum of fiddling about, and plotting Trader Joe's into the onboard GPS, Katz pulled out into the quiet, wide street and allowed the car to direct him to the huge store with its ample parking lot in front. They took a shopping cart that looked large enough to house their car inside it, let alone anything they picked up in the store, and they went inside.

Massive, wide aisles greeted them. There was so much on sale that the two of them felt dizzy within a few seconds.

"Too much, too much," moaned Yael, looking around. "I want to go home."

They looked at each other. She hadn't specified where "home" was, but somehow, Katz didn't think she meant the ranch house with the swimming pool.

"It's been a long journey and you're injured," he said, trying to be fatherly and soothing. "Let's just whiz around and pick up some groceries and go straight back. We can do a more detailed look-see of this place another time."

Yael nodded. Just looking for the food department was a job in itself, but eventually they found it, and two whole aisles dedicated to kosher groceries. As Katz dropped items into the cart, Yael couldn't help thinking that there was more choice there than in most kosher grocery stores in Golders Green. And this was in the so-called middle of nowhere!

Katz peered into a freezer and picked out some packaged schnitzels made in Israel. "Look!" he said triumphantly. "It's got a decent hechsher! And some sausages too!" Another package dropped into the cart.

Yael looked into the cart wryly. "Somehow I don't think we're going to starve," she said.

String cheese, yogurts, cereals, and even *chalav Yisrael* milk was added. Crackers, jam, peanut butter, and some toiletries, tissues, and cleaning stuff followed.

"Can we actually afford all this stuff?" Yael asked when the pile in the cart threatened to peek over the edge.

"It's all courtesy of Shabak," Katz replied.

"You're going to bankrupt the whole country." Yael laughed, then winced as her shoulder protested painfully.

"This should last us a while," Katz said, embarrassed, as he loaded up the car. Yael could do little to help him, but lifted a few lighter bags with her good arm. "The fruit and veg don't look quite up to Israeli standards, but I suppose they'll have to do."

Katz realized that he'd neglected to program "home" into the GPS, so he had no idea how to get back. After driving around aimlessly for a while, getting increasingly panic-stricken at his inability to take care of his daughter properly, he was ready to give up, when Yael saw a familiar street. Her sense of direction, however flawed, still outweighed her father's, and soon they were back in the driveway of the ranch house.

Once they'd unloaded and unpacked all the groceries, they stood in the kitchen and looked at each other.

"Dinner?" he asked her.

"Yes, please," she answered.

And they both waited.

Finally, he said, "Can you cook?"

"Nope," she replied, "can you?"

"Nope."

Another silence. Then Yael said, "What was that you said about us not starving here?"

Katz looked sheepish. "A true case of 'Water, water, everywhere, but not a drop to drink,' I think! Didn't you ever cook back in London?"

"I'm an absolute whiz at opening cans of soup and adding sliced sausages to it," Yael said. "And I can boil up pasta and pour sauce over it, and add shredded cheese. That's about as far as my culinary expertise goes."

"Well," Katz said, staring into the cupboard, "we have cans of soup and those frozen sausages. So I guess we're good to go."

"I need two hands to cut up sausages, and there's no way I can open a can of soup with one hand either. You'll have to help me. Did we get a can opener, by the way?"

"Uh…"

So they ate crackers and peanut butter and jam for supper.

After supper, Yael wanted a shower but it was too complicated, so she washed as best she could and maneuvered herself into bed. Her father came in to say goodnight and found her looking miserable.

"What's up, baby girl? Is your shoulder hurting? Shall I get you some more Novocain?"

"Well, yes, please, that might help me sleep," she said. Not wanting to tell him that what was really bothering her couldn't be fixed by a thousand shots of Novocain. But for now, oblivion seemed like a good option to ease the pain that was much more in her heart than in her shoulder.

CHAPTER 52

YAEL SPENT A restless night. She was sleeping alone and unsupervised for the first time in a while, and the pain kept waking her up. As she felt uncomfortable calling out for her father, she just put up with it and stayed awake.

The following morning, Katz came in to check on her. He looked relaxed and rested; he'd obviously not been disturbed all night. He found her red eyed and exhausted. Guiltily he ran for the Novocain.

"Why didn't you call me when you needed a painkiller?" he asked.

"I didn't want to disturb your beauty sleep," Yael said with a martyred air. "And look, it obviously worked. You slept like a log, while I slept like a baby—woke up every two hours screaming."

Katz laughed, but Yael wasn't laughing with him; the pain was too draining. He administered the Novocain and as it slowly took hold, she relaxed.

"Only half a dose again," he told her. "I want you up and about. We have things to do."

"Like what?" Yael asked with little interest.

"Like finding ourselves work. Shabak has set something up."

"What Israeli secret service work can there possibly be to do in Albuquerque?" she asked.

"Well, none, obviously, although they told me there have been some murmurings of terrorist activity in the background looking for us, so we have to stay very alert. But we have jobs nonetheless. We're working together. It's better that we stay close. In case."

He didn't have to spell out "in case what." Yael looked vaguely curious as to the job, so Katz spared her the words by telling her.

"We're working in the gym," Katz continued. "I'm pretty well set up to be a personal trainer; I've trained long and hard myself, so I can give classes—to guys, obviously."

"Oh, great. For you, that is. What about me? I'm not trained in anything except being a sleuth, and working in a gym is *really* ideal for me right now," Yael said sarcastically.

Katz looked slightly embarrassed. "I know you can't do much, but actually there's a fantastic physical therapist there. She said she'll work with your shoulder while you do your work."

"Which is?" Yael pressed.

"You'll be working in the café. It happens to be a Chabad place, we're both lucky."

"Working in the café? What, making coffees and juicing oranges with one hand? Please."

Katz shifted a little. "No, just wiping tables and cleaning up. I know it's not prestigious, but there's not a lot you *can* do with one hand, as you so rightly pointed out."

Yael sighed. Try as she might, she couldn't think of anything she could do one-handed, that wasn't being a sleuth. And even that. How could she shin down drainpipes and follow suspects with her left shoulder giving her trouble all the time and requiring regular doses of numbing medication?

"I hope the therapist is as good as you say she is," Yael said resignedly. "I really want to get back to normal ASAP."

"It won't be that quick," Katz warned her. "Shoulders are very complicated joints with lots of different movements to get back. You'll have to be patient."

"Well, as you say, I can have the physical therapy when I'm not wiping down tables and being a general dogsbody," Yael said miserably.

"Cheer up," Katz said. "It's a gorgeous day out there and we're going to have breakfast, then head out to the gym. It's a beautiful ride, apparently."

She looked pointedly at him. "Have you put your tefillin on today?"

Katz showed her the strap marks on his left arm and the slight indentation on his forehead. "Done and dusted, ma'am."

She gave him a weak thumbs-up.

"Shall I help you getting up and ready?"

The very idea made Yael shudder. "I'll manage," she said. He left her, discreetly. She got up and struggled to wash and dress herself with the sling and the pain getting in the way. Brushing her unruly hair without the other hand to hold it in place was also a challenge, but eventually she looked reasonable. She davened and joined her father in the kitchen for breakfast.

He'd laid out quite a spread, but she had no appetite, and opted for a coffee and a banana. He ate with gusto.

"You'll get fat if you eat like that three times a day," she commented.

"I'm very active, and I'll be more active working at the gym," he defended himself.

"I'm usually very active, but right now I can barely move, so I'd better watch what I eat," Yael said, nibbling at her banana.

"You need protein to heal your injuries," her father told her sternly. "I'll make you some eggs."

The pans were all new. He made her a plate of scrambled eggs, and Yael found herself eating them hungrily. "These are actually very good," she admitted.

After breakfast, Katz cleared up and Yael practiced clearing tables for her upcoming work at the gym. It wasn't nearly as easy as she imagined, but she managed a creditable job of it.

Once the house looked decent, Katz jangled his car keys and they went out into a cold, crisp, sunny morning. Yael put on sunglasses and looked around at the mountain scenery with a sharp blue sky as backdrop.

"Gorgeous," Katz said, "isn't it?"

"Mmm," Yael said noncommittally. She eased herself into the car and he plotted the gym into the GPS, this time remembering to add "home" for later. They set off, driving slowly down the wide streets so as not to jar Yael's shoulder.

The Powerflex gym had a couple of branches, but the one they had been assigned to was small and uncrowded. It had a small coffee shop, and it was there that Yael had to struggle into an apron (with the help of another waitress) and be shown the ropes. The other waitress, whose name was Kirsty, was friendly and didn't ask too many questions as to how Yael had come by her injuries, although maybe she'd been prepped. Yael noticed that Kirsty had a full face of makeup, while she wore none at all. Kirsty did comment on this, and offered to help.

"It's part of the job to wear makeup," Kirsty said. Sighing, Yael submitted to having makeup and lipstick applied as she sat in one of the coffee shop chairs. Afterward, Kirsty handed her a mirror, and Yael had to admit there was a definite improvement.

"Don't you ever wear makeup, even when you had two hands?"

Kirsty asked as she put the mirror back in her handbag.

"Nope," Yael said.

"Is that a British thing?"

"Nope, it's a me thing."

The therapist who came to introduce herself was called Gemma and was brisk and businesslike, but also kind enough to know how much pain Yael was in.

"We'll have a session during your break," she told her. "We have a lot of work to do, to get movement back into that joint and also to reduce the pain. Unfortunately, making it move will also cause you pain, so you'll have to bear with me on that one."

"Looking forward," Yael said with gritted teeth, adding "not" under her breath.

"Heard that!" Gemma said in a singsong voice, smiling, as she left the coffee shop.

Alan Katz came in to see how Yael was getting on. He was wearing the gym's uniform of Lycra and looked ridiculous, but Yael thought she'd probably get used to seeing him in it.

The morning went by fairly quickly. Yael wiped tables and cleared cups and plates with her right hand, fielded questions about how her shoulder had come to be in a sling ("It's a sporting injury, I was wrestling," she told everyone, and they looked duly impressed), and she chatted with Kirsty, who was really a lovely girl, even though she seemed happy to be stuck in Albuquerque.

"Why don't you get out of this place?" Yael asked her.

"I like it here!" she said. "An' anyway, where would I go?"

Yael didn't understand that. "What do you mean, where would you go?" She waved her right hand expansively. "There's an entire world out there beyond those mountains! Cities, oceans, other countries… I lived in London. I lived in Jerusalem for a short while. Where have you been?"

Kirsty thought for a moment, then said, "Well, I've been to Phoenix once. An' my daddy said he'd take me to Vegas for our vacation next year…"

In Yael's studies of where on earth New Mexico actually was, she'd elicited that Nevada and Arizona, along with Texas, were all neighboring states, so Kirsty was hardly ambitious in the spreading of her wings.

"Is London in England?" Kirsty asked, awestruck.

"Yup, sure is," Yael said in a southern drawl, wiping the tables like a pro.

"Wow. I'd sure like to visit London. Do you get to say hi to the Queen?"

"Not personally, no. She doesn't mix with us common folk much."

Kirsty nodded. "I'd sure like to see the Queen one day," she said in a dreamy voice.

At lunch break, Gemma took Yael into what Yael later came to name "Guantanamo Bay." It was a small room with various pieces of instruments of torture, otherwise known as physical therapy tools. There wasn't a movement she could do that didn't hurt. Gemma started with some gentle massage, but quickly saw the area was far too raw for that.

"We'll have to concentrate on healing and strengthening," she told a yelping, tearful Yael. "And healing will be faster if the circulation is better in that area, and it's not going to improve unless you use it a little bit. It'll hurt, but we won't do anything that'll impede healing."

Yael was in so much pain she couldn't talk or reply, but as the session progressed, to her surprise, the pain lessened without Novocain. By the end of it, she could, and did, hug Gemma in gratitude for making things improve, even this little bit.

On their way home in the car, Katz asked his daughter how her day had gone.

Yael hadn't wanted to be there, but at the same time, it hadn't been nearly as bad as she'd thought. But she didn't know how to tell him that without him thinking she was happy to stay.

CHAPTER 53

ON THE WAY home, they stopped off and bought a can opener. That night they ate Yael's chef's special: canned soup with cut-up sausages in it. Along with a hastily thrown-together salad, it made a fairly decent meal. Katz pronounced it delicious and his daughter beamed with pride.

"Even though I had to cut up the sausages myself," he said. "So that was my contribution, along with opening the can."

"Don't I get any credit?" Yael said.

He grinned. "I guess I'm not used to handing over the reins," he admitted.

"Neither am I, actually. What a pair we are!"

Katz helped Yael with the dishes, and after supper, they sat on the couch and she told him about her life so far. It was only after an hour or so of easy conversation that she realized she hadn't had a dose of Novocain for over six hours. The pain was receding. Previously she'd been begging for more meds after only two hours. She smiled to herself. Things were looking up.

She found herself yawning. "I think I'll head off to bed," she told her father. "It's been a long day. And I haven't been sleeping that well, for obvious reasons."

"Do you want some meds before you turn in?"

Yael considered it. "I'm not in pain right now," she said. "Amazingly enough. As long as you don't mind me calling you in the night if it gets bad, I think I'll try and do without for now."

Katz gave her a thumbs-up. "Do you need help?" he asked.

"If I do, I'll holler," she said. "I might try and give myself some semblance of a shower."

"Good luck."

While she was in the shower, Katz sat quietly, thinking about what had happened in his life—in their lives, and how they had irrevocably changed in an instant. One minute he didn't know Yael existed, and now there they were, in Albuquerque of all places. Far from everything familiar. Far from home.

A slight noise outside. An animal, maybe, rustling in the bushes outside the house?

But Alan Katz was Shabak, trained to be on the alert at all times. He took out his gun, and, crouching, went to the window, hidden by the curtains, and looked.

A dark figure was skulking outside. It wasn't an animal. It was human, and armed. Katz could see the pistol in his hand as he crept around the house, trying to peer in the window.

For a second, the man turned his head and the street light caught his face. It was Ibrahim ibn Mustafa, the Egyptian who had been looking for them at the airport.

It seemed like he found them. How was that even possible? They had been so careful.

Obviously not careful enough. Or Ibrahim was cleverer than Katz had given him credit for.

Katz sank onto the floor, trembling. Normally this kind of thing was all in the line of work, and wouldn't faze him in the least. But now things were different. He had Yael to consider.

Pull yourself together, man, he told himself. *This has happened! Deal with it!*

Without another moment's hesitation, Katz aimed his gun through the glass of the window and pulled the trigger.

Yael hurried into the room. "I heard a noise," she said.

Katz didn't know what to tell her. He couldn't speak.

Then she saw the shattered glass of the window and went to look.

"Oh, you've shot someone! Who is it? Is he dead?"

"I think so," her father said. "I'm going out to check. But one thing is clear. We're no safer here than we were back in Jerusalem. He's managed to track us down. And it's me he's after, not you. You'd just be collateral damage."

Yael was shaking so hard she could barely speak. "But, but… he's dead now, isn't he? So it's all over?"

Katz shook his head sadly. "It's never over for me. If he's tracked me down all the way to Albuquerque, you can be sure he's told others. They'll be on their way, if they're not already here."

He went outside quietly and examined the man lying on the grass. Then he pulled him indoors and shut the door.

"You've brought him in here?" Yael was horrified.

"He can't do us any harm now," Katz told her. "But leaving him outside wouldn't be a wise move. Even though this is a very quiet neighborhood, people do come by. I'll get the glass fixed in the morning."

"But, but…?" Yael pointed at the body.

"I'll sort it out. But you're going to have to leave. This place isn't safe for you anymore. I'm sorry for thinking it was. Sorry for thinking I could bring you into my crazy, dangerous life, and you'd be okay. I'm a walking disaster and I attract this kind of thing all the time. I'm used to it, but that's when I've only myself to think about. I can't have you a part of this. So…I'm putting you on the first plane out of here, to…wherever you want to go. Israel?"

"London," Yael said. "It's home to me. But what about you? I feel terrible leaving you here on your own to face…that!" She pointed to the body on the floor. "And whoever comes after him."

Katz started dialing on his cell. "Welcome to my life, Yael Reed," he said. "Hopefully we'll meet again sometime very soon when all this is sorted out and I feel safe enough to travel to you without endangering your life as well as my own."

Now Yael was crying. "I've only just started to get to know you! I don't want to leave you now! After everything we've been through!"

"It's nonnegotiable, I'm afraid," he said. "Now I finally know what being a father really means. It means putting someone else before yourself. I've never had to do that before. It's always been about me. I can't put you in danger just so we can stay together. You go back to London, back to your old life, and I'll come and find you again. Just be sure to keep in touch. I'll leave you my contact details."

Katz spoke into his cell phone, making several calls while Yael sat sobbing on the couch.

"Go and pack," he said. "I've booked you on a flight to LA and it leaves in an hour and a half. We don't have a lot of time."

"Will you come to the airport?"

"No, sorry, I can't. We'll say our good-byes here. But be assured, unless I'm dead, I *will* come for you."

Yael went into her room. She could hardly see what she was packing through her tears. What did it matter what stuff she left behind? She was leaving the most important thing of all behind, the person she'd expended so much energy and effort finding. And he could be in mortal danger! How could she bear it if something happened to him?

As if he read her mind he was in her doorway, leaning against it, looking at her. "I'm indestructible," he told her. "Don't you worry. Just trust me, go home to London, resume your life, and keep in touch. The number I've written down is a safe phone; no one can intercept our calls or texts. And here is something for you." He pulled out a phone from his pocket.

"I already have a phone," Yael said, puzzled, looking at the phone.

"Yes, but not like this. It's a secure phone. No one can hack it. Keep it safe. It only has my number on it, no one else's, and don't add anyone else's number to it, so you know when it rings, that it's me."

"What if you never ring? No one is that indestructible," she wept, and he came forward to help her close her case.

"Look at you, chip off the old block," he said, smiling at her, "and how many near misses you've been involved in and still walked away from them. Well, I'm like you, only tougher."

Yael had nothing to say to that. There was a light at the window.

"It's your ride to the airport," Katz said, looking out. "He's safe. Shabak. We'll say good-bye here."

They'd never as much as touched each other, but now she just had to hug him. With one hand. They stood awkwardly, pulling apart.

"I'll see you soon, little girl of mine," Katz said. "When all this is over, I'll come for you."

"You promise?" Yael asked, still sobbing as he helped take her case to the door. He gestured to the driver, who came forward to help take her luggage and guide her to the car.

"You promise? You promise we'll see each other again?" she asked again, in anguish.

Katz didn't answer.

EPILOGUE

YAEL WOKE UP on her first morning back in her single-girl apartment block, unable to process what had happened to her. Her shoulder hurt like mad; she'd been assigned a lengthy program of physical therapy and other medical care, privately paid for by Shabak so she wouldn't have to rely on the delays of the National Health Service. In fact, it had been a miracle that she'd slept at all; the pain was so great that every time she moved she woke up moaning in agony. It was fortunate that each young woman in the block had their own space, otherwise she would have disturbed any roommate.

At about four in the morning, she had struggled out of bed and taken as strong a painkiller as she was permitted. Eventually this dulled the edges of her pain and allowed her a couple of hours of restless sleep, in which her dreams were full of one thing.

Her father.

Would she ever see him again?

By seven she gave up trying to sleep and just lay in any position that afforded her the least pain, and allowed her thoughts to overwhelm her. The whole quest to find Alan Katz had been surreal. The more Yael thought about everything that had happened, the more unbelievable it seemed. She tried compartmentalizing the whole episode into a box in her head labeled "Weird Goings On," and shutting the box tightly. After all, she had no idea if and when she would ever see her father again, so it was safer for her sanity to assume she wouldn't, and just focus on the side issues of her trip.

She had become closer to Nena, though she knew she had abused that closeness. Nena had told her, during a phone call at the airport as Yael waited to board her homebound flight, that Yehuda Brief had come to actually admire the spunk of the spirited young woman who had tricked her way into his home.

As for Yonina, the child had never stopped asking for her, and Yael knew she'd have to make another trip to Israel to rekindle that relationship. Despite herself, Yael had developed a closeness to the pudgy nine-year-old. She, Yael Reed, the non-maternal queen, was actually missing the company of a child! But it did make her want to go back to Israel, among other reasons.

She struggled out of bed and got her phone. She was going to call Nena, to ask her how Yonina was—and, as an afterthought, how Nena was. *How bad am I!* Yael thought with a giggle. And she found herself wondering how Esther Brief was too. All these people had wriggled their way under Yael's skin and into her heart and stayed there, making it throb with longing with every beat. They were like family. Yes, more like family than her real family— a mother who didn't want to know her, and a rather wonderful father, but one who was…what? Alive? Dead? Captured?

Sometimes it seemed safer to Yael to go back a few weeks to when she neither knew nor cared about whether he existed or not. That way her heart was protected from the pain of loss and doubt and just plain old not knowing. She sat and thought about him a while, then shoved him back in his box in her head, and opened her phone to dial Nena.

And her phone pinged. It was a text. She swiped it open.

It was a phone number, followed by the words: "I gave you a secure phone. Maybe you forgot with your painful shoulder and all. It's in your jacket pocket, I think. Call me on it. I want to hear your voice, baby girl."

Yael wondered why the words looked so blurry until she realized tears were pouring down her cheeks as she read them. Her heart melted into a flowing river of joy as she went to her jacket, retrieved the phone, which she had indeed forgotten about, and sat back down on her bed to call her father.

Nena, she decided, could wait.

ABOUT THE AUTHOR

Ruthie Pearlman, originally from England and now living in Mevaseret Tzion, Israel, with her husband, continues her work as a crime-thriller writer with this latest page-turner. She is the author of the best-selling Yael Reed thrillers, including *School of Secrets*, *Lockdown*, *Disappeared*, and *Whispers*. She writes serials for the *Aim!* section of *Ami* magazine.

DON'T MISS THESE OTHER BOOKS ABOUT YAEL REED...

MENUCHA PUBLISHERS

It's a new school year at Ner Miriam Seminary — new friends, a fresh start, and uncharted territory. But students and staff at this isolated British school are experiencing more excitement than they bargained for.

MP Simon Dean and his wife, Antonia, are visiting Ner Miriam Seminary, whose students are eager to honor the famous couple. But in a shocking turn of events, the unassuming school becomes a crime scene.

When a desperate mother turns to supersleuth Yael Reed for help in finding her missing teenage daughter, the young detective quickly accepts the case. But her investigations reveal a shocking detail: Malky Hillman isn't the first girl in her high school to have vanished.

Yael Reed has seen a lot in her short yet thrilling investigative career. But when a frantic teenager contacts her regarding the picture-perfect Simon couple and their mysterious babies, the young PI encounters her most shocking case yet.

Available at your local Judaica store or at:
1-855-MENUCHA • www.menuchapublishers.com